SARA FRASER

Tildy

Futura

A **Futura** Book

Copyright © Roy Clews 1985

First published in Great Britain in 1985 ·
by Futura Publications, a Division of
Macdonald & Co (Publishers) Ltd
London & Sydney

ISBN 0 7088 2671 7

Typeset in Baskerville by Fleet Graphics, Enfield, Middlesex

Printed in Great Britain by
William Collins, Glasgow

Futura Publications
A Division of
Macdonald & Co (Publishers) Ltd
Maxwell House
74 Worship Street
London EC2A 2EN

A BPCC plc Company

Introduction

England in 1820.
A land of Plenty.
A land of Wealth.
A land of Freedom.

The nailmakers of the Midlands possessed none of those blessings. They were 'The White Slaves' of England, and knew only bitter toil and hardship from birth until death.

But there were those among them whose pride and courage forced them to fight against the savage suffering of their existence, and their spirit refused to be broken.

This story is about a young girl, who fought back. Her name was

Tildy . . .

Chapter One

Parish of Ipsley, Warwickshire. April 1820.

The Reverend Phillip Wren, Incumbent Rector of Ipsley Parish, sighed heavily and put away from him the leather-bound book of sermons that he had been reading. Leaning back in the wooden-armed chair, he lifted his spectacles from the bridge of his nose and blinked his watery-blue eyes several times to clear their blurring. Using a scrap of soft cloth taken from the pocket of his black, club-tailed coat, he started to polish the square lenses of the spectacles.

While the short fat fingers gently rubbed the convex surface of the glass, the clergyman's mind focussed on a problem that was causing his gentle nature great concern. Matilda Seymour, his wife's maid, was pregnant, only a few weeks from confinement, and the man responsible was one of their own manservants, Thomas Crawford. There came a soft tapping on the door, breaking Wren's train of thought. He sighed again, and called out.

'Enter!'

A young girl, dressed in the tiny-bibbed white apron and plain linen mobcap of a maidservant, came into the sombre, dark-furnished room. Wren replaced his spectacles and composed his plump features into the expression of sternness which he felt befitted his position in the world.

'Yes, Matilda, what is it?'

She kept her eyes downcast and dropped a curtsey, moving gracefully despite the ponderous heaviness of her swollen body.

'If you please, sir, the churchwardens are here to see you.'

Her voice was soft and musical, with only a suggestion of rustic burr.

Wren nodded his bag-wigged, powdered head. 'Very well, show them in.'

She curtseyed again and left the study, to return, almost immediately with two stocky, ruddy-faced men, both wearing the thick fustian coats, breeches and leather gaiters of yeomen farmers, and carrying wide-brimmed, shallow-crowned hats in their work-roughened hands.

The girl would have slipped away, but the clergyman stopped her.

'Stay here, Matilda, I don't doubt but that the matter, these gentlemen have called to see me about, concerns you.'

The elder of the two men seemed ill-at-ease, and he shuffled his heavy shoes and coughed nervously, before agreeing.

'Indeed it does, Reverend, indeed it does.'

Wren, resenting their presence because it would finally force him into making a decision about the pregnant girl, made no effort to put the man at ease.

'Well, Master Whitehouse,' his stern expression became a frown. 'Let us get on with the business at hand.'

The churchwarden coughed again and, to cover his discomfiture at the rector's manner, started to bluster.

'I dunno as how it's fitten to talk of this matter in front o' this young 'ooman, Reverend. Arter all, if there's to be any dispute it don't seem right that her who is the cause o' that dispute should see her betters rowing wi' each other.'

Wren assumed a tone of exaggerated surprise.

'Oh, you expect there to be high words exchanged between us then, Master Whitehouse?'

The second churchwarden, Joseph Whittington, was of tougher fibre than his companion. Scowling, he broke his silence.

'Wi' all respect, Reverend Wren, we'em wasting time that could be better spent. You knows well why we'em come . . . We wants your decision as to what you intends doing about this wench, Tildy Seymour, here. We come on behalf o' the congregation, and as parish officers, because as you well know I'm the overseer to the poor in this parish, as well as a churchwarden.' He half-turned and pointed at Matilda. 'Now this wench here is acarrying a bastard in her belly, and by the looks on it she's nigh on her time. She arn't o' this parish, and if I recollect rightly only come to work here at the rectory last Michaelmas Hiring Fair, so she's got no settlement in this village.

'I 'udden't be doing my duty as overseer and church-warden if I allowed her to birth a bastard within the parish boundary. Her and her babby would become a charge on the poor rate, and we've enough native-born bastards to maintain as it is . . .'

While the men were speaking Tildy had stood silent, her body erect and her head held proudly even though her face burned hot with embarrassment. Eighteen years old, her dark hair and eyes, coupled with the flawless skin of her oval face and shapely neck made her a strikingly attractive girl; and despite her misshapen body she could still turn men's heads to stare at her admiringly. She listened with growing anger to the harsh words of Whittington, and felt ever more protective towards the unborn child she felt moving in her womb.

Truth to tell, Baby, I never wanted you, she thought. And I want your father not at all . . . but I'll never give you up to the hands of such as these, that I promise.

Emboldened by his colleague's bluntness, Edward Whitehouse joined in.

'There's another thing, Reverend Wren, sir, and I knows that your good lady wife agrees wi' us on it, for she's so told me. It don't do at all for you as the leader of the Faithful in this parish to give succour to them as flouts the Commandments of the Lord.

'This wench has fornicated most sinfully wi' a man, and she not wedded, or even betrothed to him. Why, it'll tempt other flighty, loose-thinking wenches to do the same if they sees this 'un being protected and cared for by a Man o' God, and allowed to go free of punishment for her sins . . . '

For a moment Phillip Wren was strongly tempted to tax the man with showing a blatant lack of Christian charity towards the fallen.

'Oh Lord Jesus, will they never realize that You are a gentle and merciful Being, and forgive most willingly those sinners who truly repent, as I'm sure this poor girl does repent?' he cried in his mind to the God of Mercy he worshipped.

Whittington's harsh voice penetrated his consciousness.

'It's true what Master Whitehouse has told you, Reverend. Only yesterday your good lady, Mistress Wren, said as how the wicked girl should be driven from here, and scourged back to the place she came from, and the man who lay with her likewise.'

Phillip Wren's mind's eye conjured up a vision of his wife's thin rat-trap of a mouth as it spewed out pious hypocrisies and bitter recriminations directed against those who transgressed her own fanatically intolerant moral code. He blotted the pinched, mean face from his mind, but with a sense of shame realized that he lacked the courage to stand out against his wife's unforgiving strictures. Angry at himself, he snapped savagely at the church-wardens.

'Damn you both! Will you never cease from hounding me about this matter?'

Both men stared, shocked at this display of temper from their normally mollifying rector. Wren saw their shock and inwardly castigated himself for allowing his feelings to openly overcome him. When he next spoke his voice was its normal, placid timbre.

'Very well, gentlemen, I believe that you both are acting as the dictates of your consciences demand of you. I pray that my own conscience will not be troubled by what you force me to do in this matter. Will you both please leave, and be assured that I shall make great endeavours to solve this unhappy problem in the best interests of all con-cerned.'

Once alone with Tildy, he rose and beckoned her to the centre of the room. Placing both hands on her slender shoulders he gently pushed her down until she was kneeling before him then, folding his fingers directly above her bowed head, he closed his eyes.

'Oh Dear Lord,' he prayed aloud with intense fervour. 'I beseech that You will guide Your humble servant, and show him how best he might aid this poor unfortunate sinner . . . ' His voice rose and fell in the sing-song tones favoured by the Anglican priesthood when they communed with their Master.

To Tildy, kneeling in acute discomfort, it seemed that the prayer would never end. The hard wooden blocks of the floor pressed relentlessly into her soft rounded knees through the thin fabric of dress and apron, causing sharp pains to shoot along her calves and up the full thighs to her hips and back. Clenching her white, even teeth she forced herself to remain still. Reluctant to disturb the man whose ample paunch was just touching her wide brow, and who, she knew, truly wished her well.

At last the prayer ended and she started to rise. Immedi-

11

ately his hands pressed on the crown of her head.

'Wait child, wait! We must wait in silent reverence for the Lord to answer our prayer.'

For endless minutes they remained motionless, until Tildy wanted to shout aloud to God to send his answer and allow her to ease the dreadful cramps that now twisted her hips and thighs. At last the rector's watery-blue eyes opened and gazed benevolently down at her.

'I believe that the Lord has vouchsafed to me the solution to the problem, my child,' Wren informed the girl happily, and helped her to rise slowly and painfully to her feet.

The immediate relief from cramp made her breathe a thankful sigh of gratitude, which the man took to be her reaction to his words, and he smiled.

'I cannot think why I did not arrive at this solution before, 'pon my Soul, I cannot! I shall make Thomas marry you by special license, without the banns being called. I can marry you myself in the church before two witnesses, and then obtain the bishop's dispensation afterwards at my leisure . . . There now, what d'ye say to that, child?'

He paused in happy anticipation for her delighted answer.

'Oh no!' The dismayed exclamation burst from her. 'No! I've no wish to marry Thomas!'

Wren's rounded cheeks wrinkled in perplexity.

'But why not, girl? When Thomas told me that he had offered to wed you before, and that you had refused him, I found it hard to believe the rogue. Then I put it down to girlish vapours . . . You need not be afraid that he will now refuse to wed you, for he knows well that as a justice of the peace I have the power to commit him to prison for bastardry . . . Come now, I declare that I think you to be indulging coy fancies. I really cannot understand you. I really cannot!'

Tildy Seymour made no reply, but a silent voice within her poured out a torrent of words.

'How could you understand, Phillip Wren? Born a man, and of the gentry, able to pursue whatever course you wished in life. My mother died giving birth to me, and my father followed her to the grave before I was yet three. I was raised by my father's elder sister, and her raving religious maniac husband, who regarded a smile on a child's face as a mortal sin. All I knew all my days was drudgery, glumness and Hellfire sermonizing. I never knew laughter or comfort or pleasure. Even as a child I swore that someday I would make my escape, and that I did, the day before last Michaelmas . . . '

It had been her eighteenth birthday, and seizing upon the absence of both her aunt and uncle, the girl had taken her pitifully few possessions and had fled from the isolated country cottage to the nearest town, Redditch.

When she arrived there, the first day of the Michaelmas Hiring Fair was in full swing, filling the town's streets and alleys with a roaring, laughing, haggling, drunken bustle of packed humanity. There she had joined the long lines of male and female servants offering themselves to prospective employers. She had been engaged and given the Hiring Shilling by Reverend Wren, who was accompanied by Thomas Crawford. As was the custom, the girl was then free until the following day to remain at the fair and take her pleasure.

Once Crawford had been released from duty by his master he had gone to search for the pretty new maid. Although only five years her senior in age, Crawford was immeasurably older than Tildy in experience. Flattered, confused, excited and totally out of her depth, the virgin girl had been an easy mark for the worldly-wise man.

Early the next morning, head pounding and stomach churning, still giddy from the effects of the gin and ale he had pressed upon her, she had awoken, her naked body clasped close to his on a narrow bed, in a stale-smelling room above a sleazy alehouse . . .

'Think well on what you do, girl.' The rector's voice

13

brought Tildy back to the present. 'Consider the dreadful alternatives that lie before you. If you refuse to wed the fellow, then your child will be born a bastard; and will carry that stigma like the Mark of Cain for all men to condemn until the end of its days.' The watery-blue eyes blinked rapidly and the man's voice grew troubled. 'You cannot stay beneath this roof with a bastard child in your womb . . . ' He raised his hands palms uppermost in an apologetic gesture. ' . . . If it were humanly possible, and it were left solely to me, then I would allow you to remain here. But . . . ' He shrugged helplessly. 'You have heard the opinions of the parish officers, and I fear that my lady wife is adamant that you be sent from this house . . . Really, my dear child, you have no choice in this matter. Would you be so cruel as to force the innocent soul that you carry within you, to pay for your transgressions all its days? Imagine what its life would be like if it were born in the poorhouse, or under a hedgerow, fatherless and kinless . . . Unprotected . . . Why, death would be a merciful release for the poor mite!' Wren shook his head in doleful acknowledgement of his own prognosis.

As Tildy listened, her own doubts and fears resurfaced overwhelmingly in a tide of confusion. How often during the past months had she lain sleepless in the chaff bed she shared with two other servant girls in the attic of the house, agonizing through the long dark hours on what was to become of herself and the child? During the early stages of pregnancy, when her belly was still quite flat, she had been able to push away her fears, and hope that something would occur to solve all her problems. Now, with the birth so close, her fears had become too strong to be pushed away, and too great to be buried beneath layers of deliberate forgetfullness.

'Perhaps the rector is right,' she admitted to herself. 'Perhaps I should marry Thomas Crawford? At least it would give the baby his father's name, and there would be no slur to carry on its innocence.'

Wren continued urging her to marry, and although Tildy still rejected his urgings, yet her resolve was fast weakening. In her innermost heart, she was already conceding defeat . . .

Chapter Two

'Ohhh Tom, that's lovely . . . Ohhhh Tommm.' The woman groaned the words and writhed in pleasure as she felt the man thrust deeply into her body. His hands roughly mauled her breasts, squeezing and pinching the large brown nipples. He grunted hoarsely and his teeth bit at her neck and throat, then his hands moved down to her buttocks and thighs, grasping and kneading with urgent greed. The delight the woman experienced became laced with pain and she panted into his ear, protesting weakly.

'No, Tom, no . . . Doon't hurt me, Tom . . . Goo easy!'

'Shut your rattle, you old bitch!' His voice was cruel, as cruel as the hands now frantically tearing at her body.

'No! No! Noohh!' She tried to push him off, arching her hips then jerking them back in an effort to expel his rampant maleness from inside her.

'Lie still, Goddam you! Lie still!' He gritted the words through hard-clenched teeth. 'Lie still!' His own hips pounded against the soft inner flesh of her thighs as his motions suddenly quickened. 'Lie still, you bitch! Lie still, lie still, lie still!' His clutching fingers dug deeper and deeper into her breasts and buttocks and she squealed aloud as she felt the long fingernails breaking her skin and drawing blood.

'Lie still, bitch! Lie still!' He was sobbing the words, the breath gusting in and out of his lungs in time with his plunging body.

'Oh Christ!' The woman was shrilling loudly now. 'Oh Christ no! Nooo! Youm bleeding killing me! Nooo, you bastard! Ha' done, will you! Ha' done!'

His mouth came down on hers, smothering her noise, and though she threw her head from side to side in an effort to free her lips, still the man's teeth and lips bit and clamped on hers.

A final frenzied paroxysm shook his body and then he collapsed and lay upon her, drawing long shuddering breaths through his open mouth.

'Oh Christ Almighty!' the woman moaned in complaint. 'Youm a cruel bugger, you am. I'll not bed wi' you agen, that's for sure . . . Not for a king's ransom will I bed wi' you agen.'

Thomas Crawford rolled from her and, without a word, began to gather up his clothing from its untidy pile at the side of the heap of straw, and put it on. The woman turned her head to watch him pull the fine cambric shirt over his shoulders, and retie his lacy starched cravat, while her hands gently explored the fluid-weeping weals and deep gouges his fingernails had scored on her skin. As he replaced the green and gold footman's tailcoat on his tall sinewy frame, and checked that his white silk stockings were pulled taut and tucked fully beneath the tight knee-straps of his white breeches, Crawford whistled a lively tune and did not even glance at the woman, still lying on her back in the straw.

Her mouth twisted. 'I dunno why I loves you so, Tom,' she told him indignantly. 'I must be mad, because being rogered by you is like being a bloody she-cat rogered by a

17

tom-cat.' She realized what she had said, and cackled raucously. 'Theer now, that's a good thing I just said, warn't it? That was a joke that was . . . Tom Cat, Tom Crawford!'

For the first time since their congress he looked directly at the woman. His face was handsome, swarthy-complexioned with short-cut black hair and long sideboards twisted up below the cheekbones in carefully clipped vanity curls. But there was weakness in the puffy mouth, and a shiftiness about the black eyes. He chuckled appreciatively.

'You're right in what you say, Poll. That's a good joke, that is.'

His gaze roamed over the pendulous breasts, big-paunched belly, and flaccid, blotched thighs dominated by the bushy triangle of grey hair.

'God strike me!' he swore silently under his breath. 'What possesses me to block this old hag, I'll be buggered if I can tell. She must be fifty, if she's a day.' Aloud he said lightly, 'Now don't you get all fired up at me, Poll, my love. I knows I'm a bit rough in the rogering, but it's just that you gets me so bloody excited. I gets carried away wi' the loving feelings I holds for you.'

She came to her knees, her long grey hair tumbling in matted swathes about her face and shoulders, and reached for him.

'Come here then, sweetheart,' she begged eagerly. 'Let's have some kisses from you afore you go.'

He fended off her seeking fingers and laughed gaily.

'You get away now, Poll. I'll see you next week, that's a promise . . . Get away now!' He slapped hard at her hands as they clutched for him again.

A flush of annoyance mottled her weather-beaten skin.

'That's right! That's you all over that is, Tom Crawford. You'se had what you wanted and now youm off like a bloody stoat running from the keeper . . . It 'ud serve you right iffen I opened my mouth in the village about what goes on between us.'

He forced another laugh, but this time it held a note of tension.

'Don't talk so bloody silly, you old cow!' The note of tension deepened into threat. 'You'll not tell anyone about us, that I know . . . And you knows well that I have to get back sharp to the rectory, or Mother Wren will be ranting and raving at me for the rest of the week.'

'Goo on then, and bollocks to you! You'll get no more of what's between my legs,' the woman cursed, before slumping back into the straw, muttering aggrievedly to herself.

The young man was happy to make his escape without further argument, and quickly left the tumbledown shed, which stood by itself in a corner of the fields surrounding the scattered hamlet of Ipsley.

He strolled along the straight narrow lane known as the Icknield Way, upon which the metalled sandals of the Roman Legions had once echoed. He breathed deeply of the clean, fresh-scented spring air, happy to rid his nostrils of the lingering, ruttish smell that Poll carried impregnated in her skin.

A mile or so ahead to his left he could see the squat square tower of the Ipsley church crouching behind the bright new foliage of the oaks and elms that surrounded both it and the three-storied Ipsley Court, home of the poetic Landor family, on the low hill. Over on his right, at the same distance and some hundred odd yards east of the church, stood the old rectory, its small clock-tower perching on its ancient gables.

Thomas Crawford smiled as he strolled. He was contented here at Ipsley. He enjoyed wearing the livery and riding on the seat of his master's carriage, lording it over the poor farm labourers in their work-stained smocks and bully-cock hats who comprised the greater portion of the parishioners.

Of course, Ipsley parish extended as far as Redditch town some two miles to the westward, and even took some areas of that rumbustious settlement with its savage-fighting needle-pointers into its boundary. Thomas took care not to go to the town too often in search of his pleasures. He knew well that he could easily become a butt for the fierce pointer-lads, and although he was not averse to a fight, he had no wish to tackle those wild men. He could find his pleasures far more safely in the hedgeside drinking dens and willing arms of local drabs closer to the rectory.

His chest swelled, straining against the lacings of his shirt and waistcoat buttons.

'God strike me! I did the right thing when I left the bloody Sidemoor,' he told himself. For a brief moment he dwelt on his youth and childhood in that district of the Parish of Bromsgrove, some twelve miles or more to the south-west, where the only trade for man, woman or child to follow was that of making nails by hand . . . 'God strike me! I'm well out of that bloody hellhole.'

In fact as he reviewed his present existence there was only one cloud in the clear sky of his happiness . . . Tildy Seymour!

It wasn't her pregnancy that bothered Crawford. It was the fact that since the night he had made her helpless with drink and seduced her, he had not been able to make love to her again. Henceforth, she had repulsed his advances, thrown back at his head his gifts of ribbons and sweetmeats, and rejected out of hand any suggestion that they walk out together.

The black eyes narrowed angrily as Crawford re-visualized the memory of the way her body had looked, with the wavering light of the candle bathing the proud thrusting breasts and flowing lines of the richly rounded hips and thighs. His fingers had been shaking and he had hardly been able to restrain himself as he drew the clothes from her, while she lay semi-conscious, not really knowing what was happening to her . . . . Even today, tired from lovemaking with Poll, Crawford's breathing quickened and his mouth grew dry with lust as he re-lived the moments of possession of Tildy's beautiful body.

'God strike me, but she was a lovely piece!' he muttered aloud. 'And still is, even carrying that babby. The next morning was a bugger, though . . .'

He had been lying in the bed with her slender, yet full-breasted body held tightly to him. Tildy had woken and stirred. Instantly, the feel of that satin-soft skin moving against his own had made him ready to enter the girl again. But Tildy had not allowed him the opportunity. She had stared with wide eyes, first at him, and then at her own nudity. The soft brown eyes had filled with tears, but the gentle, red-lipped mouth had tightened in fury. Without a word she had dashed her tears from her eyes and twisted free of his arms. Before he could fully comprehend what was happening she was dressed and gone; and the next time he had seen her she was already at work in the rectory. He shook his head regretfully.

'And never a touch, or kiss, or smile have I got from the little bitch since.'

When the footman reached the rectory, he was told that the master wished to speak with him in the study. Thomas wasn't perturbed by the summons, he had already admitted to the rector that the expected baby was almost certainly his, and had intimated his readiness to marry the girl. After all, she was a sweet-tasting wench, and it was time he took a wife to share his bed. A compliant Tildy would be a joy in the night, with her long hair strewn across the pillow and her soft body trembling beneath him . . .

'Ah, there you are, Thomas, you'll no doubt have guessed why I wish to speak with you.'

Phillip Wren, who was alone in his study to receive the man, removed his spectacles as he spoke. He took the scrap of cloth from his pocket and nervously began to polish the lenses in an effort to distract himself from the unhappy feeling that he was somehow doing wrong in pressuring the girl into marrying the man standing before him.

Crawford nodded respectfully. 'Yes sir, I would think it to be about Tildy Seymour, sir. I've already said that I'm willing to church the wench, sir, and to give the babby my name.'

The rector's head bobbed in acknowledgement of the words.

'Quite so, Thomas, quite so; and your sentiments do you credit. I know that the girl indulged herself with silly vapourings previously, but now . . . er . . . I'm happy, . . . er . . . happy to say that she has seen reason. Yes, that's the word, reason. Now let me see, today is Thursday, is it not . . . er, yes . . . Thursday!

'I shall perform the ceremony tomorrow morning at nine o'clock in the church. Mrs Emmot and the gardener shall act as witnesses . . . That is all, Thomas, please be about your duties.'

The young man turned and left the room, his mind only now fully absorbing what the rector's words meant.

'God strike me! This time tomorrow I'll be a married man, wi' a child on the way.'

It was something of a shock for Thomas Crawford to realize that he was now definitely committed to marrying Tildy Seymour; and he found that he was anticipating it with pleasure.

In the great stone-flagged kitchen at the rear of the rambling house Tildy was sitting on a low stool, a large earthenware bowl on the ground before her, into which she sliced the parsnips that she was peeling. Facing her on another stool, busy at the same occupation, was Mrs Emmot, the fat, motherly-faced cook. Tildy glanced about her and took pleasure in the orderly domestic scene. The vast brick and iron range covered with cooking pots and pans, simmering and bubbling with savoury-smelling messes. The tall, many-shelved dresser and its rows of shining willow-pattern plates. The hanging bunches and strings of dried herbs and onions, and the cured hams and sides of bacon hooked to the thick black beams of the ceiling. The scrubbed cleanliness of the sanded stone floor, the tables, the chairs and the cloths airing by the range fire. Even the sounds of splashing and the high-pitched singing of young Aggie, the scullery-maid who was scouring utensils with ash and soft soap in the alcove where the water sinks stood, added to the harmony of the big room. Tildy smiled, thinking how happy she had been in this old house, despite her troubles, and the cook, peeping from beneath the broad floppy brim of her capacious mobcap, smiled also.

'Be you looking forrard to tomorrow then, Tildy?' she asked in her broad Warwickshire drawl.

Tildy's smile died and she shook her head at the other woman.

'Not really, Mrs Emmot, for he's not the type of man I would have taken for husband, if I had had freedom to choose.'

The fat woman's small eyes twinkled kindly and she chuckled from deep in her vast chest.

'That may be so, my chuck, but then, iffen us poor females had any freedom to choose I'll warrant that none on us would stay married to the same husband for more than a year at the outside . . . I knows that when Emmot died I followed his coffin to the burial yard wi' a song in my heart; and it warn't one o' they dirges neither.' She chuckled as she finished the sentence, and the fat dewlaps of her cheeks trembled in unison. Then she leered in mock lasciviousness. 'Mind you, my chuck, I don't doubt but that your man 'ull prove to be a real ram in the bed. By all accounts he's powerful fond o' woman-flesh. You'll know some joy o' nights, I shouldn't wonder, as you've done already I'll be bound.'

Tildy smiled at the remark, knowing that there was no malice behind the elder woman's words.

'You may not believe this, Mrs Emmot, but even though I'm carrying a child, I've yet to know properly what it is to lie with a man,' she stated quietly.

The fat woman's mouth gaped in a delighted cackle of protest.

'You'm pulling my old leg, my chuck, to be sure you be,' and again she chuckled richly. 'I reckon that you and that Thomas o' yourn has made the old bed to crack and creak so loud that you've been afeared it were going to break in half. Ahr, and more nor once as well!'

Tildy mentally shrugged, knowing that it was pointless to continue her denials of knowledge of a man's loving. With some bitterness she thought about what the cook had said.

Who could be expected to believe that a woman nigh on eight months pregnant couldn't even remember the moments that made her so, she ruminated. All I knew was the pain and torment next morning, and the sore places on my skin where his teeth had marked me . . . Mayhap I'll come to know joy in my bed, if so that will be something to the good. Her hand went to her swollen belly as she felt the child kick within her. But what I do, I do for you, my poor little soul . . .

'Where be you going to live when youm wed, Tildy? Did the Master say you could stop here . . . Ha' one o' the attics to sleep in like?'

The girl shook her glossy capless head, the hair neatly bound in coiled plaits.

'I don't know, Mrs Emmot, all the Master has told me is that everything shall be arranged for the best; and since I began showing the Mistress won't even look at me, let alone speak, so I've heard nothing from her. Why, she won't even let me near her. I feel sometimes that I'm a carrier of the plague.'

'Sod her!' The cook jerked her fingers in a lewd gesture. 'That's what I says to that spiteful cat. She arn't fit to lick the reverend's shoes, ne'er mind be wife to him, mealy-mouthed, pious hypocrite that she is. The curd-faced besom 'ud turn the milk sour as it run sweet from the cow, so she 'ud.'

The tirade was cut short by the appearance of Thomas, who closed the door opening from the passageway behind him and stood staring at the women, a triumphant smile curling his lips.

'Now arn't that a pretty sight!' he observed jocularly. 'My little wife-to-be busy getting me vittles all ready for me dinner.'

He crossed to where Tildy was sitting and cupped her chin with one hand. Roughly tilting her face upwards, he bent to kiss her.

She turned her head so that his lips could only find her cheek, then pushed his restraining hand down and resumed work. A spark of quick temper flared in his eyes and the smile on his mouth faltered. He glowered at her bent head, and snapped at her.

'Ne'er mind, my pretty love, I can wait 'til tomorrow for your kisses. Once we're wed you'll not refuse me them, I'll swear to that!'

Mrs Emmot, sensitive to the dangerous tension of the situation, tried to dispel it.

'Now Thomas, youm too impatient. A girl's got a right to act a bit contrary on the day afore she's wed. It's a worrisome time for her. She's concerned about her future days . . . ' The cook left the sentence hanging, hoping that the man would satisfy her curiosity as to what was to happen to the couple after the marriage. When he made no move to do so, she questioned him openly. 'What's to happen arter youm wed, Thomas? Do you stay here, or move elsewhere?'

With a shock of surprise Crawford realized that it had not even occurred to him that there might be any change of work or dwelling place. He had assumed unconsciously that he would continue in service to the Wrens, the only difference being that Tildy would be sharing his bed. Now the disquieting possibility that this pleasant and easy existence might change suddenly loomed to confront him.

'Does you know, Mrs Emmot, I never even considered

that I might ha' to leave here,' he answered, a slight frown of anxiety furrowing the smooth skin of his brow. 'You don't reckon the Master 'ull tell me to find another situation when I'm wed, does you?' he asked, seeking reassurance.

The fat woman regarded him shrewdly, realizing that the prospect dismayed him; and then, because she was not over-fond of this young man, replied in doubtful tones.

'Well, that's hard to say, Thomas. You knows well that not many o' the gentry likes to keep married servants. 'Specially iffen they's got a child wi' 'um. Might be alright for the farmhands and keepers and suchlike, but not for the house . . . Oh, I don't reckon the Master 'ud willingly ha' you leave here, Thomas. But then, we all knows that it arn't him who calls the tune in this house, don't we? It's that besom-bitch the Mistress, and you knows well how nasty her can be, don't you, Thomas?'

Her head cocked to one side, the cook's small eyes mirrored the satisfaction she felt at the obvious effect her barbed words were having on the man. She twisted the verbal knife a little more.

'She's as like to tell you to goo, as she is to spit, just for badness. Damn her hard heart!'

'God strike me!' Crawford felt a sense of real dread constrict his throat. 'God strike me! I hope she don't send me away. I'm buggered iffen I know what I'd turn to, if she did.'

Chapter Three

The brittle chaff rustled loudly as young Aggie tossed restlessly upon the mattress. The air in the tiny attic room was fuggy and stale and Tildy, lying on her back staring at the small square of moonlit sky dimly visible through the distorted glass of the skylight, wished desperately that she could for once lie alone. Dorothy, the elderly maid-of-all-work who slept between the other two, began to snore through her open mouth, and Tildy grimaced into the darkness.

'Dear God, let me sleep,' she pleaded silently.

'Be you awake, Tildy?' Young Aggie's sibilant whisper startled her, for she had thought the younger girl was asleep. 'Tildy, be you sleeping?'

For a moment Tildy debated the possibility of pretending that she was, but the need for some relief from the burden of her thoughts about her coming wedding drove her to reply.

'No, I'm not. What do you want?'

'How does you feel? Be you nervous?' Aggie's voice throbbed with curiosity.

In Tildy's mind an imp of mischief stirred, and to tease the other girl, who was not yet fourteen years old, she asked in reply, 'Nervous about what, Aggie?'

There was a pause, as the youngster searched for the words that would put the question she was burning to ask, without giving offence.

'Well, I mean . . . Be you thinking about tomorrow night? I mean, you'll not be sharing the bed along wi' us then, will you, Tildy? You'll be spending the whole night through wi' a husband instead . . . You'll not be spending it wi' us, will you?'

The elder girl smiled, amused. 'No, I don't think I shall be, Aggie. At least, not unless we can make room in here for Thomas Crawford as well as we three.'

Between the pair, old Dorothy grunted and stirred, mumbling a snatch of unintelligible speech.

'There now,' Tildy whispered jokingly. 'Just hearing about the chance of a man sharing her bed has excited Dot.'

Aggie giggled in delight, and then said, 'Well now, truth to tell, it 'ud excite me iffen I was to be wed tomorrow . . .' She giggled again and half-nervously questioned, 'What's it like, Tildy? What's it feel like? You know . . . When you lies wi' a man? What's it really like?'

The urgent whispers aroused memories for Tildy of how she had been consumed by similar avid curiosity while listening to the creaking of the leather-sprung bed which her aunt and uncle shared, and the panting, grunting, moaning utterances, the thrashing of heaving bodies, and the sobs of pain and pleasure that had filled so many hours of darkness in the single bedroom they had shared throughout her childhood in the isolated cottage.

Almost to herself Tildy replied, 'I should think that if a man and a woman had love for each other, then it could be a wonderful experience to share . . . ' She fell silent, remembering how, on the days after the noises of the night, her uncle would rant for hours in frenzied prayer, upbraid-

28

ing his wife for the wicked temptations of her body, and begging for God's forgiveness for his own weakness in succumbing to those same temptations. Tildy would peep through her fingers, frightened by the rabid features of her raving uncle, and puzzled by the weary resignation demonstrated in the drooping posture of her sad-faced aunt.

'Could it really be so wicked as her uncle claimed?' the child had wondered, 'when on so many occasions he seemed to be the one who awoke her aunt and pressed himself upon her?'

'Was it wonderful for you and Tom Crawford, Tildy? was it?' Aggie persisted.

Sensing the real need for reassurance that the girl felt beneath the façade of prurient inquisitiveness, Tildy lied to her.

'Yes, it was so. Now go to sleep, chuck, it's very late.'

The chaff rustled loudly in the darkness as Aggie settled herself comfortably, and soon the regular heaviness of her breathing showed that she slept.

Tildy's hands moved caressingly across the warm mound in which her child lay peacefully still, and then gently touched her breasts, swollen now in readiness to comfort and suckle. Drowsily, she considered the prospect of ever feeling aroused by a man's need, and felt cheated because she never had been so.

'Mayhap after I've had my baby, then things will change. I don't want to marry Thomas Crawford, and I've no love and little liking for him, but I'll try to make him a good wife. If he is kind to me and the baby, then in turn I shall be kind to him . . .'

'And if he is cruel to you?' It seemed as if an alien voice was penetrating her consciousness. 'What then, Tildy? What if he is cruel to you and the baby? What will you do then?'

She drifted into sleep leaving the question unanswered.

Chapter Four

The tiny procession approached the church with none of the loud and visible joy that usually accompanies the happy event of a marriage. There were no groom's men, bedecked with shoulder knots of bright ribbons. No bride's maidens with posies of fresh-plucked, sweet-smelling flowers. No fifer or fiddler prancing in front playing a lilting march with a capering drummer beside him to beat out the rhythm. No families laughing and shouting ribaldries as they met together to celebrate and feast. There was only the Reverend Phillip Wren, wearing his plainest surplice and cassock, leading the betrothed couple. At the rear, the heavily puffing Mrs Emmot wrapped in a voluminous cloak, her cheeks a shiny red centrepiece to the huge wings of her bonnet, accompanied the skinny-shanked, mournful-faced gardener, still wearing the blue oversleeves and apron of his trade, his boots muddied and a huge dewdrop trembling from the tip of his long nose.

Tildy wore her Sunday dress, a high-waisted, unadorned grey gown, and a black shawl about her shoulders. She carried neither posy nor Bible and the only frivolous note in her appearance was the froth of lace trimmings about the brim of the blue poke bonnet that Mrs Emmot had pressed upon her that morning as a wedding gift. Walking grave-featured at Tildy's side, Thomas Crawford had made some attempt to display an elegant turnout, with his light green cutaway coat, scarlet waistcoat, blue pantaloons tucked into a battered pair of hessian boots, and a high stock set off by a polka-dotted cravat. In his hands he carried a pair of white cotton gloves and a crescent-brimmed, low-crowned beaver hat.

No words were exchanged as the procession entered the churchyard, and indeed it seemed that even the exchange of glances was to be avoided. The day was grey and drizzly, and the interior of the small church darkly chill and damp.

For Tildy the marriage service passed in a meaningless blur, and she uttered the responses without conscious volition. Her only sharp impressions were the sobs of Mrs Emmot, who had made great inroads into a bottle of gin before breakfast, and the taste of ale and tobacco on Thomas Crawford's breath as he kissed her lightly to seal the wedding troth.

The Marriage Register was placed on a small table to the side of the choristers' stalls and the scratching of the quill pen across the yellowish vellum page as the rector filled in the details of the ceremony irritated Tildy's strained nerves. When Reverend Wren passed the quill to her and invited her to sign, she stood staring blindly at the page beneath her, and for the first time that morning felt an urge to weep. Because of the projecting rim of her bonnet neither Thomas Crawford at her side, nor either of the witnesses could see Tildy's face, but Phillip Wren was directly in front of her and with his customary sensitivity realized instantly what was the matter.

'There, my dear child, just put a cross there.' His soft white hand moved across the page and one manicured fingernail made a tiny indent upon the spot.

Tildy felt a terrible shame for her ignorance, and a rush of hot blood to her head caused the skin of her face and neck to blush with mortified embarrassment. Through a blur of unshed tears she scratched a small cross, and the rector gently took the quill from her fingers to write beneath the sign: 'Matilda Seymour, her true mark.'

Thomas too was unable to write his name, but he seemed unmoved by the fact and with bravado took the quill and made a huge cross complete with curved over ends.

Perversely the fact that her husband was also shown to be illiterate did not ease Tildy's own sense of inferiority, but only caused her to inwardly lament for her child that was to be born without even one parent capable of writing their name.

Mrs Emmot could write, however, and she signed with great panache, smiling with more than a hint of smugness as she did so.

The elderly gardener, his dewdrop dangling perilously elongated and with his tongue jutting far out of the corner of his mouth, took almost three full minutes to laboriously inscribe his signature. In the silence of the church the seconds progressed with an agonizing slowness, and a concerted sigh of relief greeted the final laying down of the quill from his peat-stained fingers.

'There now, it is done.' Behind the square lenses of his spectacles the rector's eyes regarded Tildy with anxious interest. She forced herself to smile at him, and with a sinking heart re-echoed his words in her mind.

'Yes, it is done . . . God help me!'

There was no wedding breakfast waiting for the newly-weds. Instead the rector despatched the cook and gardener to their work and took Thomas and Matilda into his study. Unhappy at his own weakness in allowing himself to be forced to act in this manner by his wife and the others, Phillip Wren took refuge in an attitude of businesslike brusqueness.

'You are now man and wife,' he stated, as he stood with his back to the room, staring out of his study window at the lushly fertile countryside. 'And Praised be the Lord, your child shall carry no slur upon its head.' He paused and glanced over his shoulder at the young man and woman waiting for him to continue. Their obvious apprehension fuelled his feelings of guilt and increased his irritation. He coughed noisily to clear his throat and turned to face them.

'I'll not beat about the bushes with you, Thomas,' he spoke directly to Crawford. 'I must tell you, that now you are wed, I can no longer retain you in my service.'

Dismay twisted the footman's mouth. 'But I don't understand, sir,' he began. 'Why cannot you . . .'

'Hold your tongue, man!' In his urgent need to have what he found to be personally painful said, Wren was behaving with a cruelty that was alien to his nature.

'I intend to pay you both a full year's wages, and further to that I shall be happy to supply references as to your good character while in my service, to any prospective employer . . .' Behind the square-rimmed lenses the rector's eyes were deeply unhappy, and even while he mouthed the words he felt a mounting shame about his cowardly surrender to the dictates of his wife and the parish officers. 'It's not I who wants to dismiss you in this manner!' he finally cried aloud. 'But I've no choice! No choice at all . . .' He shook his head in a helpless gesture. 'My lady wife insists that I send you both away from here. And the churchwardens side with her. What else can I do?' His voice trailed into silence.

For Tildy this dismissal had been half-expected, not because of any prior knowledge or experience, but because of an inner certitude that her troubles were not to be so easily dealt with by the performance of a ceremony.

For Thomas Crawford, however, dismissal came as a tremendous shock. Even though Mrs Emmot had raised the possibility of it occurring, his mind had refused to consider it for more than a brief instant. He could only stand and stare at the rector, and feel that he was being grievously wronged by the man. His long-buried gutter-devil roused within him.

'God strike me!' he burst out angrily. 'Don't you prate to me of choice, Master! You gave me little or none about getting wed! You could keep me in your service if you so wished, youm the master here not the bloody church-wardens! Or your damned wife!'

Wren blinked in surprise at his normally submissive servant, and in his turn felt that *he* was being wronged.

'How dare you address me in such a manner, Crawford?' he demanded indignantly. 'You forget yourself, my man.'

Crawford's temper was fully roused now, and he plunged on recklessly. 'Oh no, Master! T'isn't me as is forgetting hisself, but you! You stands up in that pulpit and mews out all that bloody rubbish about loving thy fellow man, and then you turns around and serves ill them that depends on your kindness. Youm a sodding old hypocrite, so you be! A sodding hypocrite! Youm as bad as that miserable old sow you calls wife!'

The rector's pink complexion drained to a chalky white-ness. Striding to the door of his study he flung it open and bellowed: 'DANIELLL! Goddam and blast you, Daniel, get here to me this instant . . . This instant, sir!'

The small houseboy came rushing to his master.

'DANIEL!' The rector roared down at the child. 'Run to the cornmill and fetch the constable up here. Tell him to come this very instant! Go on, boy, do as I bid you, Damn your hide!'

The child scurried away, and Wren stalked back into the room.

Thomas Crawford's temper still seethed, but anger was now being rapidly overlaid by apprehension. If the rector had sent for the constable, then he, Crawford, could well be in serious trouble. He started to falter out words of apology, but Wren waved him to silence.

'I've no wish to hear you, man. You'd best bite on your tongue, for it's done you harm enough already this day. When the constable arrives I intend to have you put in the stocks for your insolence, be damned if I don't. Such behaviour from inferiors is not to be borne by their betters.'

Thomas Crawford lapsed into silent misery and, standing by his side, Tildy felt fear clutch at her throat.

'Oh Dear God!' she uttered inwardly. 'Dear God, what is to happen now?'

Once again that morning a tiny procession was passing along by the church, following the track known as the Watery Lane. This time it was led by Edward Ashwin, the grim-featured, bulky-bodied constable. He was still clad in the flour-dusted smock and apron he had been wearing when summoned from the mill, and his bald head was covered by a kerchief knotted at its four corners. In his right hand he carried the long ash staff topped by the wooden crown that denoted his office of parish constable. In his left hand was one end of a short rope, the other end of which was fashioned into a slack noose around the neck of Thomas Crawford, whose own hands were manacled together behind his back.

Tildy followed the two men along the lane, which was thickly lined and overhung with hawthorn bushes carrying the white and pink blossoms of springtime. Small birds fluttered and whistled in the hedge branches, but the sweetness of their song was all but blotted out by the harsh cawing of the crows that nested in dense colonies upon the tops of the tall trees around the church. In Tildy's fancy, made macabre by what was happening, the great black birds were mocking her on this her wedding day, and hurling their hoarse cries at the bound prisoner in exultation at his ill-fortune.

The party crossed the fast-flowing River Arrow by means of a wooden bridge that flanked the brick water-

35

courses and sluice-gates of the ancient Ipsley Mill, then turning to the west began the ascent of the long sloping hill that led into Redditch Town, some mile and a half distant.

'Why be you taking me up there?' Thomas questioned nervously.

The constable didn't look at his prisoner, and merely grunted.

'Because . . .'

'Because what?' Crawford's nervousness was increasing.

'Because I've an errand to do in Redditch.' Ashwin relented sufficiently to explain. 'And them stocks next to the Horse and Jockey public house, lie in the boundary of our parish, so it's alright for me to use 'um.'

'But I could get me head smashed by them sods up there,' Crawford protested fearfully. 'There's other stocks on the bottom road to Studley village, you could put me into them. It's quiet down there at this hour o' the morning.'

For the first time during the journey Ashwin looked directly at the other man, and his grim face held contempt.

'Doon't piss your breeks, man!' he exclaimed scornfully. 'It 'ull be quiet enough up here. Most folks will be at their work now.'

Crawford's fears drove him to argue further. 'You'se got no right to lock me in the stocks, anyway. The rector's got no right neither.'

'Oh, arn't he now?' Ashwin grinned mirthlessly. 'And who d'you think is going to say him nay in this parish? And for your information, my bucko, the Reverend Wren is a justice o' the peace, and he can do whatsoever he sees fit to, with the likes o' you. Youm only his bloody serving man, and don't you forget it.'

'Not now, I'm not!' Crawford insisted doggedly.

The constable nodded positively. 'Oh yes you be, Tom Crawford.' He tapped a small lump in his apron-fold, which emitted a dull chink of metal. 'Theer's you and your missus's wages 'til next Michaelmas in theer. The reverend's told me that I'm to gi' you that, together wi' your dismissal, when I sets you free from the stocks. And until I does that, then youm still in his service.'

Tildy was finding the long climb increasingly difficult, her breathing was harsh and ragged, and a stitch pained her side. She paid little heed to the exchanges between the men, but only concentrated on keeping her balance on the rough surface of the road. They reached a cluster of cottages set about a small inn and Tildy stared about her, apprehensively searching for the stocks.

Ashwin halted to give the girl a chance to catch her breath and said, not unsympathetically, 'This here's the Kings Arms, young 'ooman, the stocks be nigh on three hundred yards further up the way theer.' He pointed directly ahead with his staff tip.

Tildy looked in the direction indicated. On both sides of the long straight slope she saw cottages, houses and the raw-red brickwork of some of the many new needle mills that were being constructed all over the district as the needle trade flourished and expanded.

'It might be best for you to wait by here, young 'ooman,' the constable went on to advise her. 'Your man is to be kept four hours in the stocks, and I don't reckon you'd enjoy seeing him pelted wi' rubbish and slops by the young varmints about here. So why doon't you goo across and sit in the alehouse yonder, and have yourself a cup o' beer, and a bite to eat. I'll let your man free the minute he's done the time, don't you moither yourself about that. Then he can come for you . . . Here . . . ' He rummaged in the folds of his short apron and pulled out a small cloth bag which he pressed into her hand. 'Theer's the money owing to you from the reverend, and here's the reckoning on it.' From the same apron-fold he produced a scrap of paper covered with the spidery crawl of the rector's writing. 'Just check that it's all correct, 'ull you, my wench?'

Tildy shook her head. 'I cannot . . . I haven't the reading,' she told the constable, and again felt the shame of her lack of knowledge.

The man grinned, but this time with some degree of kindness. 'I don't scan too well meself, my wench, but I'll try me best.' He peered at the paper and falteringly read out. 'One year's wages to Thomas Crawford . . . Four pun, four shillin's . . . To Thomas Crawford for dressing my wigs for one year, ten shillins . . . One year's wages to Matilda Seymour, now Crawford . . . Two pun and sixpence . . . ' The constable screwed up his eyes with the mental strain of adding the sums of money. 'Well, to my reckoning that's six pun, fowerteen shillins and sixpence you've got in that little bag, and that's a tidy enough sum. You can afford to sit in the Kings Arms and take your pleasure all week, if you've a mind to.'

'She'll not sit nowhere taking her pleasure like a bloody doxy while I'm bloody suffering in the stocks!'

Thomas Crawford's indignation at the other man's suggestion had momentarily driven out his fear of the coming ordeal, and now his swarthy face was dark with temper.

'She'll stay by me, and do her damndest to stop the bastards astoning me, that's what she'll do . . . And I'll thank you to stop giving your advice to my wife, Edward Ashwin.'

The constable shrugged his heavy shoulders. 'Well, my wench, you must suit yourself. But I know what I'd want my wife to do, if I was in the stocks . . . And that 'ud be to keep well away.'

He turned towards the town and jerked hard on the rope, causing the noose to burn hotly against the skin of his prisoner's neck. 'Come on you, the sooner I gets you in 'um, the sooner you gets out on 'um.'

By the time they reached the stocks a small crowd accompanied them, and stood watching with eager interest while the constable clamped and padlocked Thomas Crawford's ankles in the rounded holes of the split-planks, and freed his arms from the manacles.

'What's he done, Master Ashwin?' Quiney, the sallow-complexioned landlord of the Horse and Jockey wanted to know.

The constable did not answer straight away. He tugged on the hasp of the lock and double-checked that Crawford was securely held at the ankles, then went over to the landlord, who was standing outside the entrance of the small half-timbered inn.

'Just between you, me and the gatepost, Master Quiney, the cove's done little enough. He's the Reverend Wren's servant, and him and the reverend had a bit of a dispute.'

'How long's he to stay for?' Quiney was already computing how much extra trade this unlooked-for happening might bring him. It was thirsty work baiting a man in the stocks, and people were always glad of a drink after an hour or so spent doing it.

'Four hours,' Ashwin told him.

The landlord grinned happily and rubbed his hands.

'Should make a nice bit o' profit for you, Master Quiney.' The constable nudged the other man with his elbow. 'And I'm thinking you'll not be ungrateful to a man as was thoughtful enough to use these stocks here, instead of one of the other places.'

Quiney winked knowingly. 'Would you care to step inside, Master Ashwin. I've a keg of finest Geneva, which I fresh broached this morning.'

The two men disappeared into the inn, leaving the disconsolate captive to the tender mercies of the rapidly increasing crowd.

Tildy stood with her back to the side wall of the inn, some eighteen yards from the stocks, which were set in a clear space on the Ipsley parish side of the roadway, and took in the scene before her with frightened eyes.

Her husband was sat, arms folded and shoulders slumped dejectedly, his crescent-brimmed hat drawn low on his forehead and his head bent forward so that this face was all but hidden from view. Across the road, almost directly opposite the stocks, was a large pool, green-scummed, evil-smelling and stagnant. Its surface covered with refuse, human excreta and several gas-ballooned corpses of dogs, cats and rats. Terraces of mean cottages and workshops backed onto the pool and more terraces, alehouses and shops led westwards up a slight incline towards the town Green and chapel of Saint Stephen, its low cupola just visible through the gaps in the crooked-gabled roofs of the intervening buildings.

The composition of the crowd was fast changing. At first it had been mostly ragged, barefoot urchins with one or two old men, shawled crones and the odd lounger. Now others were hurrying to join them from the town's alleys and courts. Neatly-clad, basket-carrying housewives, and respectable artisans hefting bags of tools. Shopkeepers, and clerks with inky fingers. A man carrying a great hammer and wearing the chest-and-thigh-covering fringed leather apron of a blacksmith. A trio of young bloods reined in their mounts, adding a touch of elegance to the gathering with their fine grey hunting coats, high-crowned broad-peaked caps and highly polished riding boots. More women came, some with hands and arms still sudded and wet from the wash. More men, grimy from work. The crowd spread out and pushed inwards until they formed a circle some ten yards in diameter around the captive man.

To begin with they were content to merely ask jeering questions, and vent jibes and catcalls. Requesting Thomas Crawford to tell them if he was comfortable? Did he need a cushion for his backside? Would he care to take a glass of ale, or sup of wine? Was he there for killing a mouse, or having sexual connection with a rooster?

Some of the bolder children, laughing and excited by their own temerity, amused themselves by prancing almost to within touching distance of the prisoner and putting out their tongues, or chanting and wriggling their whole bodies in derision before scampering back into the safety of the crowd. Then another group of men appeared on the scene, and Tildy drew her breath in sharply as she saw them, and muttered a prayer.

'Dear God, let them not be drunk!'

This new group had come from the nearest needle mill, and wore sleeveless leather jerkins, rolled up aprons and square hats fashioned from thick brown paper. They were needle-pointers, the most savage element of the town's notoriously savage community. Men whose work, the dry-grinding of needles by hand, killed them within ten years as the inhaled dust of stone and steel tore their lungs to shreds. Knowing that they were doomed to an early and hideous death the pointers gave full rein to every animal instinct that they possessed, and were feared by all men. Tildy felt her own fear increase as she stared at them, and in her heart called on God for help.

Yet it was not a pointer, but a fresh-faced, clean-aproned housewife, who hurled the first missile. A rotten egg which smashed on the crown of Thomas Crawford's hat and left a glutinous mess of greenish-yellow yolk sliding down the crescent brim. The captive cried out in fright and lifted both arms to shield his head.

'You windy bugger!' A huge-framed, gap-toothed pointer bellowed in derision at the gesture of self-defence as a storm of jeering cheers burst from the crowd to acclaim the woman's aim. Tildy's heart pounded against her chest wall, and she also lifted her hands to cover her face, as if she could make her husband's ordeal disappear by blotting it from her sight. The child within her moved and kicked viciously and for a fleeting instant the young girl imagined that her own dread had communicated itself to the baby, and it was seeing what was occurring through her eyes.

Now rotting vegetables and more bad eggs found their mark, staining and sliming Thomas Crawford's wedding finery. A young pointer dashed through the barrage of missiles and jerked the hat from the prisoner's head.

41

'That's better, that is,' the pointer laughed to the crowd. 'We con see the bugger's yed now, that's a better mark to aim for.'

With a sweep of his arm he sent the hat sailing over the heads of the crowd and it swooped to splash into the green-scummed pool. Another roar of jeering applause greeting his action.

Made wild by terror, Thomas Crawford lifted his head and, shaking both fists at his tormentors, howled like a mad-man. 'I'll kill you! I'll kill you all, you bastards! God strike me, I'll kill you!'

They howled back their delight at his outburst, and dead cats and rats were promptly fished from the stagnant pool to be hurled at the man in the stocks. A swollen furry body exploded against Crawford's neck and chin, and the foul stench from its poisonous entrails caused him to retch and choke as he scrabbled with desperate fingers to claw it away.

The first stone came hurtling through the air and struck the edge of his cheekbone above the jaunty curl of side-whisker, gouging a small but deep cut. The bright red blood spurted, and at the sight of it the crowd's jeering became a deeper-pitched, menacing baying as the atavistic bloodlust took hold of them.

'That's it, lads!' a pointer exhorted. 'Let's spill his bloody claret for him, the flash bugger!'

'No! No! No!' Tildy saw the blood and her fear was over-ridden by a sudden fierce anger. 'That's my baby's father they're trying to hurt! That's my baby's father!' She spoke to herself, as if she had discovered the fact at that very moment. 'That's my baby's father, and if they're not stopped, they'll kill him!'

More stones were joining the volleys of rotten veget-ables, dead rats and human excreta, and Crawford twisted his body and ducked his head in a frantic attempt to escape the painful impacts. Tildy's fury blazed at white-heat, and she ran into the inn. She found Ashwin and the landlord standing together, sipping full glasses of gin, and laughing at the scene through the leaded bay windows of the low-ceilinged bar-parlour. Both men turned at her noisy entrance, and to Ashwin's credit he had sufficient delicacy to take the pleasurable smile from his face.

'My oath, young 'ooman, I never thought you was still about here!' he exclaimed. 'Why in all creation, didn't you do what I said, and goo and wait down at the King's Arms?'

The young girl ignored his words. 'Will you stop those beasts out there, Master Ashwin? Will you stop them afore they kills my husband? They're like loonies from Bedlam, so they are! They'll kill him if they're not stopped!'

Troubled by her distraught manner the man hesitated before replying, seeking for words to soothe her.

'Will you stop them?' Her voice rose to a higher pitch, and tears of rage and distress brimmed in her eyes.

Ashwin shook his head. ' 'Tis naught for you to moither yourself about, my wench. They'm only having a bit o' fun wi' your man. He'll not be really harmed.'

A sudden thunder of roaring cheers from outside caused all three to turn and look out of the window.

Two of the needle-pointers had somehow managed to drag the hugely bloated body of a large dog from the pool and, lifting it between them by the paws, they came stumbling towards the stocks with the streaming mass of putridity.

Something seemed to snap in Tildy's head, and all that hammered through her brain was the compulsion to save her baby's father. Without another word she snatched the constable's staff from the table where he had placed it, and ran from the inn.

'*Stop It!*' she screamed. '*Stop It!*' She hurled herself at the crowd, using the heavy wooden staff to batter a way through the close-packed bodies. In sudden alarm men, women and children shouted warnings, fighting and jostling to escape the wildly swinging blows of this raging fury. Within a matter of seconds, Tildy was confronting the two pointers, still stumbling onwards with their stinking burden.

Crack! Crack! Crack! Crack! The heavy wooden crown whipped viciously against their skulls, sending them reeling, crying out in pain and shock. Tildy went after them, her whole being consumed with the lust to destroy this many-faced, many-formed monster that, in its multitude of bodies, was threatening to make her child fatherless.

'Stop it! Stop it! Stop it! Stop it!' She shrieked the words without knowing that she was doing so, and through the red haze that veiled her sight could only discern a succession of distorted, inhuman faces that rose before her for brief instants and fell away under the crashing blows of her staff. A wave of darkness thickened the red haze and a terrible weakness engulfed her limbs. Biting agony tore at her belly and she felt herself whirling giddily into blindness, and falling, falling, falling into a black, bottomless pit . . .

'God strewth! Her arn't dead, is her?' a man muttered, and all those around him were hushed and fearful as they peered down at the motionless body of the pregnant girl who had so suddenly staggered and fallen. Hands that moments before had lifted stones and hurled them to hurt and maim, now gently lifted her limp form and carried Tildy into the bar-parlour of the inn. A blanket was spread on the floor and she was carefully laid upon it with a cushion beneath her head, her hair still covered by the pathetic finery of her lace-trimmed, poke bonnet. The bonnet was removed and the neck of her grey gown loosened. Men chafed the nerveless hands and a woman bathed the white clammy-sweated forehead with fresh cool water.

'The poor little wench!'

'God ha' mercy on her!'

'She's real heavy pregnant, the poor little bugger is!'

'Ahr, if I'd known that, I'd not ha' come here this day!'

'Nor me, that I'll warrant.'

The low sussuration of voices pierced Tildy's consciousness and slowly her full senses returned. She opened her eyes and stared up at the serried faces above her, which swam giddily in her sight. No longer the rabid, bestial features that had confronted her only minutes before, but now metamorphosed into simple, homely people.

'Are you feeling better, girl? Does you want a surgeon fetching?' the woman bathing Tildy's brows asked gently.

The girl closed her eyes again, and fought down the nausea that was close to overwhelming her. Gradually, the churning of her stomach ceased and the jerking of her sight steadied. She was able to shake her head and reply.

'No, I thank you, I'm perfectly well now.'

The lack of any recrimination heightened the sense of shame that many of those present were now experiencing. With muttered apologies the people in the room quickly shuffled away and returned to their own concerns, not even glancing at the bruised and fouled Thomas Crawford still huddled in miserable captivity.

Edwin Ashwin helped Tildy to rise and led her outside.

'Listen, my wench, I'm going to set your man free.' The constable's grim features were troubled, and he could hardly bring himself to meet her soft brown eyes, so guilty did he feel over what had happened.

Tildy nodded. 'Thank you,' she said simply. Words of blame for his lack of action trembled on her lips, but she left them unsaid, knowing how useless it would be to give vent to them now.

'If you'll take my tip, girl, you and your man 'ull get away out of this town. They'm all shamed by what they done at this moment, because o' you being pregnant. But it might be a different story when the pointer-lads gets a few drinks into their bellies.'

45

Ashwin unlocked the padlock and lifted the top half of the stock-board to free Thomas Crawford.

'Alright, my bucko, you can thank your missus here for this, and for saving your bacon like she did. She's a good 'un, she is, and you wants to remember that.'

Crawford, fast recovering from his earlier terrors, glared with intense hatred at the other man, and without a vouch-safing word to either of them he walked away, trying to scrape some of the stinking filth from his head and clothing as he moved. Tildy sighed sadly and wearily followed some paces behind her husband. He led her through the town and out along the track that stretched across the gorse-covered wasteland of the Brideley Moor to the west. For some two miles he walked in silence, and then halted by a small stream. Stripping off his clothing, he plunged naked into the cold clear waters and repeatedly doused his head beneath the surface, scrubbing with both hands at the caked-on slime that plastered his hair and face. Once cleansed, he stepped onto the bank and addressed Tildy.

'Try and wash some of the muck off me clothes. They can dry on me while I'm travelling.' His voice and expression were surly, as though he held *her* responsible for his ordeal. Then he held out his hand. 'You can give over the money, as well.'

Tildy's fingers went to the side pocket of her gown. It was empty.

'Oh no,' she moaned softly, and burst into tears as this final blow struck home, tearing at her strained emotions. 'It's gone, Thomas, it's gone . . . ' she choked out. 'The money's gone!'

'Gone? What d'you mean, gone?' His black eyes became almost demonic with temper, and he stepped towards her, fists clenched, ready to hit out.

Tildy was unaware of anything other than her grief at this last bitter event. Her wedding day, which to most women was a day of happiness, had been a long purgatory to Tildy. With her face buried in her hands she released all the pent-up emotions of months, and her sobs tore from her throat.

Something in the posture of the girl, so beaten and defenceless, caused Thomas Crawford to lower his raised fists without striking a blow. For a while his lips spewed out a torrent of verbal abuse at her, but this was more a mechanical reflex than anything else. He lapsed into a moody silence and crouched on his haunches, staring into the stream.

By the time Tildy's sobs had quietened, the man had accepted what must be done, faced with this hopeless situation.

'There's naught else for it,' he acknowledged bitterly. 'We'll ha' to go back home. Back to the soddin' Sidemoor . . .'

Chapter Five

The tall-spired church of John the Baptist soared on its high hillock above the small town of Bromsgrove, creating a massive black shadow against the clouded backdrop of the midnight sky.

Thomas Crawford halted outside the oak door of the church's tower and stared back down the gloomy slope behind him.

'Tildy?' he shouted irritably. 'Tildy, carn't you move faster?'

The shapeless blob of darkness that was the girl climbed slowly towards him, and he could hear her laboured breathing as she struggled upwards. For a brief moment pity softened his impatience, but he pushed it away from his mind, and swore at her pettishly.

'Bugger me if you arn't apuffing like an old sow! God strike me, wench! We've only covered half a score o' miles this day. Anybody 'ud think it was nearer half a hundred the way you keeps lagging behind.'

Tildy made no reply. Her lungs and throat rasped too

painfully for her to speak, and her back and hips felt numb and dead from the weight of her ponderous body. She finally reached the spot where her husband stood, and thankfully halted, her legs trembling from the strain of the steep ascent.

The clouds parted and bright moonlight lanced across the churchyard, silvering the gravestones and etching into sharp relief the man's handsome face and weak mouth. For a few moments, while the moon still lanced through the rifted clouds, the couple stared at each other. Tildy deliberately kept her face expressionless, hiding the contempt that was rapidly burgeoning inside her for this man whom she had taken as husband in the sight of God.

Thomas Crawford, hot and uncomfortable in the damp, stained finery of his wedding suit, scowled at his young wife.

'God strike me! Why in Hell's name did I ever agree to marry you? What use are you to me in this state?' he demanded cruelly as his eyes moved over her once slender body, now so misshapen by the child she carried within her. 'I wish I'd never rogered you, it's bin my ruin so it has . . . Come on,' he ordered roughly, and began to turn away.

Tildy reached out with one delicately shaped hand and caught his sleeve.

'Cannot we rest awhile? I'm sorely tired,' she questioned, her soft-toned voice betraying her total weariness.

'Look theer.' He pointed westwards to where, some half-mile distant in the shallow valley that surrounded the sleeping town of Bromsgrove, lights were flickering redly. 'That's the Sidemoor, where we'em heading for. It's not even a mile away. You can rest when we gets there. Besides, I don't know what youm whining about being so tired for, it warn't you as was in the bleedin' stocks getting near stoned to death.'

Tildy's stubborn pride would not allow her to beg with the man, and forcing her shaking legs into movement she silently followed her husband's tall figure down the hill towards the lights.

The road's slope flattened abruptly as the couple neared the village and the way grew harder, because the deep ruts and potholes in its beaten-earth surface multiplied and worsened, causing them both to trip and stumble frequently.

'God strike me! It arn't got any better since I been away!' Thomas Crawford complained in loud disgust. 'They'm still living in the same dammed midden-heaps, only there looks to be more on 'um.'

They had reached the first building of the Sidemoor: rows and tight clusters of two-storied red-brick hovels, behind each of which stood the source of the flickering red lights seen from the church – the leanto workshops of the nailmakers who populated this place. Although it was now well past midnight on a Friday the air throbbed with metallic thuds and the ringing of hammerheads against iron. Tildy stared about her with amazement. A fiery glare lit the inside of every low-roofed workshop, and she could see half-naked men, women and children crammed together inside the tight confines, their faces and bodies forming a constantly shifting frieze of sweat-greased, work-grimed, flame-reddened flesh. White-hot showers of metal flakes flew, iron clanged and rang, babies squalled, children shouted and cried, women shrilled and men cursed and roared. Each nailer driving his helpers to work ever faster, ever harder, ever more frenziedly. All around the workshops lean-backed pigs rutted and snuffled and grunted among the heaps of rotting ordure. Scrawny fowl stalked, pecked and scratched in the barren dust, and mangy, stick-ribbed dogs snarled and fought to win stinking bones. A thick smell of unwashed bodies, middens and stagnant water hung reeking over the dwelling places, and Tildy held her nostrils closed with her fingers while she fought to subdue the gagging in her throat.

Her husband glared around him with an expression of

virulent hatred, then swung to confront his wife.

'Yes, you might well hold your nose, my fine lady!' He spat the words at her. 'But it's thanks to you that we'em here.'

Tildy focussed her sight on his lips, livid and writhing like snakes in the reflected glow of the glaring fire-hearths.

'And you'd best get used to the stink, my lovely bride . . .' the lips mouthed, 'because it's all you'll ever know from here'on. This is home for you now, my wench. Home, for the rest o' your days . . .'

'What in Hell's name do you do here?' Enoch Crawford's voice was hoarse, and his gaunt, dirty-white body, covered only by a filthy leather apron and torn breeches, glistened with rivulets of sweat in the glare from his forge as he moved to confront the new arrivals in the low-lintelled doorway of his workshop.

Thomas Crawford gaped in open-mouthed astonishment at his parent.

'Don't you recognize me, Feyther?' he demanded incredulously. 'It's me, Tom, your second youngest.'

The grey-haired old man grimaced, disclosing large brown stubs of teeth, and he lifted both sinewy arms and stretched to ease his stiff muscles.

'O' course I knows you, you thick-skulled mawkin, for all that I'se bred a round dozen,' he told his son scathingly. 'Now, you tell me what youm adoing here?'

The younger man was lost for words, and his lips moved soundlessly as he strove to recover from his shock at this unlooked-for reception.

Tildy gave scant attention to the men. Tired almost beyond endurance, she was grateful for the chance to lean her back against the rough-textured wall and draw an easier breath.

'I'll not ask you agen, you gawpy bugger,' Enoch Crawford warned. 'What d'you want here?'

The son faced his father and his features twitched

nervously. To his surprise he found that the fear instilled in him as a child by this man standing before him still held its grip, and he could only blurt out a reply.

'I've come back home, Feyther, to work at the nails.'

'You? Work at the nails?' The old man jeered contemptuously.

Thomas Crawford screwed up his scanty reserves of courage. 'Yes, that's what I said, and that's what I means to do.'

The old man's head went back and he laughed long and raucously. Then stepped into the heat of the forge and made a gesture of dismissal with one work-gnarled hand.

'Goo on, boy, get back to wheer you've just come from. You'll not mek a good nailer while you've a hole in your arse. You was always too fine-mouthed and dainty for this trade, that's why you run away from here in the fust place.'

Thomas licked lips made dry by nervousness.

'Feyther, you doon't understand. I'm married now, and me wife's carrying a babby. She needs a place to sleep this night, and so does I.'

His father hawked and spat onto the waist-high, dull-glowing hearth. The spittle hissed and bubbled and evaporated in a minute puff of steam.

'So why tell me?' The old man's voice was hard and uncaring. 'My house warn't good enough for you afore, so why should it be so now. It's none o' my concern what state your missus is in. Now get off, I've work to finish, or had you forgot that today being Saturday, it's the Weigh-in for some on us?'

Tom Crawford knew from past experience that he would get no help from his parent while the old man was in his present mood. He came away from the doorway and spoke to Tildy.

'We'll find naught but hard words here, girl. Come on, we'll try at my brother Edgar's house. We was always good friends, me and him.'

He led her through a long narrow passage between rows

of cottages, then through a covered entrance passage and out into a close-huddled square of more two-storied cottages. In the centre of the square was a well, with a low, four-posted roof covering it.

'You wait there a minute.'

Crawford pushed Tildy in the direction of the well, then went to one of the cottages, from the ground-floor window of which a rushlight cast a weak glow.

Tildy sat on the low wall of the well-housing and found that there was water in the wooden draw-bucket left on top of the well. Gratefully she cupped her hands and drank deeply of the musty-tasting liquid, then bathed her hot, dusty face and neck. Too bodily tired to take any interest in her surroundings the girl could only sit with closed eyes, and doze to forget the painful rumblings of her long-empty stomach. It seemed that this welcome respite had only lasted for seconds when her husband's hand shook her shoulder. In fact over half an hour had passed, during which Tom had pleaded with his brother to give them both shelter for what remained of the night . . . Stupified with lack of rest and food Tildy followed docilely into the tiny cottage and found difficulty in focussing on the faces of what appeared to be a dense mass of children, staring at her with wide eyes in the weak glow of the rushlight.

'Lie down here, wench, and get some sleep, You looks near dead on your feet.' A woman's voice, gruff but not unkindly, instructed Tildy, and thankfully the young girl sank onto a pile of dank-smelling sacks in one corner of the room and was asleep as her head touched them.

Chapter Six

Bordering the south of Sidemoor village was a rambling collection of old buildings which comprised the establishment of the Sanders family, Nailmasters and Factors to the Trade. A light was shining from one of the lower windows of the long, high warehouse, as if to demonstrate that those who became rich from the labours of the nailers also toiled through the night hours in their turn.

'I doon't like it! I tek my oath I doon't!' Old Samuel Sanders stumped irascibly up and down the gloomy office. Jonathan Sanders, his nephew, sighed and laid down the quill pen with which he had been entering accounts in the vast leather-bound ledger lying open before him on the high, narrow desk. A tall, slender, gentle-eyed man in his late twenties, his thin, pale face showed more than a hint of impatience as he looked directly at the older man.

'What is it you do not like, Uncle?' he enquired in his rather reedy, but pleasant-toned voice.

Old Samuel's pug-featured, mottled-skinned face reddened as he halted in sudden anger and shouted: 'You knows bloody well what I'm atalking about! So doon't screw your mouth up like a prissy old maid when I arsk's a simple question.'

As he spoke the solitary oil-lamp hanging from one of the wooden ceiling beams began to splutter and smoke. Jonathan Sanders slipped from the long-legged stool and went over to attend it.

The old man's short, rotund body, made even thicker by the several layers of waistcoats and flannel shirts he habitually wore under the brown broadcloth greatcoat, tailcoat and breeches he favoured, rocked in impatience.

'Well, our Jon, be you gooing to answer, or arn't you?'

Jonathan trimmed the lamp wick, adjusting it until the pale golden light shone true and steady, highlighting the dark polish of the heavy furniture and rows of ledgers, and reflecting glints of flame from the glassed showcases of nail samples fixed around the walls of the room. Finally, when the irate tapping of the older man's clogs upon the floor threatened to become stamping, the younger man answered quietly.

'What happens between my wife and I is our own affair, and no one else's.'

'Well that's wheer youm bloody wrong, my fine gentleman! Because it arn't!' His uncle hammered the desktop with his meaty hand to give emphasis to his words. 'Her's making a bloody laughing-stock o' you, that's what her's doing . . . And you?' His voice held a sneer. 'And you moons about like a silly big Nancy and lets her do it!'

'Carlotta is still very young, Uncle, she must have some enjoyment from life while she is able.'

'What?' Old Samuel spat incredulously. 'What's that you say?' His voice rose another octave. 'Her's a married woman now, and not some silly spinster flibbertergibbittin' about through the days like a bloody butterfly. Her's married to a nailmaster, and that means summat in this district! Her place is in her kitchen, or in the bed giving you some sons of your own to follow on here when youm dead and gone.'

'There is time enough for children.' Jonathan's pale face flushed, and his tone was curiously defensive..

'Oh, is there now?' The old man sneered openly, then recommenced stumping up and down the office floor, his hands clasped behind his back and his bald, liver-flecked scalp catching greasy patches of light from the lamp.

His nephew returned to the desk and picked up his quill pen once more. Samuel Sanders stopped abruptly by the younger man's shoulder, and when he spoke the anger had gone from his voice, leaving the slight tremulousness of age in its stead.

'I was really proud when you got wed to Carlotta Tinsley. Does you know that, boy? Really proud, that a nephew o' mine, that I'd always loved like he was the son I was never blessed wi', really proud that he should be marrying into the Tinsleys of Oldhill. Marrying one of Eliza Tinsley's kin no less, the greatest nailmasters in the kingdom . . . Why, I could see the day when wi' her connections the firm o' Sanders 'ud rise to equal Tinsley . . . And another thing, I thought I'd have the holding of babbies belonging to my own blood agen. Strong, lusty boys to carry on our name . . . ' He shook his head disgustedly. 'And look what's happened? You've been wed for more than a year and there's still no sign of her whelping a pup.'

Jonathan, despite a fast-growing feeling of distress, forced a laugh.

'Before God! We've not had any great length of time to produce a son and heir yet. I have it on the best authority that it takes at least nine months for a child to ready for birth.'

The old man held up both hands for silence. 'Doon't laugh at me, Nephew.' His tone was a compound of anger, and bitter sadness. 'I'm an ignorant old fool, I know; and I've not had the schooling, like you've had . . . But my school was a bloody hard 'un, and the lessons I learned no one can teach you from a book. Does you think I carn't see

56

wi' me own eyes what's ailing that lass . . . Ahr! And you as well, boy. I've seen her a dozen times riding that horse of hers as though Old Nick himself was chasing her, and taking fences that a madwoman wouldn't take . . . I say nothing about the way she spends and wastes hard-earned money, that's only natural in a young, high-spirited wench . . . But there's a sight more than that . . . It's clear to them as can see, and I can see, Jon.' He paused, and gusted a heavy-hearted sigh. 'God's curse on me! I can see it all too plain, boy . . . Youm not man enough for her.' Shaking his head he abruptly left the room.

Jonathan Sanders stared unmovingly at the ledger in front of him for several long minutes. The neatly entered rows of figures began to dance before his eyes, then suddenly blurred.

'I fear that I'm not a man at all, Uncle,' he murmured, and put his fingers to his eyes, as if by rubbing them he could erase the torment and anguish of his marriage from his mind.

Some considerable time elapsed before a series of sharp knocks on the office door roused him and brought him back to awareness of his surroundings.

'Come in,' he called.

The door opened and a diminutive, white night-gowned figure, its head swathed in a bulky sleeping turban, slipped into the room.

'Please Master Jonathan?' It was Harriet, his wife's child-maid.

'Yes, Harriet, what is it brings you from your bed at this hour? You're not ill, I trust?' he enquired kindly.

'Please sir, I'm very well. It's the Mistress, she wants to speak with you . . . Straight away, she says.'

Jonathan smiled down at the solemn little face. 'Very well, Harriet. Is your mistress in her bedchamber?'

'Please sir, yes.'

'Thank you, Harriet, I'll go there immediately. I want you to go to your bed, it's almost time to rise as it is.'

'Please, sir.' The tiny maid bobbed a curtsey and slipped away.

Jonathan felt a sense of foreboding, knowing that such imperious summonses invariably presaged impossible demands from his wife, and refusals from him – which in turn led to displays of tantrums and cruel words. Absently he lifted the powder-shaker and waved it above the already dry ink of the ledger. He blew the surplus powder from the page and, closing the book, left the office. He emerged into the large courtyard of the warehouse and stood there for a moment, breathing deeply of the soft night air, gazing at the sky from which faint stars blinked down at him. He felt strangely comforted by their very remoteness and mystery.

My troubles must seem exceedingly petty to the Creator of those distant worlds, he thought.

The thudding of the treadle hammers still sounded from the nearby nailers' workshops. He frowned.

'Long past midnight, and still they work, and many will not finish before dawn, it being a Weigh-in day. Even nigger slaves on the sugar plantations would be abed by now.'

Footsteps approached echoingly through the high-arched entranceway to the courtyard. It was Dick Suffield, the warehouse foreman, making his customary nightly check on the premises.

Jonathan called a greeting to him. 'Suffield, come here will you.'

The foreman stopped, startled by the unexpected command, then, smiling confidently, he walked across to the doorway where his employer waited.

'Yes, Master Jon, what is it you want?'

The young nailmaster regarded the man with distaste. The foreman was in his mid-thirties, of medium height and burly build. To a stranger's eyes he would have seemed a genial, easy-smiling man, although the rusty-black clothing he always wore was similar to an undertaker's, down to the sombre-hued linen shirt, and high-crowned, narrow-

58

brimmed hat. But Jonathan disliked the man. He could recognize the hectoring bully and cheat hidden behind the jovial façade, and had frequently intervened when Suffield tried to browbeat and do down the nailers and their families. Although Jonathan Sanders fully accepted the fact that in a hard, competitive trade such as nailing there was no room for weakness, he tried to conduct his business with some degree of kindness.

'I understand that you wish to prosecute Edgar Crawford,' Jonathan stated quietly. 'Why?'

Suffield showed large yellowed teeth in a knowing grin. 'Didn't your uncle tell you why, Master Jon?'

The young nailmaster felt the familiar surge of irritation at the foreman's manner, which, although always stopping short of open insolence, somehow always verged on its edge.

'What passes between my uncle and myself is naught to concern you, Dick Suffield. I want you to answer my question,' he snapped curtly.

Jonathan's relationship with his Uncle Samuel was a delicate balance at the best of times. Originally, his father had been his uncle's partner in the business. When his father died Jonathan had taken his place as full partner to his uncle, and by his own prodigious efforts had greatly increased the firm's share of the district's nail trade. Despite this, in his uncle's mind he was still only a callow youth who didn't really know the business. It was only by the constant exertion of tact and forebearance towards the old man that Jonathan managed to avoid repeated quarrels over the running of the firm. Dick Suffield, who possessed extremely acute shrewdness, did his best to play one partner off against the other to his own advantage.

If it had been left solely to Jonathan, then Suffield would have been dismissed. But Old Samuel would hear nothing against the man, pointing out quite rightly that he knew the trade well, and was an efficient foreman. So, for the sake of peace, Jonathan usually tried to hold his tongue.

'Come now, Suffield, I'm awaiting an answer,' the nail-master pressed sharply.

The insolent grin left the other man's face, and he replied sullenly.

'Edgar Crawford took a sixty pound bundle of iron from us more than ten days past, and he's still not worked it up. You knows the rules well enough, Master. Iffen the iron arn't worked up in eight days, then the nailer is to be prosecuted.'

Jonathan gnawed worriedly at his lower lip. 'Has he given any reason for the delay?' he asked. 'Because I've no wish to get a man put in prison for three months for the sake of a couple of days' tardiness in delivery of the work.'

Suffield shook his head, and answered scathingly. 'He reckons his missus was took badly and that her couldn't work at the forge, but bugger that for a load of old abdab! He's got his old feyther, and a rake o' bloody kids; they could have helped him iffen he'd had a mind to finish the work.'

The nailmaster felt increasingly unhappy about the situation. He knew Edgar Crawford and his father, Old Enoch, and had always found the old man at least to be a fine workman, and the son to be passable. It took only a moment to reach a decision.

'You'll take no action on this matter, Suffield. You can tell Edgar Crawford that he has until next Weigh-in day to complete the work, but emphasize that it must be done by then, and no excuse will be accepted for failure to deliver.'

The other man's insolent manner returned in full force.

'Your uncle might not agree to that, Master,' he gritted out.

Jonathan jerked his head in dismissal. 'Get about your duties, Suffield. I'll not argue the matter with any under-ling.'

For a brief moment Suffield looked as if he might flare

out in open rebellion. Then, with a visible effort, he controlled himself and nodded.

'As you say, Master.'

'Yes, Suffield, it is to be as I say . . . On this occasion and on any other,' his employer told him curtly, and walked away under the arched entrance.

As the nailmaster disappeared from view an expression of pure hatred twisted Suffield's features.

'May the curse o' the Devil fall on your head, you arrogant bastard!' he muttered vindictively, then smiled. 'But then it already has, my fine cockerel, for Old Nick's given you me for an enemy, and that loose-living strumpet for a wife . . . '

The Sanders' large house fronted the roadway and the grim grey-facing blocks of its walls complemented the gloomy interior, with the high-ceilinged cheerless rooms filled with funereal drapes and wall-hangings, and the musty, graceless furnishings which Samuel Sanders refused to change in any way.

Only in Carlotta Sanders' bedroom, to which her husband now went, was there any warmth or colour. The young nailmaster knocked softly at the door and entered without waiting for a response.

'So there you are at last, panting in your ardour to reach me . . . La! What a dashing beau I have for husband, to be sure.'

The tuneful voice that greeted him held mockery tinged with contempt.

Jonathan's heart thudded uncomfortably and he felt the same shock of surprise he always experienced at every fresh sight of his young wife's flamboyant beauty.

Carlotta was sitting on the side of her bed, dressed in a long bedgown of scarlet satin. The rich colouring of the gown heightened the slight flush of her olive-complexioned cheeks, and her long raven hair, a legacy from her Italian grandmother, hung loosely about her shoulders while

Harriet, the tiny maid, gently brushed it. When Jonathan did not answer his wife peeped from under her thick lashes, her green eyes sparkling with mischief.

'You are allowed to·speak to me, husband,' she teased maliciously. 'I am not yet a divinity.'

'I was thinking how beautiful you look,' he remarked simply.

She mock-sighed, causing her full, firm breasts to strain against the thin fabric of the bedgown.

'Oh, what it is to be worshipped so!' she declaimed, then added spitefully, 'it is a pity that the worship is always on such a spiritual plane.'

Jonathan was embarrassed by his wife making such remarks in front of a servant girl. He felt the impulse to upbraid her, but realized that this would merely satisfy her sense of mischief, so he replied calmly.

'As to that, madam, there are many women who would be happy to be the object of spiritual worship, for that is truly a most pure and sincere emotion.'

She laughed at his unconscious pomposity, and ran the tip of her tongue across her small white teeth, causing them to glisten in the soft light of the multitude of scented candles that burned in their elaborate chandeliers and wall-holders.

'I am sure you are right, husband, but I fear that the type of woman who is satisfied with that sort of emotion can only be found in a nunnery.'

The maid had now finished brushing her mistress' hair, and she moved to loosen the bedgown from the shapely shoulders.

'Perhaps you would prefer me to return when you have completed your preparations for sleep?' Jonathan asked diffidently, having previously been teased and rated a voyeur by his wife because he had loved to watch her unrobing when they were first married.

'There is no need for you to go, Jonathan,' Carlotta said quickly. 'I know that the sight of my body will not excite

you into actions that would cause Harriet to hide her eyes
. . . Indeed, it never has done, has it?'

Her goading finally achieved the desired effect, and he
rose to it.

'God dammit, Carlotta! You go too far with your
remarks.' He spoke stiffly; and knowing as he said it that
he sounded like a pompous old man, he added, 'If you wish
to converse in such a loose manner, then at least have the
courtesy to send your maid from the room.'

Wicked delight danced in his wife's eyes. 'La! I declare!'
she exclaimed. 'What a fiery temper he displays! The man
is a lion when roused . . . Harriet, leave the room at once! I
fear that he might do you an injury if you remain here a
moment longer.'

The tiny maid bobbed a curtsey. 'Please, ma'am,' she
whispered, her face pale and drawn with tiredness, and
slipped away. When the door closed behind the girl
Jonathan remonstrated angrily.

'Why must you keep the child working so late? She's
weary beyond belief . . . And while we are speaking of
servants, why do you continually try to make me appear
the fool before them?'

A flash of temper flared in Carlotta. 'I do not try to make
you the fool, husband. You need no help from me in that
respect. And what I choose to do with my maid is entirely
my own concern. Do I ever try to tell you how to conduct
your business?'

He shook his head wearily. 'For the love of God, Carla,
let us not quarrel now. My head feels as if it's ready to
burst.'

For a few seconds she stared at his wan face and for the
first time noted the dark, pain-shadows about his eyes. Her
volatile temper softened, and in a kindlier tone she said,
'I'm sorry. Truly I am . . . Come, sit down here.'

She held out her hand and when he clasped it she drew
him down beside her. He sat staring at the thick carpeting
beneath his feet and so dejected did he appear that

Carlotta's softening deepened to genuine pity and remorse. She stroked his palms with her soft fingers.

'Poor Jon,' she murmured. 'I am such a shrew with you. And yet I really do not wish to be so. It is just that . . . '

'I know,' he broke in, his voice strained. 'I know what drives you to behave as you do; and I know also that it is my fault. I am no use as a husband. If I had known that I would be the way I am, then I swear that much as I loved you, and love you still, I would never have asked for your hand . . . Never!' He turned to her and all the torments of an inner Hell showed in his eyes. 'Forgive me, Carla, please forgive me!'

She lay back across the bed, pulling him with her and cushioning his head on her breasts as she would a small child's.

'Do not suffer so,' she told him softly. 'I know that you cannot help it. Do not torment yourself, Jon, I'm not worth it. It is you who should forgive me . . . '

Her fingers stroked his hair and cheeks and she felt the wetness of his tears. The minutes lengthened into hours, and imperceptibly they drifted into sleep.

Chapter Seven

The sounds of a heated altercation woke Tildy as the first palings of dawn could be seen on the eastern horizon. It was Edgar Crawford and his wife, Annie, who were quarrelling and Tildy opened her eyes just in time to see the man punch his wife violently in the face, sending her crashing into the battered old table that was the centre-piece of the sparsely furnished room. Annie Crawford lay slumped across the tabletop crying with harsh, hiccuping sobs. Edgar Crawford, a slightly older and more haggard version of his brother Thomas, shook his fist at the weeping woman.

'Now perhaps you'll gi' me some peace, you nagging sod!' he shouted.

Beside Tildy on the heap of sacks, Tom Crawford stirred and sat up.

'God strike me! Carn't a man get any sleep at all in this house!' he grumbled.

His brother, still glowering at his wife, answered him angrily, snapping, 'I'se not had a wink o' sleep all night, our Tom, what wi' this bleeding sod nagging at me.'

Annie Crawford pushed herself off the table to stand upright, a bump caused by the blow already swelling and discolouring above her right eye. She was barely twenty-eight years old, but appeared twice that, with her shabbily clothed body made shapeless by ceaseless childbearing, her teeth mostly missing and her hair dank and lustreless.

'I'se got good cause to nag at you, Edgar Crawford,' she shouted back defiantly, the words choked out between sobs. 'Today's the Weigh-in, and you'se not struck more than twelve pounds o' nails all week. There's not a penny-piece in the house, and me and the childer have not tasted a bite since yesterday morning. We'em all clemmed nigh to death, so we be.'

Her husband's haggard face was momentarily downcast, then it flamed with temper again as he retorted.

'And me? What about me? I'se ate naught either, and I was working all day and half the night at the bloody block, while you was alaying on your back upstairs, moaning and groaning that you was dying.'

'T'is not my fault I'm badly, Edgar Crawford,' his wife stated angrily. 'You kept on putting babbies in me belly even when it was near killing me to bear 'um. You wouldn't be denied your pleasure, even when summat went wrong wi' me insides wi' that last one I was carrying.'

'Oh yes, we all knows that well enough,' the man sneered. 'It's bloody obvious summat went wrong, arn't it. 'Specially when it was born dead.'

'And a good job it was, as well.' Annie Crawford's hiccuping sobs were lessening, and her speech becoming clearer. 'For what wi' your drinking and wasting, there's ne'er enough money coming in to feed them as we got already.'

'Oh for Christ's sake shut your rattle, 'ull you woman!' The man's anger suddenly deflated and he turned from her, pulling on his threadbare coat.

'Wheer be you going, Edgar?' she demanded anxiously.

'Out!' he told her flatly, and slammed from the cottage.

The woman's shoulders slumped defeatedly, and moving slowly and painfully she went to the narrow staircase that led up to the sole bedroom and tiny landing space where she, her husband and their seven living children all slept in an area not more than fifteen feet square.

'Come on down, you kids,' she called. 'You can come down now, your feyther's gone out.'

The children descended in a rush. Half-naked and shoe-less, hair uncombed, noses running, bodies unwashed, they spanned the age groups from two to twelve years, and Tildy felt pity for their undernourished, scabby bodies and spindled arms and legs.

'What's to ate, Mam?' the eldest girl wanted to know, and watched without surprise as Annie Crawford sank down onto one of the three broken-framed chairs that completed the room's furnishings, and gave way to a fresh outburst of sobbing.

Tildy had sat quietly absorbing all that had happened, and now she turned to her own husband.

'Tom, we must get some food from somewhere for the children,' she whispered urgently.

'What wi', bloody buttons?' he asked with grim facetiousness.

Tildy slipped off the wedding ring that he had placed on her finger the previous day. 'There's this,' she told him. From the bodice of her dress she removed the only other piece of jewellery she possessed, an old silver brooch she had had from babyhood. 'And there's this also. You can get a few shillings for these, easy enough.'

The man felt the hunger pangs in his own belly, and the simple kindness of her action touched a softer chord in him.

'You've a good heart, my wench,' he said simply, and smiled at her. 'I reckon we con raise the wind wi' these alright.'

Tildy, who had been expecting her husband to dispute her wishes, experienced a feeling of gratitude and warmth towards him for his easy acceptance, and she smiled back in her turn.

Thomas got to his feet and knocked the dust of the sack bed from his badly creased clothing.

'Come on, Annie, my duck!' he ordered jocularly. 'Let's you and me goo and see what we can get for these to fill our bellies wi'.'

Annie Crawford dried her tears, pouring out her profuse thanks to Tildy and, pulling a ragged shawl about her shoulders, left with her brother-in-law.

Tildy straightened her own clothing, then left the children playing and squabbling in the bad-smelling room to go in search of fresh air. Even at this early hour, with daylight not fully come, the surrounding workshops were noisy with the ringing of hammers against iron.

Reaching the well in the centre of the square she drew water in a wooden bucket and washed her face and hands and the inside of her mouth, gargling away the stale taste left by the night spent in the fetid atmosphere of the hovel. She used her handkerchief to dry herself as best she could, and felt greatly refreshed by the cool water. From some of the cottage doorways slatternly women, hands and bodies deep-grimed with the smuts of their work, their infants held to their breasts or tugging at their skirts, stared curiously at the stranger. But the day being what it was none could spare time for talk, or even to stare for more than a few seconds, and they quickly went about their tasks.

Tildy found the close-huddled square unpleasantly confining, and to escape the reek of the slops and ordure that liberally covered the muddied earth, wandered on through the long passageway she had traversed the previous night.

Passing by one workshop which stood on its own, she heard a female voice singing cheerfully, and stood for a while to listen.

Jeremiah blow the fire, Puff, Puff, Puff!
Jeremiah turn the rod, Hot, Hot, Hot!

Jeremiah use the hammer, Clink, Clink, Clink!
Jeremiah blow the fire, Puff, Puff, Puff . . .

Amused by the words Tildy went closer to the workshop and shyly peeped inside to see the singer.

It was a lone young girl, her hair bound up in a kerchief and her upper body naked, with a sacking apron covering the long drawers which were all she wore on her lower half, except for heavy wooden clogs. She was working busily at making small nails, and Tildy watched with interest.

In the centre of the workshop was the waist-high hearth with its hot glowing bed of small coke or breeze. A big bellows pointed into the back of the hearth, its funnel a leather tube tipped with a metal rondel which stuck into the heaped coke. At each side of the hearth were embedded a pair of stout wooden posts, which carried the axle of the treadle-hammer, the large-headed Oliver. Beneath the Oliver was the nail-block, a two foot cube of solid iron with holes bored through it for slotting-in the different dies for the various types of nail. This block also was held between the posts by adjustable iron rods, screws and handled-bolts. A series of long thick, springy willow boughs hung by chains across the low beams of the roof to act as control springs for the Olivers, and pumping-handle for the bellows, by means of long connecting rods of thin iron.

From the shoulder-high pumping handle of the bellows, nicknamed Teasers, a crudely constructed cradle was hanging. Inside, a small baby lay gurgling and crooning his delight as the young woman pumped the handle up and down, jetting a stream of air through the burning coke to intensify the heat, and chanting as she pumped.

'Jeremiah blow the fire, Puff, Puff, Puff!'

Two long thin iron rods were lying across the flaring coke and she lifted one of them, holding its cold end with her left hand. Tapping the heated end against the outer wall as she turned to shed the white-hot flakes of scale from its surface. With the two-pound hammer in her right hand she battered and shaped the tang and point of the nail on a small anvil to the left of the block, and cut the metal halfway through at the desired length on the chisel, the Hardy, fixed to the anvil, bending the length to right-angles. The bent end went into the bore of the die in the block. She twisted the cold iron away, freeing it with one clout of the hammer and, with a stamp of her foot on the narrow wooden trigger-platform at the base of the block, she brought the Oliver thudding down on the die, flattening the small protrusion of the hot metal against the die-top to form the nail head. Another blow with the Oliver, then a tap on a lever called the Paddle caused a tiny steel rod to drive upwards into the underside of the bore and eject the finished nail, so that it flew out and landed onto the heap of completed nails at the right-hand side of the block. The entire intricate operation took only seconds, and the young woman moved with a skillful dexterity that Tildy could only marvel at.

Jeremiah blow the fire, Puff, Puff, Puff!

Jeremiah turn the rod, Hot, Hot, Hot!

Jeremiah use the hammer, Clink, Clink, Clink!

Work the bellows, turn the iron rods in the flame, twist to face the block, tapping off the scale. Smack! Smack! Smack! with the hand hammer, bent end into die-bore and clout the cold iron free. Smash! Smash! with the Oliver. Tap the Paddle. Pump the bellows, turn the rods, twist to the block, shed the scale . . . the smoothness of the operation exerted an hypnotic effect on the watcher, and Tildy lost all track of time. At last the young woman smiled at her, displaying good white teeth which shone in her smutty features.

'Now then, Mistress, bist looking for work?' she asked banteringly. 'I shouldn't look too hard for it here, if I was you . . . In case you finds some.'

She dexterously fashioned more nails from the glowing iron, using a pair of nippers to hold the rod lengths when they became too short to be held by hand. When both rods were finished she threw her hand hammer onto the block and, wiping the sweat from her face with the back of one hand, came to the doorway.

'Well they'm done, thank the Lord! And ready for the Weigh-in once they'm cooled.' She grinned at Tildy. 'Youm a foreigner here, arn't you, Mistress. Where bist you from?'

'From Ipsley parish. I came here last night,' Tildy informed her. Then, realizing from the girl's blank expression that she was none the wiser, explained, 'Ipsley's just across the county border from Redditch town.'

The young woman shrugged, causing her full round breasts to bounce. 'I'se never bin theer,' she said cheerfully. 'Come to that, I'se never bin anywhere, 'cepting here and Bromsgrove. My name's Janey Porter, what's yourn?'

'Matilda Sey . . . I mean Matilda Crawford, but everyone calls me Tildy.'

'Crawford! You'll be married to one of old Enoch's kin then?' Janey Porter scratched her slender waist where a runnel of sweat trickled down from between her firm breasts to tickle her.

'I'm wife to Thomas Crawford,' Tildy told her. 'Mayhap you know him?'

The young woman grinned again. 'Not really, lovey, there's a whole slew o' that family, I gets mixed up wi' 'um . . . But what brings a dainty-looking wench like you, to be marrying a scruffy Crawford from the Pleck Square?' She glanced slyly at Tildy's swollen body, and chuckled. 'No, ne'er mind. I doon't need telling the reason why . . . ' At a tangent she asked, 'Be you come here to the Sidemoor to work at the nailing?'

'Yes, I hope to do so,' Tildy told her, feeling an increasing liking for this cheerful young girl, and a wish that they could become friends.

'Oh, you hopes to do so, does you!' Janey Porter laughed long and loud. 'I'll lay a wager that afore many more dinners introduces themselves to your belly, you'll be

71

hoping not to do so!' Her laughter died away and, with a look of sympathy, she quietly told Tildy, 'It's hard toil and small reward for nailers, Tildy Crawford. We sweats our guts out all week, and the bloody foggers cheats us out of most of the few shillings we manages to earn . . . You'll not know what a fogger is, I'll warrant. Well, you'll find out soon enough, my lovey. The nailmasters and market-masters be hard buggers, the Lord only knows, but the foggers be the worst bastards that God ever put breath into.'

All the cheerfulness had left Janey Porter now, and her voice was charged with hatred and loathing.

'When I copped for that babby in theer, me and me sister got behind wi' our work. In the end the nailmasters 'ud give us no more iron, so we had to goo to the fogger for it . . . And we been slaving for them bastards ever since, and getting deeper in debt to 'um every month.'

She paused and then with vehement intensity told Tildy, 'You hear me well, Tildy Crawford. Iffen you ever gets into the clutches of the bleedin' foggers, then pray to the Devil and sell him your soul if needs be to get free of 'um. For if you doon't get free, then your life 'ull not be worth the living.'

With that final sentence she unslung her baby's cot from the bellow's handle and went into a nearby cottage, leaving Tildy to dwell on what she had been told with foreboding.

Chapter Eight

From six o'clock in the morning the warehouses of the nail-masters had been open for business; and from that hour the nailers of the Sidemoor, Bromsgrove, Bourneheath and the Lickey End brought the fruits of their hard labour to the Weigh-in – some trudging with sacks of nails on their backs, others dragging their loads on small wooden sledges. Pounds, Hundredweights, Tons of Rose and Flemish tacks, Fancy Welsh, Clasp Hobs, Fine Brush, Common Battin, Long Clasp, Tips, Round Heads, Spikes, Horse and Counter Horse, Rivets, Clinkers, Fine Tuckers, and nails known by a score of other names were examined, haggled over, weighed and paid for, or rejected as inferior products.

From the warehouses of nailmasters such as Eliza Tinsley, Brighton, Juggins, Sanders and Roper, the nailers took their wages in silver and copper coins of the realm. But from the back-alley sheds of the rapacious nail-foggers the men came away with credit notes to be cashed in only at the Tommy-Truck shops and tippling-houses owned by these same foggers or their relatives.

The established nailmasters, proud of their reputation for good products, accepted only well-fashioned, well-tempered nails. The foggers would take the inferior work, but deduct anything up to thirty per cent from the accepted price for it; and then compound this virtual robbery by the high prices they charged in their truck-shops and drinking dens for the low-quality goods exchanged for their credit notes.

Jonathan Sanders stood in his warehouse watching over the Weighing-in being conducted by Dick Suffield and a couple of helpers. The nailers and their families queued to await their turn at the big brass weighing pans which were set just inside the high double-doors of the building, talking together in low voices. Since the vast majority of them had worked into the small hours of the morning, and some all through the night, they had little energy left for any display of high-spirits – even the children were dull and lethargic. The young nailmaster strolled out into the yard and looked down the queue. Few of the people had washed, and all of them wore the clothes they had worked in. They presented a uniform spectacle of drab dirtiness, and smutty, pale-tired features. While Jonathan Sanders felt a fleeting pity for some of the more obviously worn-out women and children, the scene as a whole made no deep impression upon him. The lot of the poor was a hard one. It had always been so, and would continue so; and he knew well that if his own business acumen was to falter, then he would also find himself part of a similar queue.

From inside the warehouse there came the sound of voices raised in angry dispute. Dick Suffield was arguing with a sinewy old nailer named Elijah Troth. As Jonathan re-entered the warehouse he saw the old man brandishing a fist full of long-stemmed Fancy Welsh nails under the warehouse foreman's nose.

'What's you mean, Suffield, these arn't no good?' The old nailer growled ferociously, baring his blackened teeth as if he was preparing to sink them into the throat of the man standing before him. 'They'm blue as harebells, they am. I uses only best breeze on my hearth, straight from Rowley Regis and full threepence a scoopful it corsts me . . . Me nails be blue as harebells, use your soddin' eyes and see 'um, then deny it iffen you can.'

Dick Suffield's genial grin was forced. 'Now, 'Lijah, I'm not saying they arn't well-tempered. All I'm saying is that there's some that arn't more than a quarter over the five inches; and you knows that I wants the full half-inch over five for the best Fancy Welsh.'

'I knows what I knows, you grinning bugger! And I knows what I knows a bloody sight better nor you. I'se bin striking these nails for more nor fifty years, man and boy. Youm just a bloody sprag at the trade compared wi' me!'

The old man's voice was shaking with resentful fury that anyone should dare to impugn his craftsmanship.

'What's the trouble here?' Jonathan Sanders intervened. 'Come now, let's get on with the business, there's more than two score people waiting.'

'This bugger's the trouble, Master.' The old nailer turned to Jonathan. 'He wants to count thirteen hundred to the thousand, because he reckons that some o' me work arn't right. Well, I says bollocks to that! I ought to get a count of eleven hundred, ne'er mind thirteen. There's naught but a couple o' pun allowed for waste as it is . . . And you knows well enough, Master, that there arn't a nailer wi' a better blow than me for making the Fancy Welsh in all the bloody trade. I can goo to any warehouse for me bundles of iron, even up-country to Stourbridge or Dudley if needs be, because all the masters knows my worth.'

The young nailmaster considered the problem briefly. It was the custom for the masters to give out the iron rods in bundles of sixty-pounds weight to the nailers, and receive back the finished nails within eight days. An allowance for wasted metal was made varying from a pound to thirty pounds a bundle, depending on the type of nail being made. To compensate for this wastage the masters operated a system of payment known as the Long and Short Thousand. When the nailer brought his nails into the warehouse he gave the master twelve hundred nails and received payment for only a thousand. Some masters, and all the foggers, would try and browbeat the workman into handing in thirteen or even fourteen hundred nails for each thousand paid for. They justified this by claiming that the standard of work was inferior . . . This was the Long Thousand.

The Short Thousand was when the masters re-sold the nails. They gave the customer eight hundred and charged him for a thousand, increasing their profit margin this time at the expense of the buyer.

Jonathan Sanders took time to consider his decision because he did not want to lose the old nailer, whom he knew without doubt to be the best maker of these particular nails in the entire district.

'Listen Master Jon,' the foreman urged low-voiced. 'If you gives in to Old 'Lijah, then the rest of the buggers are going to say that youm looking arter favourites, and it'll make 'um twice as hard to handle. They'll all come asking for a short count . . . They argues the toss too much as it is.'

The nailmaster let his intense dislike for Suffield influence his judgement. 'Give Elijah Troth a count of eleven hundred this time,' he ordered. 'And let's get on with the Weigh-in.'

Dick Suffield opened his mouth in angry protest, but Jonathan would not listen to him.

'Do as I say, damn you! Or you can find another position Suffield!' he shouted, and walked back into the yard.

Old Troth cackled with triumphant laughter. 'You heard what the lad said, Dick Suffield, gi' us the eleven hundred count and ha' done wi' your bellyaching. It arn't your money youm paying out, is it?' He made a great show of removing the grease-thick ancient tricorn hat he wore, and scratching his head. 'Now let me see, there's five and a half pun weight to the thousand for them, and at tuppence ha'penny a pun that makes eleven pence the thousand you owes me. And theer's more nor eighteen thousand on me sledge . . . '

The foreman's bluff features creased into their normal easy smile, but deep in the depths of his eyes there flickered a rabid fury.

'Never fear, Old 'un, you'll get what the master ordered as a count,' he answered the man civilly enough. Inwardly, however, he marked up yet another grudge against Jonathan Sanders, for which, when the time came and it was coming soon, he would extract a full reckoning.

'God strike me! That was bloody good, that was!' Thomas Crawford swallowed the last mouthful of fresh-baked bread and fried salted bacon, then lifted the crock bowl from the table in front of him and drained it dry of the rich brown ale it held. On the opposite side of the table Edgar Crawford was still chewing his own bread and bacon. Not able to speak because his mouth was too full, he could only nod his head and slap the table top with his hand in happy agreement with his brother's sentiments.

Thomas leaned back, causing the broken-backed chair he was sitting on to creak dangerously, and searched in his pockets for the twist of paper that held tobacco. On the table lay a new white-clay churchwarden pipe, and he picked it up and stuffed its bowl full of the black-brown leaf. Over his shoulder he bellowed: 'Tildy! Bring a live coal!'

The brothers were alone in the cottage, all the children and the two womenfolk being in the workshop across the narrow dirt yard, where Annie Crawford was busily and happily frying more slices of bacon in a cast-iron skillet upon the breeze fire of the hearth. At the sound of the man's voice she handed Tildy the nippers used to hold the iron rods.

'Here, my duck, take these.'

Tildy smiled her thanks and, using the nippers, carried a burning piece of coke into the cottage. Her husband lit his pipe from it, puffing out grey-blue swirls of rank-smelling smoke about his head. When the pipe was well lit he nodded to his wife.

'That's all, my wench. You goo on back wi' the rest of 'um. Me and our kid got some business to talk about.'

Silently she obeyed. When she was gone Edgar Crawford, his own food eaten now, leant across the table and tapped his brother's hand with spatulate fingers.

'My oath, Tom! That missus o' yourn is a rare sweet piece, arn't her! I 'udden't mind tupping her, even wi' her belly as big as it is.'

Although he grinned as he spoke to make light of what he said, yet there was serious intent behind his words.

Thomas Crawford took the long curved stem of the pipe from his mouth and pointed it at his brother's face.

'Mark this well, our Edgar,' he warned. 'That woman o' mine only opens her legs for me. Doon't you forget it.'

The other man was quick to placate him, knowing that there was still money left from the pawning of the ring and brooch and not wishing to lose the chance of a share in it.

'Now don't take on, our kid, I was only joshing you.'

Tom Crawford's handsome face was grim, and even his weak mouth had hardened into something approaching strength.

'I hopes you were only doing that, Edgar. But I arn't forgot what it's like in the forges, what wi' brothers rogering their sisters, and fathers their daughters, and men other men's wives. There's many a Simple Simon walking about these parts today because the blood that birthed him got too thick . . .

'But that woman out theer is for me, and me alone.'

His brother shrugged. 'You didn't find me objecting to you blocking my missus did you, afore we got married,' he grumbled sulkily.

Tom shook his head. 'That's neither here nor there, is it?' He was obdurate. 'Because it's in the past. So let's get it straight and plain afore we goes any further. My missus is only ever going to open her legs for me . . . Understand?'

Edgar Crawford shrugged once more. 'So be it, Tom. So be it! Now what says you to going down into Bromsgrove for a sup o' gin?'

The younger man demurred. 'No, I wants to get fixed up wi' a cottage and a workshop, and get some iron from one o' the masters before this day's done.'

His brother grinned at him. 'Well, that's easy fixed, that is. My 'ooman arn't fit for the work now, so I've a spare block and Oliver at my hearth . . . Why not be my staller?'

Tom wasn't keen on the idea. To be a staller meant to be a sub-tenant, paying rent for a workplace to the tenant of the forge, and also paying for part of the cost of the firing. This custom of stalling and firing was invariably worked to the unfair financial advantage of the nailer, who was the tenant of the forge.

'No, Edgar, I'd sooner rent a workshop meself. I've got to get Tildy working at the nails straight away, and there's only two blocks in your place, so she'd have nowhere to strike. Besides, your woman arn't gooing to be badly for ever, is her? And that eldest girl o' yourn must be all of twelve years. You carn't tell me that she arn't able to blow out her share o' tacks for you. We was made to afore we was six, ne'er mind bloody twelve . . . No, I'll have a look about and see what's going. Be you still taking iron from Old Sam Sanders?'

Edgar's haggard face became worried. 'I was, up to a couple o' weeks ago. But I'm a bit late in working up the last bundles and that bleeder, Dick Suffield, is athreatening to put me up in front o' the Beaks, and you knows what that'll mean.'

'I ought to know,' Tom nodded. 'I've seen enough poor coves get three months in the Bridewell, and a whipping as well if they was unlucky . . . But listen, I used to be a mate o' Dick Suffield's years ago. How about if I goes and has a word wi' him? Perhaps a couple o' shillins in his hand 'ull sweeten his temper towards you?'

His brother's features became alight with hope. ''Ull you, Tom? 'Ull you do that?' he begged eagerly.

His comfortably full stomach, and the ale he had drank, made Thomas Crawford feel expansive and confident.

'O'course I will, arter all, youm me favourite brother arn't you? Come on, we'll goo up to the warehouse now. I'll take Tildy wi' us. It'll give her a taste of what she'll have to do from now on.'

Suiting his actions to the words he jumped to his feet and led the way out of the cottage.

'Tildy?' he shouted. 'Come on wi' me, wench. I'm going to introduce you to your new trade. That'll fetch some o' the fat from your bones, I'll wager.'

Inside the forge Annie Crawford stared at the young woman's swollen body and shook her head in disgust.

'Men be real bad bleeders, arn't they, my duck?' She sighed in resigned indignation. 'That bloody husband o' yourn ought to be flogged at the cart-tail for starting you to the nailing in your condition. That bleeder o' mine was just the same. He kept me hammering until the birth pains was on me . . . Bad luck to all men, I says!'

'What's that you says, you useless cow?' Edgar Crawford had heard some of his wife's words through the open window of the workshop.

The woman kept her gaze fixed on the small child she held on her lap.

'Nothing, Edgar. I said nothing,' she answered submissively.

Tildy handed what was left of her own bread and bacon to the children clustered about her, and they immediately began to scuffle over its division. She rose painfully, her back and hips aching badly, and without a comment went after the two men. As she walked she felt the child moving in her womb and she spread both hands upon her lower body in a soothing caress.

'Ne'er mind, Baby,' she murmured softly. 'Your Mammy will do whatever she must, to make sure that you come into the world with a roof over your head, and a warm cot to lay in. She'll do whatever she has to, to ensure that . . . '

When they reached the entrance of the Sanders warehouse Tom Crawford beckoned a small ragged boy to him.

'Goo and tell Dick Suffield that there's a gentleman wishes a word wi' him in private, and ask him to step out here,' he ordered imperiously.

The urchin, not more than eight years old, didn't look at the trio. Instead he lifted his hands and cupped them around one eye, acting as if he were peering through a spyglass.

'Didn't you hear me, jackanapes?' Crawford demanded.

The urchin grinned cheekily. 'O' course I did, but I'm looking for the gennulman.'

Tildy giggled at the child's engaging mischievousness, but her husband scowled.

'I'll put my boot to your arse, you little bastard!'

'No you wun't!' the child was unafraid. 'Not today you wun't, because me Dad wun't let you.'

Crawford's scowl deepened. 'Oh, won't he? And who might he be, when he's about?'

The tiny snub-nosed face radiated delight as the man fell into the trap. 'King George, you fool!' He whooped with glee, and agilely dodged the kick Thomas Crawford let fly at him. 'King George is me Dad, you bloody mawkin!' He ducked under Edgar Crawford's outstretched hands and went whooping down the street to safety.

Tildy turned away to hide her amusement, but her husband had already noticed her smiles.

'Well, since you finds it so funny,' he snarled, 'you can get in theer and fetch Dick Suffield out.'

For a moment Tildy's own sorely tried spirit flared at his tone and manner, and an angry retort leapt to her tongue.

But she held it back. She was a married woman now, and in her world husbands were the unchallenged masters of their wives.

'How shall I know him?' she asked quietly.

Her husband, satisfied with his apparent domination over her, grinned.

'Doon't worry about that, my wench. Youm a strange face, and a pretty 'un. Dick Suffield 'ull make himself known to you a bit sharpish. When he does, tell him that Tom Crawford wants to do him a bit o' good. I knows him of old, that'll bring him wi' you, never fear.'

Tildy went under the arched entrance and into the warehouse yard. Only a few people were waiting now and the pace of the Weighing-in had slackened. She stood at the double doors of the building and peered in. Dick Suffield, bending over the weighing pans, noticed her immediately and whistled softly in appreciation. Gesturing to his helpers to continue without him, he approached the girl.

'Well now, my pretty, what can I do for you?' He paused and stared meaningfully at her bulging waistline. 'Not much more than as already been done by the looks on it,' he leered.

The young girl blushed with embarrassment, but met his lascivious stare without flinching.

'I want to speak to Dick Suffield,' she told him.

For a few moments he made no acknowledgement of her request. Instead he let his gaze travel slowly from her glossy neat-braided hair, to her small shoes and back again – noting the good quality of her simple clothes in passing.

'You'll not be a nailing lass, my honey-lamb,' he observed loudly. 'Youm too sweet and tidy . . . Er? . . . Now let me have a guess . . . I should think by your clothes that you'se bin in service to the gentry. They'm of good cut, even though they've seen better days. Would I be correct in that?' He assumed an air of grave and respectful interrogation.

'Please! All I want is to find Master Suffield.' Tildy's

embarrassment was increasing as she heard the sniggers and lewd comments of the onlookers, who were enjoying Suffield teasing her. 'Will you tell me where I can find him?'

The man's bluff features reddened with suppressed laughter.

'Why does you insist on him, my pretty, won't I suit you? I knows I don't look like the Prince Regent, better I should call him King now though, with his old dad being dead since January last, God rest him . . . But I arn't such a bad-looking cove, am I?'

I'm not caring how you look!' the girl retorted sharply.

Suffield held up his hands to ward off her annoyance.

'Calm down, my pretty, it's only my bit o' fun. I'm the man you seek.'

'Are you sure you're Suffield?' Tildy had no wish to be teased further.

He gave her his assurance, and sensing that he was speaking the truth, she gave him the message from her husband.

His face showed surprised, and he looked keenly at her.

'What be you to Tom Crawford?' he wanted to know.

'I'm his wife,' Tildy replied.

A calculating gleam passed across his eyes, and then he grinned and said easily, 'Very well, Mistress Crawford, lead on, and I'll goo wi' you and have that word wi' my old friend, Tom.'

As the pair moved across the yard Jonathan Sanders looked out from the office window, and noticed Tildy.

She is a pretty girl, he thought casually. For a brief moment he mused on who she might be, and what she was doing with the foreman, then put the matter from his mind and returned to his work at the ledgers. Yet later, without any deliberate volition, the memory of the young girl was to re-enter his mind with a curious persistence throughout the remainder of the day and night.

The reunion between Thomas Crawford and Suffield

was, on the surface at least, very cordial. After the usual greetings and some preliminary talk, a few coins passed into the foreman's hand, and he agreed to give Edgar Crawford a little more time in which to work up his iron – neglecting to inform the nailer that Jonathan Sanders had ordered him to do so already. Then, with that matter settled and his brother walking away from them, Thomas Crawford brought up his own affairs.

'I wants to start back at the nailing, Dick.' He tried to appear bluff and open. 'Truth to tell, being in service doon't really suit me. I'd sooner work as me own man agen.'

The foreman nodded understandingly, while his mind took full account of the bedraggled appearance of the other man.

'You looks as if the position you held in service was a good 'un, Tom,' he remarked, with scarcely veiled sarcasm. ' . . . judging by the quality o' your togs. There's precious few nailers as ever wore such fine-cut cloth.' The small shrewd eyes flicked to Tildy. 'And your young missus there looks well-clad and bonny wi' good living, not like our poor worn-ragged nailing wenches. I must confess, my old cully, it surprises me that you should want to come back to this trade. Especially since you seems to have a good bit o' money wi' you, judging by the easy way you slipped me them few shillins to keep your brother from the Bridewell.

'Surely you'd do better to set yourself up as a Master o' some sort . . . Open a shop, mayhap?'

Although Thomas Crawford was inwardly raging with resentment at the way the man was baiting him, he forced a sycophantic smile. 'Truth to tell, Dick, I've not got more than a few shillings, my bloody missus saw to that.' He could not prevent himself from glaring at Tildy. 'That's why I wants to get summat arranged as quick as I can; and what's more natural than for me to come and see you first, seeing as how we'em such old friends.'

Suffield sneered openly. 'I takes that statement as a real

kindness, Cully. Now let me have a guess . . . You needs me to help you, is that it?'

The other accepted the humiliating sneer. 'Yes, I does,' he answered, a noticeable note of pleading now entering his voice. 'You knows my mettle of old, Dick. I'd do anything you wanted me to, and you'd not regret your kindness in helping me, that I'll promise.'

Again the foreman's small eyes flickered to take in the young woman. Despite her misshapen body he found himself desiring her strongly. Suffield was a man possessed of considerable imagination, and he could easily visualize how desirable this young woman would be once she had borne her child and regained her figure.

She's a rare sweet piece! His thoughts moved with their customary rapidity to consider how best he might turn this situation to his advantage. The foreman had long cherished plans for becoming a power in the nailing trade, and those plans also encompassed the ruination of Jonathan Sanders as an added bonus. He could certainly think of ways he could make use of Thomas Crawford in the furtherance of his plans. The fact that the man now possessed a wife who so powerfully excited Suffield's sexual and sensual desires was an added incentive to bind Crawford closely to him. The foreman drew a deep breath . . . 'Alright, Tom, you tell me what your needs be, and I'll see what's to be done to help you.'

Thomas Crawford's relief banished all anger and resentment and made his caution disappear. He overwhelmed his benefactor with thanks and promises of loyalty. His wife, however, retained doubts which had increased by the minute during the foregoing exchanges.

Tildy had read what was in Suffield's eyes each time he looked at her, and she felt a strong premonition.

He'll prove no friend to us at all, she told herself, and her anxiety burgeoned. We'll have to pay a hard price for Dick Suffield's aid. Or rather, *I* will . . . That I'll wager . . .

Chapter Nine

Dick Suffield took the couple to a cottage that he owned in a small square known as the Tinyard. It was a standard dwelling, with one small room and a minute pantry downstairs, and a bedroom and narrow landing upstairs. Adjoining the rear of the cottages was a row of leanto workshops, and between each pair of workshops was a brewhouse with a bricked-in copper for washing and brewing. At the end of the terrace stood the communal privies, and next to those the midden-heap. Tildy was grateful for the fact that their cottage was in the centre of the row, sufficiently distant from the privies and their attendant heap to escape some of the stench they emitted.

The couple entered their new home late on Saturday afternoon. Suffield showed them the workshop with its pair of blocks and Olivers, hearth and anvils, and then the living quarters. With his eyes on Tildy he addressed her husband.

'Now normally I'd be asking three and a half shillings rent for the house and forge, and that 'ud be weekly and in advance. But seeing as how we'em old friends, Tom, I'll just take three shillings for it, and you can pay me next Weighing-in day. Is that fair enough?'

Thomas Crawford, fingering the scant few coins left in his pockets, accepted with alacrity.

'What say you, Mistress Crawford?' The foreman smiled genially at her.

Tildy looked around at the cramped, stone-flagged living room, and thought how lucky she was that it didn't have a dirt floor such as Edgar Crawford's cottage. With a bucket of whitewash and a good scrub she could at least make it clean and fresh. Aloud she replied:

'Yes, Master Suffield, I think it a fair rent.'

'Good! You'll find I'm a very fair man in all my dealings, Mistress, and I'm always ready to oblige them that obliges me.'

She imagined that she could detect a double-edged meaning in his words, then silently scolded herself.

Don't be so foolish! Why must you imagine that all men are drawn to you, you silly, vapouring idiot! It's only the man's usual manner, surely it is. He means nothing more than what he says.

There was some further talk between the two men concerning the supply of hand-tools, iron rods and firing to start Thomas Crawford at the work; and Suffield agreed to sell him the tools and breeze and take the debt back at so much weekly. The iron rods would be issued from Sanders' warehouse in the normal way. They spat on their palms and slapped them together to seal the bargain, then Suffield took Thomas Crawford away with him to collect some of the articles, leaving Tildy alone in the cottage.

She looked about her, and suddenly realized what was nagging away at her . . .

'Dear God above, we've not even a candle-stub to give us light when it gets dark, let alone a bed to lie on,' she exclaimed.

For a moment her heart sank and she felt a deep despondency, then she drew a long breath and forced herself to shake off the feeling. 'Surely Tom will buy what's needed after he's fetched the other things!'

She went to the back door of the forge and leaned against the side-post, gazing out into the square. It was surprisingly quiet. Traditionally, after their work had been weighed-in, the nailers took the remainder of the day and the Sunday as a rest period. Most of the men went to the alehouses and drinking-dens that abounded in the district and drank and gambled away whatever money they had been able to avoid giving their wives for the household expenses. The women and elder children snatched the opportunity of a respite from the grinding labour of their lives and lay down to rest for a few hours. Even the most house-proud wives would put off the cleaning and cooking until Sunday morning. Only those children who were too small to work at the forges had the energy to play and skylark; and now there were a few toddlers clustering about the well-house in the centre of the square, engrossed in a game of their own creation.

Tildy watched the tiny ragged-clad children and daydreamed how her own child would also play about the well-house in the years to come. It became a disquieting dream, for she would not relish seeing her own child with its stomach distended by malnourishment, its legs crooked with rickets, and complexion pitted by the scars of smallpox that so many of the children about the well had borne from their earliest years.

'There must be some way of improving my child's life,' Tildy told herself. 'But how? I can't read or write. I'm ignorant of the world, and I'm married to a man who is likewise without education.' She smiled ruefully. 'To think it was only yesterday morning that I was wed. It seems like years ago.' Apprehension stirred within her. 'Tonight we shall lie here alone in this house as man and wife.' Her hands moved to shield her swollen belly. 'Tom didn't touch me last night. He couldn't, could he, with us both being so weary? But tonight he'll not be so weary . . . Surely he'll not want to do anything to me, what with me being so near to birthing the baby.' Her breathing fluttered nervously. 'Surely he'll leave me be? Surely he will?'

'I takes it youm me new neighbour?'

The gruff-toned question startled Tildy into awareness of the woman standing outside the next cottage's door. She was tall and raw-boned, her middle-aged features badly pitted with bluish smallpox scars. On her greying hair she wore a man's bullycock hat, and her only clothing was a man's old sleeveless waistcoat barely covering her shrivel-led breasts, a long pair of cotton drawers and a sack apron which reached from her middle to her iron-studded clogs.

She grinned to show a completely toothless mouth and spoke jokingly, 'You'll know me next time you sees me, I'll tek me oath on it.'

Tildy, made aware of her rudeness in staring as she had been, became flustered.

'I beg pardon!' she blurted out. 'I meant no offence.'

The pale-pink gums were in clear view as the woman laughed. 'Don't moither none, my wench, there's plenty more who looks like me around these parts. You'll have your fill o' gawkin' at 'um in double-quick time, that's a surety, that is . . . I teks it youm Tom Crawford's new-come wife.'

Tildy's obvious surprise at the other's knowledge made the woman laugh again.

'Don't be so shook-up at me knowing that, my duck. News travels like bloody lightning down here in the Sidemoor. I'm Hester Lammas, wife to Ikey Lammas. He arn't here to bid you welcome because he's in the bloody alehouse swilling down the porter like the pig he is. I 'udden't mind that, but he ne'er thinks to bring his own true, sweet-loving young wife a flagon or two back to gargle wi'.'

Tildy had to giggle at the woman's droll manner, and

found herself readily answering the rapid succession of questions that Hester Lammas put to her. The pleasantly ugly face softened as the story of the glum wedding, the ordeal at the stocks and the loss of the wages all came out; and Tildy herself experienced a tremendous easement in being able to pour out her troubles to a sympathetic listener.

At last Hester Lammas had heard enough. 'Just you wait theer a minute, my duck,' she told the girl, and disappeared into her cottage, to reappear some minutes later carrying a large bundle in her muscular bare arms.

'Here you be, this is a good flock bed. It'll do for you until you get one o' your own. Then you con gi' it back to me.'

The unexpected and unasked for kindness brought a lump to Tildy's throat.

'My thanks to you, Mistress Lammas,' she said haltingly.

'You call me Hester,' the woman instructed. 'And talk no more o' thanks, 'tis little enough I'm doing for you. I arn't used this bed since me boy died on it last Whitsuntide.' She chuckled gruffly at the instantly suppressed frown of doubt on the younger woman's face. 'Doon't you fret none, he didn't die o' naught that's catching. He allus was sickly, the poor cratur, since the day he was breached. His yed was allus too vast for his body, and it just kept on aswelling like a great bladder-ball as he got older. Thanks be to God, he died afore it could burst right open. It 'udden't half a made a mess if it had a done.'

While still talking she pushed past Tildy and carried the flock mattress up the narrow staircase to lay it on the plank floor of the tiny bedroom. While she was inside the house Hester Lammas' faded, red-rimmed eyes moved all around the bare interior, and when she came back to Tildy her gaunt features were compassionate. With one work-calloused hand she stroked the girl's soft smooth cheek.

'Youm a mite short o' house chattels, I see . . . Never fret none, we'll soon get that remedied.'

She encircled one slender wrist between finger and thumb and led the young girl upstairs, disregarding her protests.

'Say no more, my duck. You lie down on this fine bed and rest awhile. Just think on that babby that's acoming. It needs you to rest so that it can draw strength from you.'

Gently but firmly Hester Lammas made Tildy lie down on the mattress. As the soft loose flock moulded to her weight and gave malleable support to her aching back muscles, Tildy sighed with pleasurable relief.

'There now, that's nice arn't it!' Hester Lammas' toothless mouth smiled down at her. 'Now you just shut your peepers and take a nap. I've some errands to do. I'll not be long away.'

For the first time in many long years Tildy experienced what it felt like to be the recipient of maternal tenderness, and like a small child she felt utter trust. She let herself relax completely, and with that relaxation came an all-pervading drowsiness. Softly and easily she fell into sleep.

Oh they called her Jenny Bligh, Jenny Bliiiggghhh.
Oh they called her Jenny Bligh, Jenny Bliiiggghhh.
Oh they called her Jenny Bligh
'Til a Flash went in her eye,
And they brought her home to die, Jenny Bliiiggghhh . . .
Arms around each other's shoulders, Tom Crawford and his brother Edgar came singing, staggering and stumbling through the long narrow covered-entry into the Tinyard. From side to side they wove, shoulders hitting the walls and bouncing their bodies against each other.

She was born to making nails, making naiilllsss.
She was born to making nails, making naiilllsss.
She was born to making nails
With all that that entails,

91

Youm a loser, Heads or Tails, making naiilllsss.

The song's bitter lament echoed through the muddy square and Tildy came awake with a start. She lay still for a moment, trying to identify what had woken her, her eyes staring into the darkness of the night.

Oh they called her Jenny Bligh, Jenny Bliigghhh,

Oh they called her Jenny Bligh . . .

Tildy recognized her husband's voice.

'G'night Edgar, me old cock! See you in the morn . . . Oh they called her Jenny Bligh, 'til a Flash went in her eye . . . And they brought her home . . . '

BANG! The back door was kicked open.

. . . to die, Jenny Bliiiggghhh . . .

CRASH! Wood splintered and broke and the dull thud of a body falling brought Tildy upright with a jerk, her heart thumping rapidly.

'God strike me! What the bleedin' . . . ? God strike me! *Tildy*? Wheer the Hell be you? TILDYYY?' Tom Crawford's roars seemed loud enough to rouse the entire village.

Tildy levered herself up from the mattress and felt her way across the landing and down the stairs.

'Be quiet, I'm coming,' she called.

In the living room the small window let in enough moonlight for her to see that a few pieces of furniture had been brought into her home while she slept: a table, a couple of chairs and a stool, and several sack-wrapped bundles and wooden boxes. In the wreckage of one of the latter Thomas Crawford was sprawling face-down. The young girl's rush of warm gratitude towards her new neighbours was paralleled by her angry disgust for her drunken husband. He pushed himself upright and, still on his knees, peered about him in puzzlement.

'Wheer's this bleedin' lot come from?' he demanded aggressively. 'Have you bin scoring up a tally wi' a bloody cheapjack?'

The injustice of his attitude stung Tildy.

'How could I score up a tally with anyone?' she asked indignantly. 'You took all the money we had out with you. I've not got a ha-penny. I think it was Hester Lammas who brought these things here. She's given us a bed as well, and she expects no payment, she's done it out of kindness.'

Using the wall to support him, he came laboriously to his feet.

'Who d'you say?' He stood swaying. 'Who give us a bed?'

'Hester Lammas, she lives next door,' Tildy repeated.

'Lammas? Lammas?' He blinked owlishly, then nodded. 'Ahr, I knows her . . . Old Ikey's woman . . . Yes, she's the good heart, that one . . . A good heart.'

He swayed violently, and would have fallen if Tildy had not stepped forward and grabbed his arms to steady him.

'And you, did you get the tools and things from Suffield?' she wanted to know.

He grinned lopsidedly, and essayed a grotesquely exaggerated wink.

'O' course I did, my sweetheart.'

'Well, where are they?'

'I've left 'um at the Mitre alehouse for safe-keeping.' He winked again, as if to demonstrate his sagacity. 'Johnno Dipple is a good landlord, for all he's a bloody fogger. He'll watch 'um for me until I can fetch 'um out agen. Wi' any luck I'll have them out first thing tomorrow morning. Won't corst me more than a shillin'.'

'Why should it cost you anything at all?' Although she felt a dismayed certainty as to what the answer would be, Tildy was still driven to ask the question.

'Well, that's a daft thing to arsk, that is!' Her husband was scornful. 'It'll cost me a shillin', because I popped 'um to him for a shillin . . . ' He paused to belch loudly, then went on. 'Arter all, a man's got to buy his round o' drink, arn't he? He's got to stand his corner . . . Everybody knows that.'

Tildy's dismay was overlayed by exasperation, but that fresh emotion was tempered by the knowledge that at this moment in time she was helpless to rectify the situation. Not only had he drunk away all their money, he had even pawned the tools that he needed to earn a living. She shook her head, and felt near to tears, but knew it was pointless to prolong the conversation.

'Come, I'll help you up to bed,' she told him.

Grinning vacuously, Crawford let himself be led up the stairs and placed on the flock mattress.

Tildy pulled off his boots, and lay on her back beside him. Since they had no blankets both of them stayed fully clad.

For a while they lay silent, then he moved so that he lay close-pressed against her, and Tildy felt his hands on her body. She stiffened involuntarily. Crawford's fingers unbuttoned her bodice and then his hand was inside her dress, cupping the firm milk-swollen breasts, fondling the sensitive nipples. She tried to push his hand away.

'No, Tom, don't!' she whispered.

His breathing quickened, and his thigh clamped across her own, while his mouth crushed down on hers. Tildy jerked her head back from the beer-thick, tobacco-laden breath.

'What about the baby, you'll hurt it!' she warned, a feeling of desperation stealing over her.

For the first time he answered: 'It'll be alright, sweetheart!' His voice was hoarse and the words came jerkily as the lust to possess her surged through him. 'We'em man and wife now, my wench. You carn't refuse me!'

His mouth went to her breasts and greedily slobbered and sucked at the erect nipples. With rapid movements he unlaced the codpiece of his pantaloons, freeing his engorged maleness, then with the same hand began to pull her long skirt up about her waist.

In Tildy's womb the baby kicked hard and painfully. Desperately she fought to keep the man from her but, driven wild by his violent hunger for a woman's body, Thomas Crawford forced her arms above her head, using one hand to pinion both slender wrists. Brutally he bludgeoned his legs between the girl's thighs and, despite her by now frantic efforts to evade him, he entered her.

In anguish Tildy bit her lips until they bled. 'Oh my baby! My poor baby!' The silent cries reverberated through her being . . .

Afterwards, when her husband had done and was snoring beside her in drunken slumber, Tildy rearranged her clothing and made her way downstairs. In the living room she slumped onto a chair. At first she could feel only a terrible sense of degredation, as well as self-contempt at her failure to prevent him from abusing her body. This slowly passed, and it was as if a vacuum within her had swallowed all emotion and metamorphosed it into its own nothingness. No tears moistened her eyes, no sobs tore from her throat. Then, almost imperceptibly, the vacuum was filled with a cold, implacable resolve.

'If that animal upstairs has harmed my baby in his rape of me, then I'll destroy him as a man, and as a human being. I swear it! Before God, I swear it!'

The oath calmed Tildy and she went through the forge and out into the moonlit night. Drawing water from the well, she bathed her violated body. As the cool liquid laved and soothed her flesh, Tildy felt wonder at her rapidly growing feeling of inner strength.

'I know that I cannot match a man in bodily force,' she admitted. 'Nevertheless, I now know that no man will ever crush my spirit, and nothing will ever make me give up and surrender without a struggle.' Her lips parted and she smiled up at the stars, sardonically amused by the wayward fancy that had just entered her mind: 'I'm like the Iron Duke, I'm become unbeatable . . . '

Tildy's sense of invincibility only lasted until the full realization of her predicament flooded through her mind. The tools and iron obtained from Dick Suffield on credit were in pawn!

'Dear God!' she swore softly in sudden despair. 'There's no money to fetch them out! No money for anything . . . Tom's drunk it all away!'

For long, long minutes she remained sitting on the low wall of the well, head bowed, hands moving restlessly across the rough stone coping. Suddenly the child in her womb stirred, and from the depths of her being Tildy found fresh resolve . . .

The Mitre alehouse stood in the long straight road that was Bromsgrove town's centre. The weathered sign swayed and creaked above Tildy's shawled head, and the wind moaned in lament as she willed her pounding heart to slow and calm. The town was shuttered and still, and the front of the tumbledown alehouse showed no sign of life. However, from a solitary side window a lamp shone, and shadows were thrown into wavering silhouettes on the wall of the neighbouring building, as people rose and moved within the lighted room.

Summoning her courage, Tildy stepped up to the front door and hammered on its thick unpainted boards with clenched hands. In the silence of the early morning her blows reverberated thunderously and for a brief instant Tildy's tormented nerves almost failed her. The door was still vibrating from her furious assault when it swung inwards and a hoarse voice growled threateningly.

'Bist looking for a broken yed, you noisy bastard?'

Tildy involuntarily stepped back so that the moonlight enveloped her, and the hulking figure in the doorway swore in surprise.

'Blast my eyes, who the bleedin' hell be you?'

Fighting to keep her voice steady, she told him. 'If you please, I'm Thomas Crawford's wife . . . and I've a wish to speak with Master Dipple.'

For a few seconds there was no reply, then the hulking figure moved towards her, and became a huge-bodied, shaven-headed man, whose features, etched by silver moonlight into sharp relief, were the epitome of brutal menace.

Tildy drew breath sharply in fear and shrank back as this fearsome man loomed over her.

'What does the likes o' Tom Crawford's missus want with Johnno Dipple at this bloody hour o' the morning?'

His foul breath gusted against her face as he bent forward, and her voice shook as she faltered out, 'It's about the tools . . . and the iron . . . I've got to have them . . . we've no money . . . nor food . . . and . . . and . . . we've . . . ' Her lips trembled uncontrollably, and to her own mortification, she burst into tears.

A second man appeared at the alehouse door and stood watching the weeping girl. After a few moments he tapped the shaven-headed man's shoulder and jerked his own head in a gesture of dismissal. His huge companion grinned and winked salaciously, then went back into the dark entrance passage of the house.

Dick Suffield waited until the other was out of earshot, then moved quietly to stand directly in front of Tildy, who remained unaware of his presence in her distress.

'Now then, Mistress Crawford, dry your eyes. Things can't be that bad, I'm sure.'

Hearing the bluff-toned voice Tildy experienced an eerie recognition of an inevitable happening. She knew with utter certainty that this man was to play an important role in her life. For fleeting instants she seemed to be on the verge of remembering some previously held knowledge of exactly what that role would be, but even as her mind strained to recall it, that knowledge eluded her, and it was as if a veil had fallen to prevent her mind finding what it sought.

'I reckon I know what's amiss, my pretty.' Suffield went on speaking, and now his voice was soft and gentle. 'That husband o' yourn has popped the tools and iron I give him . . . That's it, arn't it!'

Wiping her eyes on her shawl, Tildy nodded.

Suffield's yellow teeth showed in a fleeting grin of satisfaction, then he assumed an expression of sympathy and patted the girl's slender shoulder in a fatherly gesture of comfort. 'Doon't you fret yourself any more, my pretty. I'll help you all I can. Dick Suffield's not the man to stand by and see a decent young 'ooman grieve herself, if he can do ought to prevent it . . .'

Tildy looked squarely into his face. 'And what do I have to give you, in return for your help, Master Suffield?'

The man smiled kindly at her, and shook his head slowly from side to side.

'Doon't moither yourself, honey-lamb. There's no price to be paid for my help. I arn't a cove who trys to take advantage of a wench's troubles. You'll ha' to repay me whatever it costs me, o' course. I'm not able to afford to give money away. But the repayment can wait until youm earning sufficient and above for your needs . . .' He paused to let the full import of his words be absorbed then, lowering his voice to a conspiratorial whisper, finished, ' . . . and whatever I give you now, we can keep a secret atween the two of us . . . Just you and me . . . No one else need ever know . . .'

Coins clinked together as he pushed them into Tildy's hand and gently closed her fingers upon them.

'Goo on home now, Tildy,' he urged softly. 'Tomorrow morn you'll find tools, iron and breeze on your forge.'

He turned and went back into the alehouse.

Tildy stood staring at the closed door, her mind a confused jumble of emotions, then wearily began to trudge back along the rutted road to the Sidemoor.

Behind her, in the hot, reeking air of the Mitre's side-room, Janey Porter's gin-flushed face glared at Dick Suffield, sitting on the opposite side of the bottle-strewn table.

'Youm getting up to your bleeding tricks agen, be you?' she accused furiously.

98

The man smiled genially, and took a long swig from the stone gin bottle he held in his hand.

'Ahhhh, that was good!' He gusted his satisfaction, and winked at the angry girl. 'Doon't you fret yourself, my honey-lamb. You knows well that youm my sweetheart.'

'Just you remember it!' she snapped. 'And remember whose bastard I gi' birth to, and am acaring for.'

Suffield leaned back in his chair and roared with laughter.

Chapter Ten

The sun was high and hot next morning, and the only moving creature in the Tinyard square was a starving cat, rooting among the stinking heaps of refuse in search of food. Hester Lammas was in her workshop stirring a mess of porridge in the iron pot suspended above the glowing hearth. Using the wooden spoon she tasted the thick gruel and, satisfied with the result, lifted the pot easily in her tough-sinewed arms and carried it into her living room. Moments later she reappeared in the square carrying an earthenware bowl full of the porridge, and went to her new neighbour's cottage.

Opening the door, she peered into the fusty-smelling room. Her gaunt features scowled, then softened. Tildy was sitting upon a broken-backed chair, her upper body slumped across the table and her head pillowed sideways upon her arms. Hester Lammas studied the dark smudges of dried tears upon the sleeping girl's cheek and clucked her tongue sympathetically. Through the thin jerry-built partition wall she had heard Tom Crawford's homecoming and subsequent rape of his wife the previous night.

'I fear you'se got yourself a bad bugger theer, my poor wench.' The woman shook her head and sighed heavily. 'But then, where be you likely to find a good 'un in this bleeding hell-hole? Tildy?' She spoke aloud, gently shaking the young girl awake. 'Tildy, I'se brung you a bite to ate.'

Tildy reluctantly dragged herself to consciousness and smiled her gratitude. 'You're very good to me, Mistress Lammas!' she murmured, and full remembrance of the night's happenings abruptly returned to her. She felt in the pocket of her skirt for the coins and pulled them out. There was nine shillings and eight pence in silver and copper. She spread the coins on the table and addressed the elder woman.

'Please, Mistress Lammas, let me pay you something towards the furniture and other things you've given me.'

Hester Lammas' toothless mouth pursed in doubt and burgeoning offence, and Tildy hastened to placate her.

'I pray you, don't be offended . . . ' She went on to explain how she had come by the money.

The older woman listened intently and made no comment until the story was finished. Then she said merely, 'Eat your vittles afore they gets cold, and put that money away somewhere's safe. I'll be but a second.' She opened the rear door of the room and looked into the adjoining forge, then turned back to Tildy. 'Well, you'se got your tools, iron and breeze alright in your shop.'

Tildy experienced a surge of gratitude towards Dick Suffield. 'He has behaved very kindly towards me,' she told her companion. 'But I must confess that when I first met him I doubted his character and motives.'

The other woman cackled with laughter. 'Then keep on doubting the bugger, my duck. Dick Suffield's character and motives am plain enough to them as knows 'im as well as I does. Youm a rare pretty wench, and when you'se birthed the babby you'll be a sweet enough armful for any man's bed. No, Dick Suffield's a real crafty sod, and knows well what he's about.'

'And what might that be, Hester Lammas?'

Unnoticed by the women Tom Crawford had awoken and come silently down the stairs. Bleary-eyed and unshaven, still reeking of stale ale, he glared sullenly at his wife. 'And doon't you know, wife, that an 'ooman shouldn't go stuffin' her guts afore her husband's had a bite to ate, or even a sup to quench his thirst. I ought to ram that bloody gruel down your throat until it chokes you.'

'You hold hard, Tom Crawford,' Hester sprang to Tildy's defence. 'I brung that gruel in for your missus. The poor cratur needs a bit o' care, being so far gone wi' that babby. If you had any decency in your bones you'd ha' got up and made sure she was alright instead of lying stinking in your bed, whiles the poor wench was having to sleep on a tabletop like a bloody tramper, 'ooman.'

The young man was disconcerted by this attack. Hester Lammas had a well-deserved reputation as a ferocious brawler and braver men than he hesitated to cross her.

'God strike me, woman! Give a man chance to wake up,' he grumbled, but in a placatory tone. 'I've not got me yed working proper yet.'

'Well I 'as.' His opponent pressed on relentlessly. 'And I'll tell you this . . . Youm a lucky cove to have a good little cratur like this 'un for wife. She's got your bloody tools and iron back from Johnno Dipple so you can earn yourself a few shillings.'

Tom Crawford's devil of jealousy immediately roused itself, and he scowled accusingly at Tildy, whose head was bent, and face half-hidden from him.

'So, you bin down at the Mitre getting up to God knows what wi' Johnno Dipple, as you?' His drink-lacerated nerves caused his temper to flare. 'God strike me; I'll bloody well do for you iffen I gets to know that you'se bin sportin' with another man.'

The older woman acted to prevent the threatened explosion of violence, knowing from bitter experience what could happen to Tildy once she was left alone with her husband.

'She's bin sportin' wi' nobody, Tom Crawford. I went down to the Mitre with her, and I give her the money to get the stuff back from Johnno Dipple.'

His bleary eyes swung to the coins still lying on the table, and his tobacco-stained fingers trembled as he pointed at them. 'Then how the bleedin' hell did her get that theer? Was it earned by lying on her back wi' her legs open?'

'Don't talk like a bloody fool!' Hester Lammas spat out. 'That theer is my money, and be thankful that I'm good enough to lend it to you. Or you'll find out sooner than you'd like to what it's like to slave your days out at the nails wi' empty guts.' She saw uncertainty register on his features and seizing her advantage went on. 'Still, if youm too proud-livered to take my help, then I can bloody well take the offer back quick enough.'

She jerked her hand out as if to snatch the coins up, and Crawford automatically reached to prevent her.

'No Hester!' he blurted. 'No! I'm sorry I spoke as I did!' He flushed deeply as he babbled out his apologies.

The woman, satisfied with her victory, heard him out in silence.

' . . . well, I just wants to say that I'm really grateful to you, Hester . . . ' he ended lamely.

She grinned, disclosing pink gums. 'Let's hear no more talk of whores and doxies then, young Tom.' She was magnanimous. 'I knows youm not a bad cove at 'eart, and you'se got a real fine little wench for a wife. just you remember that, and treat her well.'

With that parting admonition she left the couple alone.

Tildy pushed her scarcely tasted gruel away from her. 'Would you like this, Tom? Only I've naught else to offer you until I can get out and buy something.'

The thought of eating caused a wave of nausea to flood through Crawford. All he craved at this moment was a drink to quieten his tormented nerves, and to still the churnings of his stomach. He forced himself to smile at his nervous wife.

'No sweetheart, you ate it. It'll do you and the babby good. I'll just take a couple of shillings and goo and buy a pie or summat.'

Tildy, afraid of provoking any further outbursts of rage from him, allowed him to take some of the money from the table without protest, and watched him leave with a sense of relief.

Alone once more she forced herself to face an unpalatable fact! She was terrified of his violence, and the harm it might bring to her unborn child.

I must learn to be meek and unoffending, she told herself. ' . . . But what if that avails you naught?' a tiny voice whispered in her mind. 'What then, Tildy? What then?'

Chapter Eleven

Oh for a closer walk with God.
A calm and heavenly frame.
A light to shine upon the road
That leads me to the Lamb . . .

The Sidemoor's tiny Emmanuel Chapel was full and the voices of the congregation rang out powerfully to fill the air with music.

Hester Lammas and Tildy, carrying food and flagons of ale, paused outside the red brick walls to listen.

'Be you a Methody, Tildy?' Hester Lammas wanted to know.

The younger woman shook her glossy-haired, bonnetless head, a fleeting bitter memory causing her eyes to darken. 'My uncle was though. He was a true Ranter. But I fear he was such that he turned me against his faith.'

The toothless mouth before her pursed and clucked in agreement. 'Ahr, I knows what you means, child. But some of the Methodys down here are good souls, and trys to help them that needs it. Jacob Ashfield preaches a rare good sermon. I'se bin and listened to him manys the time

. . . And truth to tell there's bin times when I'se wished I was a Methody meself. It must be nice to have a faith like them, and to have a sober, God-fearing man for husband, instead of that drunken, wasting bugger I'se got.' The woman abruptly cackled with laughter. 'But then, iffen your man is sober, how be you going to take a drop o' Mother's Ruin when the thirst torments you?'

Tildy laughed with her. The beauty of the warm sunny day had lifted her earlier low spirits, and Hester Lammas' company was more than welcome to her loneliness. It was still only morning and the pair had been into Bromsgrove to buy provisions from a dealer.

'You must learn to act as we does,' the older woman had instructed. 'As soon as you gets money, then buy food for the week, and pay your rent. Doon't gi' your man chance to spend everything in the alehouse. Because that's what the buggers does. Manys the time my Ikey has worked like a slave for a week or more, and made me work wi' him, and then he's took all the Weigh-in money and gone off on the bleedin' drink, and not left me a penny-piece to feed the children or mesen . . .'

She resettled the broken-brimmed, low-crowned man's hat on her mass of tangled hair, and chuckled wryly.

'Still, you knows what they says, doon't you?'

'No.' Tildy smiled.

The older woman chuckled again. 'Why, they says . . . Iffen life gets hard, then you must get harder.'

Tildy laughed in appreciation.

> So shall my walk be close with God,
> Calm and serene my frame.
> So purer light shall mark the path
> That leads me to the Lamb.

The hymn came to an end, and Hester Lammas jerked her head.

'Come on, let's goo and listen to a bit o' the sermon.'

Tildy demurred. 'What if Tom should be waiting at home for me?'

106

'Doon't talk daft, wench!' her friend scoffed. 'The bugger 'ull be drinking as long as the ale is for sale. He'll not be home until the night.'

Tildy allowed herself to be led into the chapel. It was austere, as befitted the Ranters, or Primitive Methodists, with a small raised pulpit for the preacher and a simple altar table. There were no ornate fixed pews, merely rows of rough-hewn wooden benches, which to Tildy's mind complemented the rough-hewn appearance of the congregation. A stocky, white-haired, black-clad man was in the pulpit, and as the two newcomers unobtrusively seated themselves he began to read hoarsely from the open Bible on the lectern.

'For I was envious at the foolish, when I saw the prosperity of the wicked. For there are no bands in their death but their strength is firm . . . '

Tildy heard the words without giving thought to their meaning, instead she let her eyes rove about her. Most of the people present were tolerably well-clad, the men in dark broadcloth coats and breeches, their womenfolk wearing plain dresses with clean white aprons and mobcaps. Here and there were dotted the rags of the very poor, but Tildy noted that even these unfortunates had made some effort to cleanse and tidy themselves for their appearance before their God.

' . . . They are not in trouble as other men, neither are they plagued like other men . . . ' The preacher's voice rose angrily, as if he felt personally affronted that the wicked of the world should be so blessed.

On the front bench, Jonathan Sanders sat hunched forward, his hands cupping and hiding his face.

' . . . Neither are they plagued as other men . . . '

The words echoed in his mind and conjured a mental vision of his wife's face.

She plagues me, the young man thought sadly. Or rather, my love for her plagues me . . . Dear God, what is wrong with me? Why cannot I act the man and make love to my own wife? Why am I impotent? Why?

Hester Lammas had seen the nailmaster, and nudged Tildy to draw her attention to him. Tildy glanced with interest at his slender figure. The elegance of Sanders' plum-coloured morning coat, and high-collared shirt with its carefully arranged cravat contrasted glaringly with the crude-cut clothing of the other men, and rendered its wearer's presence in this humble chapel even more incongruous.

'Master Jon is the only nailmaster who worships in chapel,' Hester Lammas whispered. 'All the rest play the fine gentry and goo to St John's.'

At that moment Sanders straightened his body and glanced about him. His eyes met Tildy's and for a brief moment their gazes locked and held. Then, suddenly aware of how shamelessly she was staring, Tildy became flustered and dropped her head. But as her momentary embarrassment subsided, she experienced a sense of pity for the young man.

His eyes were tortured, she told herself. The poor man is enduring some dreadful torment . . .

When Jonathan Sanders returned home from the chapel he found two saddled horses tethered at the side of the house. Both bore signs of having been hard, even mercilessly, ridden, their flanks bloody from spurring and their glossy coats sweat-lathered and dust-clotted. His sensitive features twisted in distress. He hated cruelty towards dumb beasts, and to drive a horse to the limits of its endurance was cruel indeed . . .

'It'll be that dammed scapegrace, Jervis, come to tempt Carlotta into more excesses . . . ' Jervis Tinsley was Carlotta's twin, and possessed all her faults in abundance without, in Jonathan's opinion, any of her better traits. Even as he opened the front door he could hear Jervis' affected high-pitched drawl.

' . . . and so I told the cove that if he wished to cut a

swell, he would be better doing so away from my vicinity; and with that, I'm dammed if the impertinent blaggard didn't up and cock a snook at me.'

'And pray tell me, Brother Jervis, what happened then? Don't keep me in suspense any longer!' Carlotta broke in laughingly.

'Dammee, if I didn't fan his arse for him with this! Dammee, he was soon begging for mercy, I do assure you.'

Jonathan entered the sombre-furnished drawing room to witness Jervis Tinsley brandishing his riding crop in demonstration. Jonathan nodded brusquely.

'Good morning, Jervis, I trust all is well.'

The three people in the room regarded him without any visible signs of welcome, and Jonathan coolly returned their regard.

Carlotta, wearing a simple white morning gown, her hair dressed in the fashionable, ringletted Grecian style, looked, as always, beautiful. Her two male companions presented the appearance of rakish Dandies, both in olive-green, full-skirted, frock riding coats, with nipped-in waists, extra high collars and cravats, skin-tight white pantaloons and tasselled and spurred hessian boots. Jervis was a remarkably handsome male replica of his sister in colouring and features. The other man was taller and broader, favouring the French-style moustache and side-whiskers, and his eyes were a cold blue in the deep-tanned hard-featured face.

This one is a tough-looking fellow, Jonathan mentally acknowledged, judging the man to be in his late thirties.

'Captain Cassidy, allow me to present my husband, Jonathan.' Carlotta archly performed the introduction, and both men bowed.

'I am honoured, sir.' Cassidy's voice held no hint of dandyish affectation, and was deep and mellow.

'Your servant, sir.' Jonathan straightened and looked down at his seated wife. 'Have you ordered refreshments for our guests, my dear?' Even as he spoke, Jonathan cursed himself for his unconscious crassness, for his question implied that she did not know the obvious duties of a hostess.

Carlotta bridled immediately. 'Indeed I have, husband. Do you think me lacking in social grace?' she snapped pettishly, and launched her counterattack. 'But as always in this house, your servants are woefully lacksadaisical.' She tilted her shapely head and flashed a warm smile at Cassidy. 'It was not so in my own home, Captain Cassidy, and I'll warrant that in your house in London the servants are somewhat prompter in obedience, are they not, sir?'

The man's strong white teeth gleamed as he laughed and replied easily, 'If you think that to be the case, ma'am, then I must with the utmost regret inform you that you are sadly mistaken.'

Jonathan warmed towards the man for this attempt to ease the tension, but Jervis Tinsley, hardly bothering to conceal his malice, intervened.

'Of course the servants here are devilish lazy, sister. It's what comes of your husband allowing them to behave as if Jack were as good as his master.' He addressed himself directly to Cassidy. 'You will find matters to be ordered somewhat differently in my father's house, Edward. No egalitarian nonsense is to be found there, you may be sure.'

Jonathan allowed none of his resentment at this rudeness to show. Instead he apologized to Cassidy for the delay and went to see what was causing it.

As the door closed behind him, Jervis Tinsley burst out spitefully, 'Damm my soul Carla, what possessed you to wed with that dull yokel?'

'Tinsley, I'd much prefer you not to discuss these private family matters when I am present as a guest in your sister's household.'

Cassidy's cold eyes held Carlotta's gaze as he corrected her brother, and he smiled intimately at her as he continued. 'I am quite sure that Carlotta found him to be the admirable gentleman that I also, even on such brief acquaintance, consider him to be.' He stared meaningfully at the younger man. 'I fear we are tardy for our appointment with the earl, so be good enough to go and ready our horses, there's a good fellow.'

After a moment's hesitation, Jervis bade his sister goodbye and went to do as he was bidden.

Cassidy bent, taking Carlotta's unresisting hand to his lips, then pleaded urgently, 'May I call upon you again, Carlotta?'

She felt a frisson of inner excitement, but coquettishly avoided his eyes and looked down at the floor like some shy young girl.

'You have not forbidden me, Carlotta, therefore I will call upon you again. Please make my excuses to your husband, but I am already late, and the earl does not brook tardiness in his social inferiors.'

Again he kissed her hand, and again Carlotta experienced that surge of sexual excitement.

'Goodbye for the present, Carlotta,' he whispered, and was gone, leaving her uncertain as to how she really felt about him, but increasingly aware of her desire to see him once more.

Only moments later Jonathan returned, a maidservant following him, carrying a laden dish.

'Where are they?' he questioned.

Carlotta frowned. 'Captain Cassidy had an appointment with the earl. He could wait no longer, and I for one am fairly mortified. The standard of service in your house is intolerable.' Her anger was fuelled by her pique at the abrupt departure of her new admirer. 'What must he think of us? We must appear the veriest rustics to him.' She prepared to storm from the room, snapping, 'I'm going to lie down, and I don't want to be disturbed on any pretext whatsoever.'

Jonathan could only watch her leave with a sad resignation.

Chapter Twelve

Through the month of May the sun blazed day after day in cloudless skies. The black and white plumage of house martins darted among the roofs and eaves of the Sidemoor, and larks sang over the mean terraces and squares as they spiralled upwards in the balmy air. Wild flowers blossomed and scented, and cattle browsed upon the lush meadows of the Midlands plain. For this year at least, it was truly named The Merry Month.

But not for Tildy . . . For she was serving her apprenticeship to her new trade, and for the first time in her young life was finding out what 'slavery' truly meant. Her ponderous body aching in every joint and muscle, she toiled at the forge for thirteen, fourteen, fifteen, even sometimes sixteen or seventeen hours a day. Her hands blistered and raw, head aching from the noise, stomach sick from the foul air, sweat streaming to blind her eyes, she existed in a man-made purgatory.

Tom Crawford was a bad workman, and a worse master. With oaths and blows he drove her, until she began to hate the very sight of him. Not fast or skillful enough to tackle the more difficult and better-paid types of nails, Crawford was forced to make the small tacks normally reserved for women and children's labour, and the cruel gibes of his fellow nailers wounded his inflated ego, and made his uncertain temper vicious. The pay was poor for tacks, and no matter how hard he and Tildy worked, they could still not earn sufficient for their needs, let alone begin to pay off their debts.

Now Tildy knew the reason why so many of the nailers' women were dirty and uncaring of how they looked. Why their food was so badly prepared. Why their homes stank and their children were so badly neglected . . . The reason was simply weariness . . . Bone-deep weariness.

For the first time in her life Tildy's hair became dank and tangled, her skin grimed with dirt, her clothing stale and unwashed. The hammer, the forge, the iron, ruthlessly drained all strength from her, leaving her spent and exhausted, able only to crawl up to her bedroom each night and collapse into unconsciousness until scant hours later she must drag her tortured flesh back to the ceaseless, bitter toil . . .

Another Weigh-in day had come, and the queues of nailers formed in the warehouse yards. Tildy and her husband stood grey-faced in the pale light of dawn, waiting their turn at the great brass scales of the Sanders warehouse . . . Scant weeks at the trade had metamorphosed their appearances, and now they were indistinguishable from their fellow nailers. Just as shabby, just as dirt-grimed, just as weary in mind and body from the grinding toil of the week.

Dick Suffield, wearing his customary rusty-black tailcoat and high top hat, stood at the pans directing his two helpers. Behind the foreman, Jonathan Sanders, muffled in a greatcoat against the chill dawn air, his top hat pulled low on his forehead, stood watching in his turn.

A small-statured nailer, ragged and broken-booted, was at the scale-pans, and as he went to place his sack-bags of finished nails on them, Dick Suffield moved to stop him.

'Wait a minute, you. Let's have a look at the colour.'

The small man assumed an aggrieved expression. 'My oath, Master. Youm wasting your time and mine. They'm blue as a summer's sky, and all to length,' he asserted confidently, but in his eyes lurked a shifty apprehension, which the foreman was quick to notice.

'Open the bags and tip 'um!' he ordered.

The apprehension showed more clearly as the nailer tried to bluster. 'It's bleedin' insulting me, you be, Master. I'm a good blow and you knows well I am.'

'Good blow you might be, Sam Latchmore, but youm a fly cove, arn't you.' Suffield's bluff features were smilingly contemptuous. 'You must think I'm a bloody mawkin.'

He grabbed the nearest bag, as one meaty arm easily fended off the small man's attempts to snatch it back. Stripping away the string which held the bag closed with an ease that demonstrated his great muscular strength, the foreman hefted the bag to head-height and upended it. The nails fell in a blue-grey cascade onto the dirt of the yard – and from the bottom of the bag a large piece of waste iron fell on top of the heap.

Latchmore swallowed hard, and tried to assume an expression of bewilderment. 'Blast my eyes, Master! I dunno how the 'ell that got in theer!'

Suffield's smile widened. 'I reckon it's the Bridewell and a whipping for you, Latchmore. That's a pound to a penny, that is. Youm guilty of embezzlement, arn't you? At least, that's what the Beaks 'ull call it.'

'For the love o' Christ, doon't charge him, Master Suffield!' Latchmore's wife, even smaller-bodied than her husband, grasped the foreman's arm in her work-calloused fingers. Tears streaming down her lined face, she begged piteously, 'Doon't charge him, Master Suffield. It warn't 'im as done it. I put the iron in theer. Me childer be sick wi' the fever, and I had to fetch the doctor to 'um, and I'd no money to pay him. So I took some o' the nails and sold 'um. My man knew naught about it . . . It was me who did it!'

It was Suffield's turn to assume an expression of surprise.

'Why now, Annie, does you fancy taking the whipping instead?' he demanded. 'Because you arn't got enough meat on your bones to cushion the stripes, my wench.' He shook his head slowly. 'Iffen I was you, I'd keep out on it.' He struck away her restraining hands and pointed his index finger into Latchmore's frightened face. 'Becos this bugger's worked this trick afore,' he bellowed threateningly, ' . . . and doon't you bloody well try denying it, you thievin' bastard. For my name is Dick Suffield, not Simon Simple. I found iron in your bags arter you'd gone two weigh days since.' He swung to Jonathan Sanders. 'Well, Master Sanders, do I send for the constable?'

The nailmaster's heart began to pound, and he gnawed worriedly at his lower lip. He accepted the fact of the man's guilt without question. But the harshness of the penalty, should he charge Latchmore, caused him to hesitate. Were a few pennyworths of iron sufficient reason to have flesh torn to the bone, and a woman and children sent to the poorhouse, if they were not to starve to death on the streets? Miserably, Jonathan stared at the sobbing woman, and at the chalk-white face of the guilty nailer, whose scrawny body was shaking with terror.

Twice the young nailmaster opened his mouth to give Suffield his assent, and twice the words would not come. The foreman's face mirrored the disgust he felt at what he considered to be weakness on the part of Jonathan, and it was that open display of disgust which at last impelled the nailmaster to act.

'I'm going to give you a chance, Latchmore. Mayhap you are innocent, as your wife claims, but I doubt that. However, I'll not charge you, although I have full right to do so. But you will get no more iron from my warehouse in future. Go now, before I begin to repent my lenience.'

Relief brought colour to the nailer's white face, and he babbled his thanks, then fell to his knees and went to refill the empty bag with the fallen nails.

'Leave 'um lie!' Suffield growled. 'They'll do to pay us back for what you've thieved afore.' The foreman's voice quivered with barely suppressed rage, and his big hands clenched into fists. Latchmore's shifty eyes flitted to Jonathan Sanders, as if hoping that the nailmaster would again intervene and overrule his employee, but the young man was uncomfortably aware that he had pushed his foreman to the limit, and shook his head in denial. Latchmore bit his lips and seemed about to burst into tears, then Dick Suffield's heavy boot crashed into his side and sent him sprawling.

'Gerroff from here, you dirty little thief,' Suffield bawled, and the nailer pushed himself up from the dusty ground and ran from the yard, his weeping wife scurrying behind him. White-lipped with temper, Suffield confronted the waiting queue.

'Iffen any more of you buggers has got ought other than nails in your bags, then you'd best get rid of it afore you comes to the pans . . . Becos I'll turn the next bastard who tries to cheat me over to the Beaks meself.' He glared at his employer. 'And neither God, Devil, or any living man 'ull stop me doing so.'

Jonathan tried to maintain an air of stony dignity, and perhaps wisely forbore from making any reply.

As the Weighing-in continued Tildy, despite her depression of spirit, could not help being amused at seeing several of the men in the queue slipping out of the warehouse yard carrying bags of nails, then reappearing a short while later with those same bags, not now quite as full as before.

In the face of Dick Suffield's bad humour no one haggled or disputed, and as a consequence the weighing went quickly. In a short time it was the Crawfords' turn at the pans. They placed their bags and waited for the foreman to note down his tally. Instead he scowled at Tom Crawford.

'Let's have them bags opened,' he ordered brusquely. When Tom complied, he lifted a handful of the tacks, and with a guttural ejaculation of contempt, hurled them to the ground. 'Bloody rubbish, Crawford!'

Tom Crawford's weak face paled beneath its grime. 'What does you mean, Dick?' he stammered.

'Exactly what I says, you fool! Your work is rubbish. They'm badly struck and badly tempered. They'll bend double at the first clout . . . Look at 'um, man.'

Crawford lifted his hands in a gesture of appeal. 'I'se done the best I could wi' 'um, Dick. I'se done . . . '

'Well, your best arn't good enough for me.' The foreman brutally cut him short.

While the exchange took place Jonathan Sanders kept his eyes on Tildy. 'She is a pretty girl,' he acknowledged yet again, and when he saw her fearful expression he felt pity swell in his breast. Only scant weeks in the Sidemoor, and she had lost all her bloom and freshness, he thought sadly. Dear God, what a savage beast the trade of the nailer is. It sucks all grace and beauty, even their very femininity, from these poor women. He moved forward, and as he did so Tildy's dark-shadowed eyes fixed on his in mute appeal. He tried to smile reassuringly at her as he asked his foreman, 'How bad is the work?'

'See for yourself, Master Jon.' The man lifted more tacks from the open bag and held them out for inspection. A brief glance was sufficient. The tacks were indeed badly shaped and badly tempered. The nailmaster regretfully shook his head.

'There's naught to be done, Crawford,' he said quietly. 'For the sake of my firm's good name, I cannot accept these.'

'Be dammed to it, they'm not all bad,' Crawford's gutter-devil momentarily asserted itself.

'Mayhap they're not.' Sanders took no offence at the

117

workman's aggressive attitude. He understood the desperation that prompted it. 'But my men cannot spend their time sorting the good from the bad. They have too much else to do.' He glanced at Tildy and saw unshed tears glistening in her eyes. Again pity surged through him. 'All I can suggest is that you sort out the good from the bad yourself, and I will accept the good.'

'But it 'ull take bloody hours to do that!' Crawford grumbled.

'Suit your bloody self, man,' Suffield growled. 'Now get out of the way. There's others waiting, and I've no more time to waste.'

For a brief second it seemed that Crawford would argue further, but the nailer realized the hopelessness of his case. His shoulders slumped despairingly, and he lifted the bags from the pans and trudged away, with Tildy carrying her own bags trailing dejectedly after him. Out on the ruts of Broad Street, Tildy could no longer hold back her tears, and her husband rounded savagely on her.

'There's no use in blartin, you useless cow. Iffen you was any good, you'd make a better job o' the tacks.'

The injustice of this assault stung Tildy, and she spiritedly defended herself.

'I do the best I can, Tom, and you know well that I do. T'is not my work that's so bad, but your own!'

Crawford's temper flared. 'Hold your tongue, you bitch!' Letting fall his bags he came at her with upraised hands, but before he could reach and strike her, Hester Lammas came running.

'Leave her be, you bullying hound!' she warned. 'Canna you see that the poor little wench is badly.'

Other bystanders now intervened.

'Yes, leave the girl be!'

'You should be shamed, hitting her wi' the babby in her belly.'

Crawford let his hands drop. 'Ahhh, youm not worth bruising me hands on!' he snarled.

One of Suffield's helpers now came from the yard and beckoned Crawford, and when the nailer went to him, whispered a few rapid sentences. Crawford nodded sullenly, and picking up the nailbags told Tildy, 'Come on, you.'

'Where to?' she queried.

'To Johnno Dipple's,' he answered. 'Suffield sent word to tell me to take 'um theer. He'll take 'um from me.'

'But Dipple is a fogger,' Tildy protested weakly, all the fearsome stories she had been told of the plight of those unfortunates who fell into the foggers' clutches rushing through her mind.

'I know he's a bloody fogger, you stupid cow,' her husband snarled. 'But what else can we do? We'se got to ate, and pay the bloody rent.'

'Oh God help us . . . ' Tildy prayed fervently. 'God help us now . . . '

Chapter Thirteen

It was June, Tildy's final month of pregnancy, and she felt weak and feverishly ill. Struggle bravely though she did, she was not physically capable of managing to work at the forge, and even Tom Crawford was finally obliged to admit the hopelessness of forcing her to continue.

'You'd best take things easier until the babby is birthed,' he told her grudgingly, after she had actually fainted and fallen one late afternoon. 'But t'is no use expecting to play the lady and do naught while I waits on you. You'll ha' to make food and keep house as best you can. I'll have to spend all me bloody time at the forge, now youm become such a burden to me . . . ' The sight of her gaunt, grey-skinned face, so different from the fresh beauty he had married, caused him a pang of guilt. 'Bugger me, if she arn't come to look like a walking corpse since she's bin here,' he muttered to himself.

His guilt metamorphosed into resentment of her ill-health. 'God blast you, what a useless, snivelling thing you be!' he sneered cruelly. 'No good for work, no good for the bed . . . Some bloody hard bargain I got, when I took you for wife.'

Tildy made no reply. What strength and courage remained to her, she hoarded like a miser his gold. It took all the inner fortitude she possessed just to survive from day to day, and even then her spirits sank so low at times that she almost wished for death to take her. But then the thought of her nearly-born child would somehow enable her to struggle on, to endure whatever she must, in order to give her child life.

The respite from the grinding labour of nailing came as an answer to her prayers, and to be able to sit and rest her aching body whenever she felt the need, was a heaven-sent blessing.

Strange to her though it was, although she and Tom Crawford were now working for the fogger, Johnno Dipple, the pressures of their life had eased a little. True, their debts had increased, but at this point in time, none of their creditors was pressing for immediate repayment. Tildy didn't allow herself to wonder at this mysterious leniency. Instead, she was only grateful that it should be so.

To work with him at the forge, Tom Crawford took his brother Edgar's eldest daughter, Martha. A thin, under-sized girl, with eyes that had witnessed too much of life, and were far older than her twelve years warranted. The child was adept at the trade, and Crawford, despite the added expense of her meagre wages, was happy enough with this new arrangement, at least for the time being.

He was happy enough also with his arrangement with Dipple. The fogger was lavish with credit at his alehouse, and Crawford took full advantage of the opportunities to drink himself into a stupor each weekend. There would, he knew, come a day of reckoning, but he would face that unpleasant hour when he must, and until then, enjoy what he could.

Another Friday night, and all through the Sidemoor

beneath a thunderous sky the Olivers thudded, and hammers rang upon white-hot iron. Tildy, her body and head hot and feverish, lay upon the flock mattress in the dark upstairs room watching the forked flickerings of distant lightning through the dirty, cracked windowpanes, her thoughts wandering aimlessly.

Memories came and went, faces loved and unloved passed before her mind's eye. Dick Suffield's bluff features loomed to the forefront, and the young girl tried to decide what manner of man he really was. Since his rejection of their work, which she accepted as justified, she had only seen the foreman on a couple of occasions in the streets of the village. Both times he had smiled and asked how she was feeling, then passed on without attempting to prolong their conversation.

People say he is bad and wicked, Tildy reflected idly. Yet to me, he has shown kindness.

Janey Porter came to mind, and a slight frown of puzzlement creased Tildy's smooth brow. She had once thought that Janey Porter might become her friend, but whenever they encountered each other, the young woman totally ignored her.

Why should she behave so? Tildy wondered.

Inevitably her thoughts turned to her husband. Following his rape of her, he had not touched Tildy in any sexual sense again. But had hit her on many occasions, particularly during her first weeks at the forge, when in her ignorance and lack of training she had made mistakes at the work. Lately his temper had improved somewhat, and he had not lifted his hand against her.

'I pray it might remain so.' Tildy wished aloud fervently, but she was a child of her time, and knew only too well that a wife was her husband's chattel, to be used by him as he saw fit. All her life Tildy had seen husbands beat their wives.

It's the custom, and always has been so, she told herself resignedly, but one portion of her mind remonstrated angrily. But it is wrong! Totally wrong! Women are surely not placed on this earth to be treated like brute beasts. We are here to be helpers and mates of man, not his slaves. Her hands caressed the mound of her belly. 'If you are born a man, then I shall teach you to treat women with gentleness all your days,' she whispered aloud, as if the unborn child could hear her, and unbidden, Jonathan Sanders came into her mind. 'You would never ill-use any woman, would you? You are too fine and gentle a man for that.' Tildy smiled.

Next instant the smile became a rictus of agony.

The pain cramped and twisted the whole of her lower body, causing her to clench her teeth to hold back a scream, and when it passed, it left her badly shaken and nauseated. She felt a hot dampness on the insides of her thighs, and knew that the process of birth had begun.

'I'll need to get Tom,' she told herself. 'He can fetch help.'

Even as she struggled to her feet another pain tore at her belly. She leaned against the wall, moaning softly.

'This cannot be right! The pains shouldn't come so close set.'

Panic threatened to overwhelm her, and she forced herself to retain control. Opening her mouth wide she tried to call for her husband, but a third onset of pain transformed her call into a strangled howl. The air seemed to become thick and tangible, and Tildy sucked desperately to draw it into her labouring lungs.

As the pain slowly ebbed she thrust herself away from the wall and laboriously clambered down the steep narrow staircase. In the darkness of the lower room she paused. Something was not normal. There was no thudding of Olivers, or ringing of hammer on iron coming from the leanto at the rear of the house.

'Has he gone to swill drink at the alehouse?' Tildy felt violently indignant. 'How could he? And me giving birth!'

123

In her distraught state the question of how Tom Crawford could know that she was at that moment giving birth did not occur to her. Energized by her indignation she slammed the door of the leanto open, then drew back in a shock of horror . . .

Tom Crawford was in the forge . . . On the floor, grunting like some voracious animal, as he rutted upon the body of the girl-child, Martha. Tildy gagged, and tasted the foul acridity of bile in her throat as she took in the scene. The girl's dress drawn high to reveal her under-developed body. Her thin legs wrapped around the man's muscular thighs. Her mouth wide as she gasped under the impact of Crawford's taut buttocks pounding furiously down, while his greedy hands clutched and mauled the tender young flesh beneath him.

Martha screamed in fright as she saw Tildy, and with an oath Tom Crawford twisted his head to find the cause. His mouth gaped open.

'What the bleedin' Hell?'

Tildy was impelled by one single, all-consuming need . . .

'I must get away! I must get away from here!' The need seared through her being. ' . . . I must get away . . . My baby can't be born in this house . . . Not in this filth, this wickedness! I must get away . . . get away . . . get away . . . ' Senses reeling, sight blurred, she stumbled from the house and into the storm-racked night.

Blindly she fought her way out of the Sidemoor and along the deep-rutted roads. Panting for breath she staggered through narrow lanes, and across wild tracts of open country. Tongues of lightning cracked and rolls of thunder reverberated through the cloud-scudding skies. Winds gusted and hurled sharp pellets of icy rain against her burning face, but still she went on, driven by her terrible need to escape.

Thick woodlands loomed in a black, forbidding mass and as she pushed through their undergrowth brambles clutched and held her long skirts, tearing the thin cloth and gouging bloody furrows in her legs, arms and body as she struggled onwards.

Another excruciating pain brought her to her knees, and throwing back her head she screamed her agony in counterpoint to the howling wind.

A bolt of lightning exploded a tree only yards from her, and the dreadful noise of its destruction left Tildy's head ringing, and her hearing deadened. She screamed again, more in terror now than pain, and that terror lifted her body and drove it on through the forest. More lightning cracked and flashed overhead, illuminating the trees about her, showing their branches waving and creaking in the wind like the arms of unearthly demented creatures.

Tildy's courage deserted her, and now no atom of courage remained. She became a demented creature herself, and could only plunge wildly on, heart pounding, lungs straining, whimpering as if she were some wounded animal.

Like a cannonade of artillery the heart of the storm crashed above the girl, and flash after flash of lightning turned the night into a livid, flickering, infernal day.

A narrow path opened before her, an overhanging tunnel of fluttering leaves that beckoned to her, promising a refuge. She entered it, another flash of lightning came, and suddenly before her a human figure appeared, its arms outstretched to grab her.

'NOOOO!' she shrieked, then her eyes rolled upwards and she tumbled forward into a yawning pit of blackness.

The man knelt by the fallen girl, and gently turned her over so that she lay on her back. The full fury of the storm diminished as its centre moved away from the woods, and in a sudden lull of the wind the man shouted out loudly.

'Tom? Tom come here, quick!'

Another figure materialized from among the close-set trees and brushwood.

'Strike me blind, Davy, doon't goo bawling like that. You'll fetch the bloody traps down on us.'

125

The kneeling man grabbed the other's trouser leg and pulled him nearer.

'Ne'er mind the bloody keepers, they'll all be sheltering in the nearest barn. Look at this wench! Her come running along the path and banged right into me. Then her fell down as if her 'ud bin shot.'

'Is her dead?' the newcomer asked nervously.

' 'Course not, you bloody wooden yed. Her's just fainted . . . Give us the glim. Let's take a proper look at her.'

From under his makeshift cloak of sacking, Tom produced a small shuttered lantern, and by its dim light Davy Nokes examined Tildy as closely as he could.

'My oath,' he muttered appreciatively. 'Her's a rare good-looker, for all her dirt, but look at her belly and her colour. Christ! She could be dying by the look on her.'

As he finished speaking Tildy stirred and moaned, drawing her knees up against her stomach as pain thrust itself through her semi-consciousness.

'The poor little wench is badly, we'll ha' to get her to shelter and get some help for her,' Davy Nokes stated decisively.

'But what if . . . ' his companion started to protest.

'But nothin'! Look at her face, man, and listen to her groaning. It 'udden't surprise me if her warn't having that babby right this minute.'

'Oh my Christ!' Tom's voice shook in nervousness. 'Wheer con we take her? The nearest doctor's at Redditch. She could bloody well die afore we could get her theer.'

'We'll take her down to the poorhouse. Theer's enough bastards birthed theer every year. They'll know what's to be done with this one. Come on now, let's not waste any more time argufying.'

Between them, the pair lifted the moaning Tildy, and half-carrying, half-dragging her, made their way through the woods.

The building and its ramshackle outhouses stood isolated

among the fields. Once it had been the house of a wealthy yeoman farmer, and its serried windows and wide entrance were mute testimonies to vanished glories. Now, tumbledown and neglected, it served as the poorhouse for the Parish of Tardebigge, the last grim refuge for the aged, the destitute, the pauper, the orphan, the bastard, the lame, the sick and the mad.

Breathing heavily and sweating profusely from the effort of carrying the girl, the two men thankfully arrived at the high, weather-beaten main door. With one hand Nokes reached out and tugged the rope bell-pull, and with a smile on his youthful, handsome face, listened to the bell's wild jangling.

'That'll fetch that miserable bastard, Morris, at the run,' he observed with satisfaction. 'He'll think it's a Divine Summons, so he 'ull.'

Again he tugged furiously at the rope until it seemed that the bell would jangle itself to pieces.

'Give over 'ull you! Youm making enough noise to raise the dead!' An angry voice sounded, muffled by the thick door, and then the door itself creaked open to disclose a tall, cadaverous man, dressed in a long nightgown and nightcap, a lighted candle held high before his pinched-featured face.

'What d'you mean by this outrage, Davy Nokes, you worthless young devil? What d'you mean by coming here at this ungodly hour and waking good folk from their slumbers?'

The young man beamed at his irate questioner. 'Why, Master Morris, my good sir, I'se brung you a new resident for these marbled halls. And by the looks on her, you'd best send for a doctor straight away, and a midwife too, I reckon.'

The poorhouse master came closer to the trio, and peered at the moaning girl. 'Who the Devil is she?'

Nokes shook his head. 'I dunno. We found her alaying on the road. Didn't we, Tom?'

127

His companion nodded vigorously.

The poorhouse master's thin lips turned downwards. 'And what was you doing out of your bed at this ungodly hour, Nokes? A bit of your usual poachin', I shouldn't wonder.'

Above them the dying echoes of thunder rolled, and rain fell afresh. Davy Nokes' easy smile gave way to a frown.

'Ne'er mind your wondering now, Master Morris. Let's get this wench wheer she belongs. In shelter, wi' a doctor to look over her. She's in a poor way, if I can judge.'

Morris' mean features were doubtful. 'I don't know as how I can admit this woman,' he protested. 'Any fresh admittance has to come by way of the overseers, or the magistrates . . . I can't just let any bloody tramper who wants a night's shelter come in here . . . Is she belonging to this parish, anyway?'

The young man's temper rose. 'How the bloody Hell should I know what parish her belongs to . . . All I know is that she's badly, and I wouldn't leave a sick dog lying out in a ditch, let alone a young wench like this. I thought you was supposed to be a good Christian, Master Morris, at least you spends enough time crawling around the bloody vicar to be so. So let's have no more nonsense about wheer she belongs . . . She belongs in shelter, and even this bloody ruin is better than a ditch . . . So lead on!'

For a moment Morris seemed ready to stand his ground, but then sensed the possible danger to himself should he continue to object, and with a very bad grace he motioned the two men to follow him with their burden.

Tildy was unaware of what was happening around her as she floated in a nightmarish cloud of fever and pain. Of incomprehensible movements, and sounds, and sensations which imprisoned her helplessly, and which periodically submerged her into oblivion.

'The overseers 'ull hear all about this, Davy Nokes,' the poorhouse master muttered, as he mounted the rickety stairs. 'You'll see if they wun't. You can't treat this place

128

like a wayside barn, or one o' them stinking low drink-kens that youm so fond of. You should ha' took her to one o' them, that's wheer she rightfully belongs by the looks on her.'

'Shut your bloody rattle, Morris.' The young man let his temper fly free. 'Or I swear to God, I'll lay this girl down, and then bleedin' well lay you out.'

Morris gulped hard, and lapsed into silence.

Chapter Fourteen

'Can you hear me, young woman? Do you understand what I am saying to you?'

The voice was faint and far away, and Tildy felt that she was floating in a sea of misty grey through which shards of light penetrated fitfully.

'Come now, girl . . . Gather your senses.'

The voice suddenly grew louder, the swirling greyness paler, and through its mist a blurred, wavering form swam into view. As Tildy blinked and concentrated, it stilled and transformed itself into a lanky, sallow-faced man wearing a tall black hat perched upon a full-bottomed tie-wig, black clothing and a ruffled white shirtfront.

'Ah-ha, you are once more present with us, young woman. My name is Doctor Pratt. I've delivered you of a son. Some hours past.' He spoke in stacatto bursts. 'A mewling, weakly thing, to be sure. But he should live. God willing.'

At first his words made no real impression on Tildy, instead she was mentally coming to terms with how she felt. Curiously light-headed and empty-bodied, as if all her inner substance had been drawn from her, leaving only a thin outer shell. Then her mind back-tracked and eagerly clutched at the word, 'Son'.

'Where? Where is he?' she demanded, and tried to push herself up from the mattress on which she lay. But the soreness of her lower body, and sheer weakness prevented her from succeeding, and she fell back.

The doctor frowned his annoyance at being so interrupted.

'You will see the dammed thing. All in good time,' he snapped brusquely. 'It is being tended to. As I said. It's a mewling, weakly thing. But should live. Though you are not able to care for it. At present. At least. That is my considered opinion. For a while you were near to death. And lost much blood. However, you will no doubt make full recovery in good time. I have played my part. The rest is God's will. Some gentlemen wish to speak with you now. I bid you, good day, young woman.'

He stamped away, leaving Tildy bemusedly gazing about her, wondering where she was, and how she had come there.

The whitewashed room was very small, only a tiny narrow window, set high, breaking the bareness of the walls. The floor was of rough wooden boards, and the only article of furniture the wooden bed on which she lay, with a coarse blanket over her, and a straw mattress beneath.

'What is this place? And where is my baby?' Anxiety for its well being coursed through her.

Heavy boots clumped upon the landing and the room filled with men. Instinctively Tildy knew what they were, even though all wore the rough clothing and leather gaiters of farmers.

'They'll be parish overseers,' she told herself. 'And I'll warrant this is a poorhouse.' Acute shame caused her pale face and neck to flush deeply. 'My poor baby has been birthed in a poorhouse. May God forgive me for bringing such a disgrace on its innocent head . . .'

131

Ebenezer Morris scowled down at the girl. 'Now, young 'ooman, youm in the Parish o' Tardebigge poor'us, in Webheath hamlet. I'm the Master here, and these gennulmen be the parish overseers. We needs to ask you some questions.'

As Tildy looked at the dour faces surrounding her, she felt her heart sink.

'Shall I do the honours, gennulmen?' Morris waited for the overseers' assent, then began to question Tildy. As her pitiful story unfolded the poorhouse master's manner became increasingly that of the bully, and even though Tildy tried to be absolutely truthful, his hectoring at times confused her, and she would give what appeared to be contradictory answers.

At length, Ebenezer Morris appeared to be satisfied.

'Well, gennulmen, no matter how her's tried to confuse the issue, it's plain enough to see that this young woman has got no rights to be in this establishment. We can inform the constable and he can take her and put her across the parish boundary this very day.'

'But how can I walk, let alone carry my baby?' Tildy protested.

'We'll have a carriage and four brought, my wench, and you can ride in it like a high-born doxy!' Morris sneered.

One of the overseers, a much older man than the others, seemed reluctant to agree with the decision. 'Now wait a minute . . . This wench says that she lived with the Wilkinsons over by Brockhill Lane from when she was a little 'un, to her eighteenth birthday. That gives her the right of settlement in this parish.'

His companions rounded on him furiously. 'Don't talk sarft, man!' the burliest of the quarter shouted. 'Her's a married 'ooman, by her own account, and her husband lives in Sidemoor. So that makes Bromsgrove her parish, not here . . . Before God! We pays too big a poor rate now to keep our own bloody paupers sitting on their arses and living on the fat o' the land. I'll be buggered afore I'll see this 'un and her babby took on the rate as well.'

Weak and sore-bodied as she was, as Tildy listened to the dispute she felt her pride reasserting itself.

I've been humiliated by others all my life, she told herself. It's time I stopped letting myself be used so. But even as the thought ran through her mind, fearful doubts assailed her. But what will I do? I can't work straight away, and I've no money . . . And God only knows how Tom Crawford will serve me and the baby if I return to the Sidemoor . . . But where else have I to go?

'It's settled then, Master Morris, don't mind what this old fool says,' the burly man declaimed. 'Fetch the constable,' he went on, then paused, as if a doubt about the strict legality of their actions had occurred to him. 'No, best leave him out of it. I'll bring a cart tomorrow morning and we'll do the job ourselves. Arter all, there's only us knows the facts of this case, or even that she's here . . .'

'And Doctor Pratt,' the elderly overseer, his unhappiness plain to see, interjected. 'He knows the poor wench is here.'

'Doctor Pratt 'ull be paid for his work, and for him that'll be an end to it,' the burly man blustered. 'Blast me, Harry King! Arn't it enough that we'em paying him out of our rates for attending to this bloody woman, as it is. I reckon we'se already showed sufficient Christian charity towards her. Iffen it hadn't bin for Master Morris being good enough to take her in, then she and her babby 'ud be laying dead as doorknockers in a ditch somewhere, instead o' being in the pink of health.' He shook his large head until his purple jowls quivered. 'We'se done enough, and she goes tomorrow . . . And that's final!'

'I'm really sorry, my wench,' the elderly man told Tildy sadly. 'But I'm feared there's naught I can do . . . I'm out-voted.'

She felt a surge of gratitude towards him, and forced a smile. 'My thanks to you anyway, sir.' Then Tildy

133

demanded as forcefully as she could: 'At least let me have my baby with me now, Master Morris!'

'You'll have it soon enough,' he snapped, and led his companions from the room.

The springless, two-wheeled cart lurched and jolted along the potholed track, and through the layers of straw which covered its floor, Tildy's body was painfully jarred and shaken. In her arms she cradled her rag-swaddled son, and he so engrossed her that she was uncaring of her discomfort. Ebenezer Morris, accompanied by the burly overseer, was leading the decrepit horse, and at the rear of the cart walked the elderly man.

'Look here, my wench,' he whispered to attract Tildy's attention, and stealthily passed a coin to her. 'Here's a shillin'. It'll buy you a bit o' food, at least.'

She nodded her thanks, and his rheumy eyes blinked hard. 'I'se got daughters of me own . . . I wish I could do more to help you, but my missus is a bloody tartar, and she'd fairly destroy me iffen I was to gi' you shelter in my house,' he told her regretfully.

Tildy sucked in a deep breath. 'Don't worry about me, Master. I'll get by, somehow or other.' She smiled down at her baby. 'I've my son to care for now, so I'll have to get by, won't I?'

The man sighed heavily and, lifting his gnarled hand in farewell, struck off across the fields.

Tildy stared about her, at the carefully tended fields and hedgerows, the well-fed, placid cattle sheltering from the heat of the day beneath the ancient oaks and elms, and tasted the warm, grass-scented air with her lips and tongue.

'It's so beautiful, is it not, Baby?' she murmured. 'Why could we not have been lucky enough to live our lives here, and have sufficient fortune to enjoy ease and plenty?'

Ahead of her, the graceful, delicately-shaped spire of the Tardebigge parish church soared above its green hill. Tildy

gazed long and hard at its perfect proportions and bitterness quirked her mouth.

'What sort of God is He, who gives so much good
fortune to so few, and so little good fortune to so many? But
then, it's not really God who misuses Man,' she told
herself resignedly. 'But Man himself.'

The cart lurched on, and eventually juddered to a halt at
the bottom of a sweeping hillside.

'This'll do us, Master Morris. We'em well across the
boundary,' the burly overseer stated, and came to the rear
of the cart. He held out his arms. 'Come, my wench. This
is your rightful parish. I'll help you down.'

Tildy wanted to contemptuously reject his offer, but,
afraid of stumbling in her weakness and endangering the
baby, was forced to stifle her pride and accept. Not
ungently he settled her on the long-grassed verge, and
addressed her gruffly.

'You may well think that we'm bad-hearted sods, girl.
But times are cruel hard and we've little choice but to act as
we does, for the sakes of our own families.'

She refused to answer, or even look at him, just sat stiffly
erect with her face averted. With a shrug of his meaty
shoulders he tossed a few pence into her lap, and left her.
The creaking cart lurched away and once it had gone she
let her stiff body relax, and tried to plan some course of
action.

'Thank God, it's warm,' was the only coherent thought
that would come to her.

The somnolent air made Tildy feel lethargic and un-
willing to rouse herself and move on. The baby was
sleeping soundly, and her reluctance to disturb him was an
added inducement to remain where she was. Occasionally
people would pass by on the road – mostly farm labourers
in wide-brimmed hats and white smocks, carrying their
tools with them, and their small wooden ale-kegs slung at
their hips. They would stare curiously at the woman and
baby, but never spoke to her. To them she was just another

dirty tramper woman, here today, and hopefully gone tomorrow.

She had breakfasted on bread and gruel before leaving the poorhouse, and was neither hungry nor thirsty. Her body was stale and unwashed, but during her time in the Sidemoor she had learned to accept dirt, so she felt no undue discomfort.

A young man came into view, walking from the direction of Bromsgrove. Although he carried a long-bladed scythe over his shoulder, he was not wearing the white smock of a countryman. Instead he wore an open-necked calico shirt, leather waistcoat, cord breeches tied beneath the knee, ribbed stockings and high-low boots – and was bareheaded. He whistled as he walked, and Tildy listened to the gay, piping air with pleasure; a pleasure enhanced by the good looks and fine physique of the whistler.

He too peered curiously at the girl as he drew near, then recognition filled his grey eyes and he walked directly over to her.

'Now then, my wench, how bist?' He smiled, and his teeth were white and clean in his sun-bronzed, clean-shaven face. He noted her puzzled expression and laughed as he ran his fingers through his thick brown hair. 'I see that you doon't remember Davy Nokes, but then, how could you, seeing as how you fainted clean away the very second we first met.'

Tildy had a fleeting mental picture of the tunnel-like pathway in the woods, the livid flashing of lightning, the human figure with arms outstretched before her . . . 'Was it you that night in the woods? Was it you who took me to the poorhouse?' she exclaimed.

He nodded and grinned. 'Ahr, it was me, and a good job for you that I come along when I did, or you might ha' died in that storm.' His grin disappeared. 'But why are you sitting here? You shouldn't have left the house so soon arter birthing your baby!'

His obvious concern, and the kindly way he spoke to her,

136

pierced the flimsy defences Tildy's pride had erected, and try as she would, she was unable to hold back the tears.

'I'm sorry!' she choked out. 'I must look a real booby sobbing like this . . . I've no wish to . . . I just can't help myself . . . It's so silly and weak.'

Davy Nokes laid aside the scythe and crouched down beside her.

'Theer now, my pretty, you'se got a right to cry . . . Arter all, you'se had a hard time on it, and women always be cryfull arter they'se birthed. T'is natural so.'

His soft country burr soothed her, and after a while she smiled, touched by his air of wisdom.

'And how would you know how a woman feels at such a time?' she gently teased. 'You're no more than a boy.'.

He threw back his head and the strong neck muscles tautened and swelled as he laughed. 'Boy, am I? I wish I still was, I'll tell you.' His laughter stilled, and his eyes gentled. 'Now then, you tell me the whole story. For knowing the miserable bastards we'se got as parish overseers, I doon't doubt but that you'se had reason enough for more tears than you've shed.'

She looked at him searchingly, and recognized the genuine concern he felt; with that recognition it was as if a dam burst within her, and all her pent-up troubles came flooding out. She talked, and talked, and talked, and as the young man listened, he found himself increasingly attracted to this girl, and was aware of a dawning appreciation of her beauty.

When the spate of words finally faltered and came to a halt, Davy Nokes plucked a blade of grass and chewed on it, his eyes unfocussed as if he were deep in thought.

Tildy, half-ashamed of her volubility, waited for him in her turn.

Abruptly he tossed the blade of grass away and grinned merrily at her. 'I reckon you'd best come and stay wi' me for a while. It'll give you time to get strong again and decide what you wants to do . . . You'd be the worst sort of fool to goo back to that bloody dog of a husband of yourn, and I shouldn't think the Bromsgrove poor'us is any better than the bugger you'se just left.' He saw the suspicion and doubt welling up in her, and hastened to assuage that. 'Doon't you be afraid to come, my pretty. I swear that you and your babby 'ull come to no harm wi' me. I'se got a little cottage down towards Stoke Prior,' he waved his arm vaguely towards the east. 'Me Mam, and me and me brother used to dwell there. Only, me Mam died two years ago next Whitsuntide, and me brother got caught by the traps last winter and sent to Van Diemens Land for seven years . . . Too fond of the earl's pheasants, our William was, God bless him . . . So I'm all by meself theer now, and it do get sore lonely at times. But there'll be nobody to moither you, and I'll not attempt to take liberties. You can lie easy o' nights. I swear to that on me Mam's grave.'

Sincerity radiated from him, and Tildy blushed with embarrassment.

'I never thought that you would try to take liberties with me,' she flustered. 'Only, what would it look like? Me, a married woman, sharing a cottage with a strange man. It wouldn't be decent!'

'Rubbish!' He scoffed at her good-naturedly. 'We shall know ourselves that nothing untoward is going on between us, and that's all that really matters, arn't it? Besides,' he added shrewdly, 'think of your babby. How sweet and comfortable he'd lie, wi' trees and flowers and fields all about him, and good clean air to fill his lungs, and sweet milk to fill his belly to bursting, and fresh eggs from my own hens to ate. Why, he'll grow as strong and sturdy as a young oak, so he will.'

Tildy's mind raced, searching for alternatives, and found none. She drew a deep breath, and made up her mind. 'Alright then, we'll come and stay with you . . . For a while,' she qualified. 'And I'm very grateful for your kindness in offering.'

Davy Nokes rose to his feet, his pleasure at her agreement shining in his eyes.

'We'll goo along nice and easy, that's if youm able.'

'I think I am,' Tildy told him uncertainly.

He helped her to rise, and a wave of dizziness caused her to sway, and cling tightly to his muscled arms.

'Forgive me, I'll be alright in a moment,' she apologized, but he expressed his doubts.

'You'll not manage the distance. 'Tis more nor three miles to me cottage.' He brushed aside her protestations of ability. 'No wench, youm plainly not able to manage it.' Then his eyes danced with mischief. 'You need only walk half a mile. Just to the next house. A friend o' mine lives there and he's got the very thing to get you home.'

And so it was that Tildy arrived at her new refuge sitting in a gardener's wheelbarrow, her baby held close, and her new-found friend singing happily as he pushed them both along . . .

Chapter Fifteen

For nine days and nights Hester Lammas had worried about the disappearance of her friend Tildy, and for nine days and nights she had badgered her husband, Ikey, with those worries. Until finally, at three o'clock on a Monday afternoon, he could stand no more.

'Goddam your bloody mouth, 'ooman! Canna you gi' me a bit o' peace?' he shouted, hurling his hammer and the iron he was working onto the floor. He glared at her and smashed his great calloused fists against his naked, sweat-soaked chest. 'What the Hell does you want from me?' I doon't know wheer Tom Crawford's bloody missus has run to!'

On the opposite side of the hearth, Hester Lammas in her turn hurled her hammer and iron to the ground.

'Suppose that bastard, Crawford, has killed the poor little cow?' she shrilled. 'What then?'

'Supposin' he has?' her massive-framed husband bellowed back. 'What does you expect me to do about it?'

'To come wi' me to the constable,' she riposted, wiping

spittle from her wide thin-lipped mouth with the back of her filthy hand.

'Why cannot you goo to the bloody constable yourself?' he asked wearily. 'And leave me in peace.'

'Oh yes! Oh yes! That's right! You hide behind me bleedin' skirts wun't you!' She was scathingly contemptuous. 'You knows well, Ikey Lammas, that Fatty Bunegar wun't pay any heed to me. He's the same as all you bleedin' men. He never 'ull listen to a woman.'

'God rot me!' the big man gritted out from between his rotting teeth and, snatching his ragged shirt from its hanging-nail, he tugged it over his brawny torso.

'Come on then, you nagging bitch . . . We'll goo together. Then mayhap you'll be satisfied, and we can get some bloody work done here.'

He slammed out of the leanto and Hester, pulling her old waistcoat over her own nude upper body, hurried after him.

As they walked towards Bromsgrove a horse and trap, heading in the same direction, overtook them. Jonathan Sanders saw their agitation and reined in.

'Is anything wrong?' he called. 'Can I be of assistance?'

Ikey Lammas' brawl-scarred features were still mottled by his recent anger. 'It's this bloody missus o' mine, Master Sanders. Her keeps on nagging me about Tom Crawford's 'ooman.'

'What of the girl?' the nailmaster questioned, and Hester Lammas hastened to tell him.

'What does Tom Crawford say?' the nailmaster wanted to know.

'The no-good bugger just says that Tildy 'as run away, and that he's well rid on her . . . And then he told me to mind me own bloody business.' The woman sniffed indignantly.

'Run-away wives are no uncommon occurrence, Hester,' Sanders remarked.

'I knows that well enough, Master Jon. But how many

141

runs away when they'm nigh on birthing a babby, and am too sick to do ought but take to their beds, like that poor little wench had to?' The woman argued vehemently. 'Answer me that, now?'

The nailmaster took her point, but could not accept her wilder accusations, and reasoned with her. 'Hester, your concern for your friend does you credit, but in all truth you cannot go to the constable and accuse Tom Crawford of killing his wife.'

'O' course you canna, you silly cow!' Ikey Lammas interjected. Then lapsed into a morose silence as the nail-master continued.

' . . . You have no proof, or even any reasonable grounds for suspecting that he has done such a thing. If you lay charges against the man, and he is found to be innocent, then you may well find yourself in a serious position.'

To forestall the woman's counterattack, Jonathan Sanders held up his hand. 'Hear me out, I beg of you . . . I will talk to Crawford myself, and also have enquiries as to the girl's present whereabouts set afoot. That is the best course of action to take, I do assure you.'

After reflection, Hester Lammas was forced to agree with him.

Tom Crawford's assertion that he was well rid of Tildy was not a reflection of his real frame of mind. The knowledge that his wife had run away, no matter for what reason, was a deep affront to his ego. At first he had expected her to return within a short time, but then as the hours lengthened he became increasingly anxious, and had searched the Sidemoor for her. The hours had become days, and the days had multiplied and still no word of Tildy came, and Tom Crawford had begun to be afraid. Supposing she was lying dead somewhere? Supposing she had died in some wayside ditch in the very act of giving birth? How would the people of the Sidemoor react to that?

Rough and brutal as the nailers were, all but the most

callous and depraved would unite in condemning him, and blaming him for it. They might drive him from the parish, and worse, attack him physically. There had been other examples of such mob violence in the Sidemoor that Crawford knew of, and he had no wish to end his days blinded, or crippled, like previous recipients of such attentions.

At times he considered leaving the village himself, but he knew that if he did so, then the already prevalent suspicion would harden into a certainty that he had done away with Tildy. In turn, that certainty would bring dire results upon his head.

Already, thanks to Hester Lammas' malicious tongue, dark looks were being directed at him, and threats and gibes shouted outside his cottage windows during the night. Even his brother, Edgar, had been affected by the fast deteriorating climate of hostility, and had stopped Martha from working with him . . .

The recently completed interview with Jonathan Sanders had done nothing to ease Crawford's mind either, with its probing questions into why Tildy had run away; and the nailer came away from the warehouse office in a surly mood. Before he could leave the yard his name was called, and he swung to face Dick Suffield.

'Well now, Tom, youm not looking so cheerful these days.' The man was his customary genially smiling self, but his eyes were cold as he looked the nailer up and down. 'No, for sure, youm looking a mite seedy. As though your cares were getting you down.' He affected an air of surprise. 'You arn't got troubles, have you, Tom?'

Crawford rose to the other's baiting. 'You knows well what my troubles be, Dick Suffield. Folks saying that I'se done away wi' my missus. Even bloody Sanders thinks so, I can tell that, for all his soft blethering, and promises to have enquiries made for her . . . Bloody bitch, that she is!' he ended viciously, and turned to walk away.

Suffield's hand grabbed his upper arm and spun him

about again. 'Doon't show me your back, Crawford, until I'se done talking wi' you.'

The mask of geniality had gone, replaced by the ferocity of a savage, and Tom Crawford's mouth dried up in sudden fear.

'I'm not answerable to you, Suffield.' He tried to tug himself free, but the fingers around his biceps were like iron bands. 'I'm naught to do wi' you now. I works for Johnno Dipple these days. You doon't like me work . . . Remember?'

'And who does you reckon Johnno Dipple works for, you thick-skulled bastard?' Suffield whispered, and his grip tightened until Crawford gasped in pain . . . . Youm mine, Crawford,' Suffield hissed, and his words burned into the nailer's brain. 'I owns you body and soul. Any time I wants to, I can get you transported, and iffen you tried to run, I can have you hunted down like a mongrel dog . . . How much does you owe Johnno Dipple? Because that's how much you owes me . . . How much as you told Johnno Dipple about your thievin' ways? Because that's how much you'se told me . . . .'

As he listened an actual physical nausea invaded Tom Crawford's body, and he inwardly cursed himself over and over again. Now he saw clearly why the fogger, Johnno Dipple, had been so accepting of his shoddy workmanship, so lavish with his credit. Why he had poured drink into him, and listened so avidly to the resulting drunken boastings about Crawford's raids on the district's warehouses, to steal the iron for working into nails. Why the fogger had accepted those same nails without a question as to their origin, but with knowing winks and nods. Crawford's gorge rose, and he felt close to vomiting with fear.

Dick Suffield stared at the badly-shaken man, smiled and let his hand drop, the ferocious savage hidden once again behind the genial mask.

'Doon't piss your britches, man, I've no wish to get you

transported, or hung,' he said jocularly. 'You and me has bin friends for too long for me to want that.'

Tom Crawford listened numbly. 'Then what does you want of me?' he queried abjectedly. 'Aren't I got sufficient o' trouble on me head as it is?'

The foreman chuckled richly. 'So you has, Tom, so you has,' he agreed. 'But I'll help you, Tom, so put your mind at rest. All you'se got to do, is the minute you gets word of your wife's whereabouts, then goo and fetch her back wheer she belongs. Here at your side, as your lawful wedded wife.'

Even in the depths of his misery, Tom Crawford's jealousy burned. 'So that's it, is it! You wants Tildy for your whore, doon't you? That's it, arn't it?' he demanded.

The other man chuckled again, and winked broadly. 'That's just so, my buck . . . That's just so.' He jerked his head in dismissal. 'Gerroff, and remember what I'se said. And remember who Johnno Dipple works for.' The genial smile vanished, and the savage glowered once more. 'You 'udden't survive in Van Diemens Land, my buck. The few who comes back reckons it's a Hell on earth, and you arn't got sufficient bottom to survive that, I know for sure . . . 'He paused to let his words sink home, then asked, 'So what's it to be, Tom?'

The nailer's shoulders sagged. 'It'll be as you say . . . When I find where she is, then I'll bring her back.' His bitterness surfaced. 'And I hope she brings you what she's brung me . . . naught but bloody evil since I married the bitch. And that's the truth on it . . . '

Chapter Sixteen

Muscles writhed beneath the satiny-brown skin of Davy Nokes' torso as he sent the curved scythe-blade whispering through the high grasses, they fell in swathes of sun-burnished greenness, the heady scents of their juices saturating the still air. Far behind the scytheman Tildy, head, neck and arms bared to the sunlight, used a long-handled pitchfork to 'ted' the fallen grass. To fluff it up and spread it so that the sun and wind could dry and entrap its rich nourishment.

The young man worked to the end of the row, then upended the scythe, planting the butt of the snaith firmly into the soft, red-brown earth. He snatched up a fistful of grass and wiped the long blade clean, then took a rounded whetstone from its sling on the rear of his broad leather belt and began to sharpen the scythe's cutting edge, working slowly from the broad base towards the pointed tip, his left hand holding the blade firm. As he worked his gaze wandered back to fix on Tildy.

It was almost two weeks since she had left the poorhouse, and in Davy's eyes the change in her bordered on the miraculous. Her skin glowed with health and cleanliness, her unbound hair was lustrous, her eyes shone with a contentment that only rarely dulled with secret and unhappy thoughts . . . Now, as she plied the slender-tined fork she sang gaily, and her voice was sweet to his ears . . . But then, everything about Tildy Crawford was sweet to Davy. In their brief time together he had fallen deeply in love, and although as yet, he realized that his love was unrequited, he still knew that, in her turn, Tildy was becoming increasingly fond of him. He allowed himself to hope that in time she would return his love in full measure. He smiled at his thoughts, muttering, 'Time? That's one thing I have in abundance . . . And what better way to spend it, than in company wi' this wench . . . '

As if sensing his glance, Tildy looked over towards him, and bantered, 'Come now, Davy, have you tired already? Shame on you!'

He grinned and, testing the blade-edge with his thumb, shouted back, 'I finds you a distraction . . . Youm looking so beautiful, that I 'as to stop every so often and fill my eyes with you for the sheer pleasure on it.'

The compliment evoked mixed feelings in Tildy. Pleasure, of course, but also disquiet, and a sense of guilt. She knew that Davy Nokes had fallen in love with her, and her guilt came from the fact that she felt she could never return his love in the way he wanted. She could care deeply for him as a friend, but not as a lover. The disquiet arose from realizing that although so far the young man had never by word or touch attempted any intimacy with her, driven by his hungry emotions, he was bound to make some such attempt sooner or later. The thought of the pain she would cause him if she rejected him had increasingly begun to trouble her.

A sense of unease marred her happy mood, and she fell to work again, tossing and spreading the green swathes surrounding her. A thin, high-pitched wailing came from the edge of the field where a huge old elm spread its masses of foliage. Tildy smiled wryly. Davy Nokes had spoken truly when he said that her baby would thrive in these surroundings. If his appetite was anything to judge by, he would grow as tall and as strong as the elm tree in whose shade he lay.

As she walked towards the plain wooden box, with its raised, tentlike awning of butter-muslin, she was aware of her swollen breasts straining against the grey bodice of her dress and silently gave thanks that she was able to nourish her child so richly. As yet, Tildy had not given him a name; to her, he was simply Baby . . . She reached the box and lifted the awning to see the child squirming on its soft padded bed. The entire interior of the box was similarly padded, and Tildy experienced a surge of gratitude towards Davy Nokes, who had spent many hours carefully fashioning the cradle for her.

Lifting the baby she unbuttoned her bodice and freed one heavy breast, guiding its erect dark nipple into the searching, sucking mouth. The exquisitely shaped lips closed and tugged greedily, and a wave of well-being soothed Tildy's recent sense of unease.

'I love you, Baby.' She crooned the benediction. 'I love you more than life itself.'

Staring fondly down at the puckered little face, topped by its swatch of black hair, she searched yet again for any likeness to Tom Crawford, and to her relief yet again could find none.

'I thank God for that,' she told herself fervently. 'Let him be solely my child. Let him be purely of my flesh and of my blood.'

Her feelings towards her husband were hostile, at times verging on hatred, but fear always accompanied any thoughts of Tom Crawford. For, as her legally wedded husband, he was in the society she dwelt in, her master. Owning her property, her possessions, her body, as he owned her child. They belonged to him, and he could do virtually whatever he wished with them.

The thought that he might find out where she was and come to fetch her was Tildy's constantly recurring dread. 'How could I stop him taking me back to the Sidemoor?' she whispered to herself. Resolutely, she fought to cast Tom Crawford from her mind. 'I'll not let myself think of such things! I'll worry about it when the time comes,' she told herself forcefully, and glanced down at her feet where a solitary honey-bee feasted upon a clump of golden-yellow cowslips. 'I'll be like you, Master Bee,' she murmured fancifully. 'And enjoy life's sweetness while I have it around me.'

While the baby fed, Tildy watched Davy Nokes working. Stripped to the waist his bronzed body was beautiful in its muscular symmetry, and Tildy found herself wondering what sort of lover he would be.

'Strong, yet tender and gentle, I'll warrant,' she decided, and detected a stirring of sexual desire in herself. 'Do not be immoral!' she inwardly scolded. 'You must not allow such thoughts to enter your mind. It's wicked, so it is.'

The baby was sleeping, and she laid him back in his box. With loving care she replaced the awning and went back to her work.

The hours passed and as the glaring sun moved across the sky the heat of the day pressed down on the land. Tildy's body was wet with sweat and the blood throbbed achingly through her head. Davy completed his current row, and laid his scythe down.

'We'll eat, and rest for a while, Tildy . . . It's scorchin' enough to fry eggs.'

Thankfully, the girl went back to the cool shadows beneath the great elm.

In an old leather saddlebag they had brought bread, cheese and raw onions, plus a small gallon-keg of beer and two horn drinking cups. The first taste of mellow cheese and pungent crisp-textured onion roused Tildy's appetite and she ate and drank heartily. Davy Nokes watched her with smiling eyes, taking pleasure from her obvious enjoyment. When both had satisfied their hunger, Tildy carefully wrapped what food was left into a clean rag and replaced it in the bag. Davy took another horn-tot of beer and savoured its taste.

'It's a fine brew, old Mother Buckley makes,' he praised. 'And thanks be to God, we've another keg still to come for this day's toil.'

Tildy looked around the half-mowed field. 'How much is there here, Davy?'

'Four acres,' he told her. 'I reckon we'll have two and a half acres cut and cocked by night-fall, and the rest finished tomorrow. If this weather holds it'll be dry enough for George Buckley to stack straight arter. That'll please the miserable bugger . . . Though, to gi' him his due, he's paying us a fair price for cutting and cocking. We'll earn near on ten shillings for this field, plus the beer allowance.'

Today was the first time that Tildy had left the environs of Davy's cottage, and although she had wondered how he earned his living, she had thought it impolite to question him about the subject.

He grinned satisfiedly at her, and artlessly boasted, 'That's real good wages, that is, Tildy. Nigh on ten shillings for two days' toil. But then, I always gets well paid, I'm a bit sharper in the head than most on 'um hereabouts . . . ' He briefly outlined the way the land was held around Tardebigge. The Earl of Plymouth owned over eight thousand acres and many farms and tenements in the district. Most of the local farmers were his tenants, as was the farmer whose land they were mowing today, George Buckley.

' . . . But I'm lucky, you see, Tildy. That old cottage o' mine is freehold, and the half-acre round it as well. My forebears has bin theer for centuries. They used to be landowners themselves, but fell on hard times and lost everything except that bit o' land and the cottage.' A fierce pride burned in the young man's eyes. 'But because of that bit of property, I'm a free man! I doon't have to call no man Master, nor bind meself to any employer. I can turn me hand to most anything, and I'm good at anything I turns me hand to, so I can take jobs on the piece.' He noted her puzzlement and added, ' . . . I mean for a price, like this bit o' mowing, for example. The hay and corn harvests are always good earners for me, because I'm the best scythesman that's e'er come out o' these parts. And come August you'll see that I'll be the Lord o' the Harvest, on any of the cornlands I chooses to go to. It'll be me, Davy Nokes, who'll settle the contract wi' the farmer. It'll be me who directs the work. It'll be me who leads the scythemen and sets the pace, me, Davy Nokes, The Lord of the Harvest . . . '

He fell silent, as though abashed by his own boasts, but Tildy was thrilled by the confident strength he radiated as he talked, and she urged him on.

'And after the harvest, what then, Davy?'

His eyes danced with mischief. 'Why, then it'll be strong ale and weak wenches until me money's spent.'

She laughed with him, but then he sobered and said gravely, 'At least, that's what it used to be, Tildy, but mayhap it'll be different this year . . . '

Tildy understood his meaning and, flustered, looked away.

Davy, sensing that he had overstepped some invisible line drawn between them, hastily continued. 'When the money's gone, why, there's all sorts o' things to do . . . I sometimes goes along the canal to Tardebigge Wharf and legs the barges through the tunnel theer. Or I'll do a bit of hedgelaying, or threshing, or potato pulling or winter planting.' He chuckled wickedly. 'Or spend me nights tormenting the earl's traps and lifting his birds and rabbits . . . Lord love you, wench, I can always meet my needs. And best of all, I'm bond-servant to no man other than myself. I'm free-born and free-living and, God willing, I always will be.'

She smiled, and told him quietly, 'I'm sure you will be, Davy. Certain sure.'

'Halloooo, be you asleep, Davy Nokes?' A burly man in a wide-brimmed, low-crowned hat, brown broadcloth coat and leather gaiters came along the grass verge of the hedge-row towards them.

'It's only George Buckley,' Davy explained, and rose to his feet.

Tildy looked harder at the oncoming man, and her heart thudded. It was the parish overseer who had carted her across the parish boundary. Davy saw her concern and patted her shoulder in reassurance.

'Don't moither yourself, honey. He'll do naught to you. Youm under my roof now, and naught to do wi' the over-seers.'

Buckley studied Tildy with interest. Despite the change in her physical appearance he had recognized her at a distance.

'Well now, young 'ooman, youm looking much improved in health,' he said gruffly. 'This rascal must be taking good care on you.'

Tildy drew on her courage and faced him boldly. 'He is, Master Buckley.'

The farmer nodded. 'Ahr, that's alright then. I'd heard you'd got this young 'ooman staying with you, Davy. Her's real bonny-looking, I'll grant you that.' His mouth gaped wide in raucous laughter, showing his tobacco-stained teeth. 'A sight bonnier than my old brood mare, and that's a fact.'

He turned his back on Tildy, and shrewdly evaluated the field before him. 'It's cutting nice and dry, Davy, you'll be done by tomorrow night-fall, I can see . . . I've another meadow for you arterwards, up along Harbors Hill.'

'I thought the Irishers were doing the rest o' your crop?' Davy queried, referring to one of the many bands of itinerant Irish labourers who travelled the county during the harvest seasons.

152

'So they was supposed to,' the farmer answered irately. 'But Agent Blascomb wants 'um for his big meadow, and what the earl's man wants, he must bloody well have. So that leaves me wi' eight acres still to cut. So will you take them?'

For a short time the men discussed prices and allowances, then they spat on their palms and slapped horny hands together to seal the bargain.

'I'll bid you good day.' Buckley took his leave and, with a final long look at Tildy, went on his way.

For some reason, the mere fact of the farmer seeing her cast a shadow over the day for Tildy, and she felt a foreboding of coming ill-fortune.

'Don't be silly,' she angrily berated herself. 'The man was perfectly civil, and said naught to cause you any concern . . . ' Nevertheless, the foreboding persisted in her mind, and the brightness of the day no longer cheered her.

Chapter Seventeen

The darkened room was dominated by the ancient four-poster bed on which old Samuel Sanders lay. Jonathan sat on a high-backed chair at the side of the bed, looking sadly down at his only surviving blood-relation. All flesh had fallen from the once rotund body, and the pug-featured face was a skull-like caricature of what it once had been. The old man was in a coma, and the breath rasped raggedly in his throat as the life-force struggled to retain its hold on the ravaged body. Despite his frequent disagreements with his uncle, Jonathan had loved him, and now he prayed silently that the old man would be spared further sufferings.

A man servant entered, and whispered into the nailmaster's ear.

'Very well, stay here and watch over Master Samuel, call me instantly if he shows sign of change,' Jonathan instructed and went to his wife's chambers.

He drew the perfumed air deep into his lungs, glad to rid his nostrils of the sickly stench of decay that hung about his uncle like a miasma. Carlotta was dressed for riding, the blue, military-trimmed habit, plumed black beaver hat and dainty half-boots setting off her dark beauty to perfection. She noted Jonathan's expression of disapproval, and snapped at him pettishly.

'Upon my soul, husband, you resemble a prune-faced old maid, the way you glare at me so.'

'I think only that you should not go abroad at this time, Carlotta.' He was unhappily aware that he sounded pompous, but could not stop himself. 'You know well that my uncle is dying, and it is not seemly that you should go racketing about the country with your brother and his cronies, while Uncle Samuel could pass away at any moment.'

His wife twisted the riding-crop in her gloved hands as if she could barely restrain herself from lashing out with it.

'I need air, and I need exercise,' she argued petulantly. 'I know well that Uncle Samuel is fast declining . . . Before God! You never for one moment let me forget the fact. But keeping me incarcerated in this house, as if I were a common felon and you the turnkey, will do naught to prevent Uncle Samuel's passing. Indeed, it will serve only to bring my own health and spirits to a low ebb.'

Jonathan was forced to acknowledge that he found some justice in her argument. 'Yes, I appreciate that, my dear,' he said placatingly. 'And, indeed, I have no objection to your taking the air, but . . . but . . . ' He struggled to find the words he wanted, and his wife was quick to take the opportunity to attack.

'You have no objections, you say! And pray, how could you hold any? I am going riding in the company of my brother and his friends . . . They are well-born, well-connected gentlemen. In God's truth, husband, my life here is dull enough, is it not? We see no one, we visit no one, we never go to a ball, or to a play, and I am starved of that Society that I was brought up to mix with. Do I object to your spending all your days at your warehouse, or in

155

that low chapel you are so fond of attending? Since I do not do so, then how in justice can you object to my finding a little innocent diversion in the company of my brother?'

Hoping to avoid yet another bitter quarrel the young nailmaster gave way. 'I pray you to say no more, Carlotta. I do not prevent your going riding . . . ' Attempting to restore an amicable atmosphere, he went on: ' . . . I hope you will enjoy the exercise. Who accompanies yourself and Jervis?'

With a feigned casualness, Carlotta told him. 'I am not sure, but I think it possible that Captain Cassidy will keep company with us.'

'Oh, I see . . . ' Jonathan took no pleasure from the information, having heard several stories of Cassidy's womanizing propensities. He frowned slightly. 'Captain Cassidy calls on you quite frequently, does he not?'

She was instantly on the defensive. 'No, not frequently by any means. At least, I would not consider three visits in a month to be frequent. Indeed, I am also forced to receive the gentleman alone, because you are always too busy to help entertain him. You must always have your nose buried in one of your dull ledgers. It is little wonder that we have so little society when you are so ill-mannered to our callers.'

He was stung to an acid reply. 'I am in business, wife. Those dull ledgers that I so ill-manneredly bury my nose in, are what pay for your extravagances.'

An angry flush dulled her olive skin. 'My extravagances, as you term them, are the sole means by which I am enabled to endure the lack of any normal relationship within the married state,' she hissed viciously.

As on so many other occasions, Jonathan Sanders was defeated by this reminder of his failure as a husband. Without another word he turned on his heel and left her.

For a brief moment Carlotta was sorry for wounding him so, but her own cruel frustrations overlayed the pang of guilt.

'It is his own fault. He should never have married me. He had no right to condemn me to such an existance.' She let her thoughts dwell on how different married life must be with a man such as Edward Cassidy, and her breathing quickened as her vivid imagination ran riot . . .

Jonathan wearily opened the leather-bound ledger and began to study the long columns of figures and annotations, but try as he might to concentrate, his thoughts persisted in returning to the problems of his marriage.

'Can I, in all justice, continue to hold Carlotta bound to me?' he asked himself, and such was his bitter anguish that his eyes filled with tears, and the neatly entered columns wavered and blurred so that he could not read them.

'What is to be done?' he whispered. 'What is to be done?'

Heavy knocking shook the office door, and Jonathan hastily blew his nose on a voluminous white handkerchief, and with an effort composed his features.

'Come!' he shouted.

Fat William Bunegar, the local constable, waddled into the room, his caped greatcoat adding to the mountainous figure he presented, and his tricorn hat balanced precariously on his tie-wigged head.

'I 'opes I'm not disturbin' you, Master Sanders?' he wheezed, his high-pitched voice issuing incongruously from the vastness of his swollen, puce-complexioned face.

'No Bunegar, you are not disturbing me,' Jonathan answered, grateful for this distraction from the painful burden of his thoughts. 'Have you news for me of Tom Crawford's wife?'

The fat man's eyes squeezed into puffy slits, as he wheezed portentously. 'I reckon I may have, Master Sanders. I reckon I may have . . . But then again, I'm not altogether certain.'

Sanders reined back the impatience that the other's

irritating mannerisms always roused in him. 'Tell me what you have discovered, if you please, Bunegar.'

'Well, Master Sanders, as you instructed, I went to Droitwich and to Kidderminster, and to Alvechurch and to Redditch, and made a lot of enemies, and it cost a fair bit o' money, I'll declare. More than the parish allows me for such matters, that's certain.'

'Put your mind at rest on that score, Bunegar. I shall fully recompense you for any expenses you may have incurred, and also reward you handsomely for your efforts.'

The hanging dewlaps quivered with gratification. 'Well, sir, I found that a young 'ooman gi' birth at the Tardebigge Parish poor'us. She's not bin named, but I found out that her 'ud bin put back across the Bromsgrove boundary arter the birth wi' her babby. The poor'us master said that her was a tramper woman, but he wouldn't set a name to her. I got a description of her off one o' the paupers, though, and I'm pretty well certain that it was Tom Crawford's missus.'

'But surely you could have prevailed upon the man to name her?' the nailmaster expostulated.

The constable uneasily shifted his crowned-staff of office from one hand to the other.

'That's none so easy, Master. You knows as well as me, that every parish tries to get shut o' paupers, and no overseer or poor'us master is fussy about how it's done . . . They don't exactly stick to the letter o' the law, and always tries to keep any such dealings hidden among themselves. My oath, I'se sin men and woman die on the cart as they bin put across the boundary.'

'And this woman, was she dying when they moved her?' the nailmaster interjected.

'Well no . . . Her was hale and hearty, so the poor'us master told me. But he 'uuden't say so more nor that, and I've no powers to compel him. Not in Tardebigge parish . . . Anyway, I made more enquiries hereabouts, but her's not been seen anywhere local, and no corpses have been reported, so I reckon someone has taken her and the babby in. And I should venture the opinion that her arn't far off neither . . . '

Jonathan reflected on this for some moments then, opening his desk drawer, he took a small purse from it and handed it to Bunegar.

'Here, this will recompense you fully, Master Bunegar. I thank you for your endeavours in this matter.'

The constable touched his staff to his hatbrim in salute, and Jonathan went on.

'You may call on Tom Crawford and tell him what you have told me. It will no doubt ease his mind to know that his wife and child are apparently alive and well. I bid you good day.'

Alone once more, the nailmaster closed the ledger and sat deep in thought.

Dick Suffield had seen the constable enter the office, and when the fat man re-emerged, beckoned to him. They talked for some minutes, more money was pushed into Bunegar's ready hand, and Suffield returned to his work with a contented smile . . .

Chapter Eighteen

The weather stayed fine. Day after day the sun blazed from cloudless skies, and the Harbors Hill meadow was quickly mowed, cocked and stacked, freeing Tildy and Davy for any other work that George Buckley might find for them until the corn harvest had fully ripened. Davy Nokes fashioned sling-straps for the baby's cradle so that it could be easily carried; and in the warm, light evenings and on their rest days, he, Tildy and the baby would go for long, easy-paced walks.

He showed her the Earl of Plymouth's great mansion, Hewell Grange, set in its arcadian parkland. The ruins of the once mighty Bordesley Abbey at Redditch. Ancient Hanbury Hall, once the seat of Admiral Vernon, 'Old Grog' himself. The sleepy village of Feckenham, where Nicholas Culpepper, Herbalist and Alchemist, had sought for miracles. More often, they would walk along the canal banks, to marvel at the series of locks that could carry waterborne vessels uphill. To stand and listen to the snorting of the steam-driven engine in its tall-walled house, that pumped the water from the Tardebigge reservoir into the upper reaches of the canal. Tildy gazed into the blackness of the tunnels that snaked their way deep beneath the hill-sides, resounding to the echoing shouts and badinage of the leggers, who by sheer muscle-power drove the heavy-laden barges through the lightless depths. Sometimes they would stop for an hour at a canalside beerhouse or wayside inn, to drink the sweet tangy Worcestershire cider, and listen to the soft burring talk of the farm labourers, or the out-landish speech of the wild, gypsy-like bargees and their families, who travelled the length and breadth of England in their horse-drawn narrowboats.

The baby thrived, and Tildy steadily regained her peace of mind. Sunlight and clean air restored colour to her cheeks, and the hard physical work of haymaking, turnip-thinning and pea-picking firmed and strengthened muscles made slack by child-bearing. Her body again became lithe and shapely enough to torment men with the desire to know its sweet secrets.

Tildy was coming to look upon Davy Nokes' ancient, thatched, wattle and daub cottage as her home, and she kept its sparsely furnished interior swept and cleaned, and filled it with masses of meadow sweet, cowslips and pimper-nels. Honeysuckle orchis and hyacinth. Celandine, colum-bine and campion, and hosts of other wild flowers that mingled their perfumes with the all-pervading scent of the wild thyme that spread its thick profusion around the single-storied cottage.

Davy had insisted that she and the baby take the only bedroom the cottage possessed, while he slept on a wooden pallet in the room that served both as kitchen and living-place. At night, tired but content, Tildy would lie on the narrow bed in the darkness, listening to the muted murmurings of the sleeping world, and give thanks to her God for granting her this respite in her troubled life . . .

'Tildy, wake up! It's gone break o' light!' Davy called

softly through the closed door, and Tildy struggled gently from sleep. Outside birds greeted the dawn with their sweet-fluting chorus and through the small-paned window the girl saw that the sky was paling. She checked that the baby was sleeping peacefully in its cradle at the bedside. Satisfied, she dressed in her petticoats and faded gown, and taking her towel, ash soap, and a small wooden box went barefoot into the kitchen.

Davy was bending at the large ingle-nook, stirring the glowing embers and adding fresh kindling and wood chips. He smiled over his shoulder, and tapped the iron pot suspended by its chain above the fire.

'I'se mixed the water-porrage, it'll not be long.'

She returned his smile and went outside to where the pump stood against the cottage wall, its stone trough forming a sink beneath the iron spout. She pumped the long handle until fresh water gouted, wetted her flannel and, opening the tiny box, dipped the wet cloth into the mixture of soot and salt it contained, and scrubbed her teeth with the tart-tasting mixture. After rinsing her mouth she soaped and washed her face, neck and arms. While she dried herself on the rough-textured towel she drew deep breaths of the pure, cold air, and felt like joining the birds in their song.

'Why, I'm happy . . . ' she realized with a sense of wonder. 'I think that for the first time in my life, I'm truly happy.'

By the time Tildy had finished brushing and plaiting her hair in the bedroom, the breakfast was ready. On the wooden table the porrage steamed in an earthenware bowl, two smaller bowls each containing milk and a wooden spoon flanked it; to one side stood two leather flagons of cider and a platter heaped with hard oatcakes and wedges of yellow cheese. They sat opposite each other on four-legged stools and ate in silence. Tildy let her eyes wander. In the ingle-nook a side of bacon hung yellowing, while over her head backbone chines from the same pig were hooked to the beams. Willow-baskets hung from beam-hooks holding oatcakes and bread, lumps of salted beef, a tub of salted butter, and small round cheeses with thick red rinds. Strings of onions dangled down the white-limed walls while in the coolest corners of the room a keg held pickled pork, another held cider, and a wooden chest contained grain-flour for baking. Outside in the garden turnips, cabbages and carrots grew and a big clamp covered with layers of straw and earth held sufficient potatoes for months to come to feed both of them, as well as the pig that, even now, snuffled and grunted in its sty at the garden's end.

Tildy compared this abundance with the frequent short rations of the Sidemoor, and silently blessed her good fortune.

Davy chewed and swallowed his last morsel of cheese, drained the flagon of cider, and got to his feet.

'I must be off. Agent Blascomb wants me to settle wi' him for taking the harvest, and I told the lads I'd meet 'um up by the Plymouth Arms.' He reached out to touch her smooth cheek. 'I wants you to rest today, honey. We'll more than likely be starting to cut the corn tomorrow, and you'll need all your strength for that. If you feels like it, come to the Arms later on. There'll be a bit of a frolic arter I'se took the harvest . . . Bye now!' With that, he was gone.

As the echoes of his whistle faded, Tildy remained seated, trying to decide if the feelings of tenderness and fondness she felt for him could be love. Even though she had both hated and despised her uncle, the long years of his puritanical rantings had conditioned Tildy's morals and mores. She believed implicitly that a woman should only have sexual relations within the marital state, and that outside that state, any sexual relationship was a sin in the eyes of God.

Now she was fully recovered from childbirth her own sexual longings were becoming stronger, more demanding. But these demands and longings of her body filled Tildy with a sense of shame and self-disgust. It was unseemly for a woman to admit to those desires, even in her own mind, and wicked for a married woman to feel them for any man other than her lawful wedded husband.

Even at this moment, Tildy's thoughts of Davy Nokes' compact muscular body, the clean fresh smell of him, the gentleness of his voice and hands, were causing pleasurable stirrings in her loins, and a will-sapping sensation of delightful lassitude . . .

'God forgive me!' she suddenly said aloud. 'I do believe that if Davy was to lay hold of me now, I'd do naught to prevent him, do naught but welcome his loving . . . God forgive me for a wicked sinner.'

In a flurry of movement she began to clear away the dishes, trying to dispel those forbidden, yet all too sweet images.

She heard footsteps approaching the door, and then Davy speaking her name as he came back into the kitchen, carrying a small handleless basket fashioned from cornstalks. He smiled at her surprised face, and held out the basket towards her.

'Here, my honey, I picked these for you last even', and left 'um out for the moon and the dew to sweeten 'um.'

The small basket was filled with tiny wild strawberries, among whose redness minute sparklets of moisture glistened.

'You must ate 'um now, Tildy, while the dew's still on them. That's when they'm sweeter than honey on the tongue.'

So strong a wave of affection for him welled up in Tildy, that it brought a lump to her throat, and tears to her eyes.

'No fruits will ever be as sweet to me, as you are yourself, Davy.'

She spoke so tenderly that the man's overwhelming love for her impelled him forward. Tildy trembled as his hands gently sought for her breasts, and his lips touched her mouth.

'I loves you, Tildy . . . I loves you more than my life.'
His voice was low and husky with wanting.

For a moment she pulled back from him, clasping his
face between her fingers, and searching his eyes with her
own. In their brown depths she saw the soft shining of his
love for her, and content with what she saw, surrendered to
her own longings.

Lying beneath him on the narrow bed, the smooth lithe-
ness of his body hot against her nakedness, the maleness of
him thrusting deep inside her, filling and satisfying her
hungry need, the clean scents of his hair and skin in her
nostrils, the taste of his mouth in her mouth, Tildy, for the
first time in her life, came to know the sweet joys of
loving . . .

The Plymouth Arms resembled a small mansion house,
rather than what it was, the inn of Tardebigge village. It
reared three stories high with a colonnaded front entrance,
wide windows and a sweep of gravelled foreground large
enough to accommodate scores of stagecoaches separating
it from the road. It faced east and was almost on the brow
of a hill. Below the inn, and almost directly opposite, lay
the basin, wharf, sheds and dwellings of the Tardebigge
canal, and from that basin a tunnel bored through the
bowels of the earth beneath the inn. Further to the east on
another hill stood the gracefully-spired parish church, and
stretching down southwards towards Bromsgrove straggled
the cottages and houses of the village.

Davy Nokes walked unhurriedly along the canal towpath
and even before he reached the steep-ascending slope that
would take him above the pathless tunnel and to the inn, he
could hear the hubbub of voices, and the rattle of ironshod
hoofs and wheelrims. The whole of the inn's foreground
was filled with men, women and children, with horses and
carts, with carriages and traps. White, grey and blue
smocks mingled with broadcloth, corduroy and velveteen
coats. Broad-brimmed billycocks and narrow-brimmed

stovepipes, mobcaps and straw bonnets swirled and bobbed about each other. Canvas leggings confronted leather gaiters, and boots, shoes, clogs and bare feet crushed and crunched the loose-strewn gravel. The doors of the inn were flung wide, and sweating barmaids and waiters carried trays of ale and cider and gin and rum to satisfy the clamouring thirsts of those outside, while from the open windows came the smells and sounds of other hungers being met and dealt with.

As Davy pushed through the close-packed throng he heard snatches of many different dialects and accents. Cheshire, Lancashire, Derby and Nottingham. Irish and Welsh. Stafford and Scots. The harvest here came early, particularly this year with its unusually extended spell of fine weather, and people would come to reap the wheat and barley and oats of Worcestershire, to gather its peas, its hops, its beans, and then go back to their own harvests in the colder counties of the north. The harvest brought good wages to its gatherers . . . It also brought back-breaking, muscle-straining, blood-sweating toil. Sometimes savage violence. Sometimes heat-stroke, fever, accidents and death . . .

The Earl of Plymouth's agent, John Blascomb, was a small middle-aged, pale-faced man who tried to compensate for his lack of inches by wearing high-heeled hessian boots and tall stovepipe hats. He strutted rather than walked and kept his narrow chest puffed out aggressively against the world. He was a native of Birmingham, but despite his town-bred background, a shrewd estate manager, who knew his business well and drove hard bargains. Now his calculating eyes were fixed on Davy Nokes . . .

'I'm not prepared to accept those terms, Nokes. You're asking a deal too much in the way of allowances . . .'

They were standing almost in the centre of the crowd, and all about them other farmers and labourers haggled and bargained. Davy remained silent, and the agent went on . . .

'The ration of mutton and drink is extortionate enough to be sure. But to ask six bushels of wheat each man at four shillings the bushel, and five bushels of malt as a gift, that's an imposition not to be borne. The wheat will sell for twice that price and more at market, and if you think that the earl would countenance me giving over a guinea's worth of malt to every manjack of your company as gift, then you've another think coming to you. There are plenty of companies here today who'll take my harvest for half those amounts.'

The younger man shrugged his broad shoulders, and replied easily. 'I doon't doubt you'll find somebody who'll take it . . . But what sort of a job 'ull they do for you, Master Blascomb? You'se got more than two hundred acre of wheat, and a hundred forty odd of barley. You might be able to chance leaving your barley for a few days, but I was over the Grange fields yesterday, and iffen that corn arn't cut a bit sharpish, then the first good wind 'ull blow the ears empty. And another thing . . . a full half o' your barley is laying badly, so badly that we'll not be able to use scythes, so it'll be sticks and fagging hooks and twice the time to do it. But I'se not overcharged you for that. So the bit of extra allowance we ask for is well worth giving . . . ' He paused, to let his words sink home, then shrugged again. 'Still, you think on awhile, Master Blascomb, but I'll tell you now, them's my terms. Mayhap we'll talk later.'

He nodded farewell, and sauntered on through the crowd. The agent's thin lips twisted in annoyance. The harvest season was the only time of the year when Jack was as good, or even better, than his master. Few farmers retained a large permanent force of labourers. They preferred to employ their people on a casual basis as and when they required them. Apart from the specialists like shepherds, stockmen, horse and ploughmen, most farmers retained only a couple of general labourers. But when the harvest season came, the permanent staff were totally unable to cope with the work, and that was when the casual labourer came into his own. For every farmer needed labour in abundance, and sufficient labour was in short supply. The men could, and did, drive a hard bargain with the masters, and Davy Nokes drove a harder bargain than any . . . But Blascomb knew Davy's boast that his company, or work gang, was the best in the county to be true. He also knew that before the day ended he would accept Davy Nokes' terms . . . Nevertheless Blascomb was determined not to be seen to give in too easily. The bargaining and haggling must be drawn out to the last possible moment. That was the way it was, always had been, and always would be . . .

The nine smock-clad men who formed Davy's company of harvesters were sitting in the meadow adjacent to the inn, and greeted him eagerly when he joined them. Their ages ranged from sixteen to sixty, their physiques from corpulent to cadaverous, but they all possessed one ability in common. They were expert scythesmen who could cut, tie and shock grain for eighteen hours a day, seven days a week, and continue to do so no matter what obstacles opposed them until the harvest was gathered in.

'Well Davy, what cheer?' old, white-bearded, withered-bodied Jas Tolly wanted to know.

Davy grinned, and spread his hands wide in a gesture of supplication. 'Shylock Blascomb arn't happy about the allowances . . . So we've no contract as yet.'

Old Jas scowled, and his stringy long beard waggled furiously. 'I tolt you, didn't I, Davy Nokes, that you was arskin' too much wheat and malt. Why 'udden't you listen to me? Damn you, we'll get no bloody contract at all, afore you'se bloody well done!'

Davy's friend, Tommy Gibson, indignantly intervened. 'Who's our captain, Jas? Who's our Harvest Lord?' He answered his own questions. 'Davy is! And you voted to elect him like the rest of us did. It's up to him what terms he makes. He's always got us good contracts afore, arn't he?'

'You canna be too greedy,' the old man persisted doggedly.

'Why not? The bloody masters be . . .' Tommy Gibson shouted, and used both hands to snatch the battered, greasy billycock from the old man's bald head and push it against the toothless mouth, adding, ' 'Ere, put this in your gob and suck it, you silly old bugger!'

Old Jas spluttered and raved and the men around him burst into roars of laughter. As the laughter quieted another of the group spoke out.

'There's one thing worries me though, Davy. Paddy Nolan's company be pretty good. They took most on the earl's hay . . . They might take the bloody harvest as well.'

'Ahr, that's right enough . . .' another man agreed. 'You knows the bloody Irish, they'll work for sod-all.'

Davy chuckled. 'Doon't fret about that, lads. I had a word wi' Nolan yesterday. He's already agreed to take Gaffer Shingler's harvest, and took the Earnest Money this morn . . . There's just them Lancashire companies left, but Blascomb doon't like the Northeners. He's had trouble wi' some on 'um afore, so there's no chance o' them taking it.'

He grinned all round, tilted his broad-brimmed hat over his eyes, and lay back on the grass. 'Put your minds at rest, boys . . . We'll take the earl's harvest alright, and at our price . . . I knows it . . . *And* Blascomb does.'

The tiny donkey laboured up the long hill, the panniers of nails slung across its withers sagging and straining under their weight of metal. Shaven-headed Johnno Dipple led the beast and by his side walked Dick Suffield, hot and sweaty in his rusty black tailcoat and tall top hat.

The nails in the panniers had been collected the previous Weigh-in day as part of their fogging dealings, and when sold would represent a tidy profit.

'I'll be bloody glad when we gets to the Plymouth Arms.'

Dipple's tongue ran across his dry lips. 'I'se got a mouth like a brick-kiln.'

'You should sell the gin, and not drink it, then you wouldn't get dry-mouthed after a bit o' walking,' Suffield told him genially.

'Will we need to goo right up to the Grange?' Dipple wanted to know.

Suffield shook his head. 'I shouldn't reckon on it, Johnno. Blascomb 'ull more than likely be at the Arms. Doon't forget they'm settling the harvest contracts today, so everybody 'ull be at the pub. We can drop the load there as usual, and he'll get his own men to carry them on . . .' His voice took on an admiring tone. 'He's a fly cove, is Blascomb. He buys the shoddy stuff from us, puts it in the account books as prime wares, and then makes the bloody tenants buy it from the estate at full price. The earl can well afford it though, robbing bastard that he is.'

The donkey stumbled and faltered and Dipple belaboured it across the head and neck with the thick ash-stick he carried. 'Cummon you bastard, gerrup! Gerrup! Bloody old bag o' bones.' He spat disgustedly. 'There's no strength in the bleedin' thing. By rights I should ha' sent it to the knacker's yard months since.'

Suffield glanced at the trembling, bony little creature and chuckled dryly. 'You ought to try feeding it on occasion, Johnno, it's amazing how a bit o' grub 'ull put strength into a cratur.'

It was well past midday when they arrived at the inn and the earlier crowds had thinned, but still large numbers were left, most of them busily drinking away the Earnest Money paid to them on acceptance of the harvest contracts.

'Hulloa Dick, how bist? Hast come to take the harvest?' a man who knew the nail foreman hailed them.

Suffield patted the panniers of nails. 'Not me, Jamie, I've already gathered my crops in . . . Have you seen Agent Blascomb hereabouts?'

'Ahr, he's about somewheres . . . Here, take a sup.' He

proffered the leather-jack of ale he was drinking from, and both Suffield and Dipple took long draughts.

'You might as well rest here a while, Johnno, and I'll goo and find Blascomb,' Suffield suggested. 'And get a couple of tankards ready for when I get back to you.'

'Make it three,' the man who had greeted them put in, and upended his empty jack. 'For you'se bloody well drained me dry.'

'Three it shall be, Jamie,' Suffield agreed, and went in search of the agent.

Blascomb was in the adjacent meadow, once again arguing the terms of contract with Davy Nokes. As Suffield neared them he could hear the agent's high-pitched voice, which, as always when he was agitated, became increasingly overlayed with the nasal sing-song accents of his native city.

'Yow'm asking too much o' me now, Davy Nokes. Yow'm floggin' a willing hoss.'

Suffield saw the good-looking muscular young man throw back his head and laugh, and so infectious were his high-spirits that the foreman found himself grinning in sympathy.

'Two gallon o' small beer or cyder has always been the drink allowance in these parts.' The agent grew increasingly indignant. 'How can you justify asking me for two quarts o' strong ale each man, each night, as well? God blast your eyes! I've agreed to the other allowances, and the rate I'm paying yow'll be earning nigh on ten shillings each man, each day, if you puts your backs into it, and now yow wants this extra as well. It's not to be borne, Nokes. Not to be borne!'

The nail foreman glanced at the rest of the men surrounding the disputants . . . 'Typical thick-skulled chaw-bacons.' He dismissed them contemptuously, but was not able to dismiss their leader so easily. The young man had a certain air about him. His manner radiated strength and confidence.

'I reckon he'll prove too much for you, Blascomb,' Suffield decided. 'He's a gamecock, and you're naught but a dunghill rooster, for all your high position.'

He came to a standstill and stood unobtrusively, waiting for the argument to finish.

Davy Nokes was not bothering to argue. He knew that the agent had no choice but to agree to his latest demand. Blascomb scowled and cursed.

'Goddam you, Nokes! Goddam you for a robber-dog! Two quarts it shall be . . . But you'll get no clause for twenty-four fine days in the contract. You must settle for the piece, no matter if it rains, hails or gales . . . You must settle for the piece!'

The young man nodded gravely. 'That's fair enough, Master. We'll take our chances with the weather.' Mischief danced in his eyes. 'But by God, youm a hard man to do business wi', Master.'

'Yow'll never get the same terms from me again, you young bugger,' Blascomb grumbled bad-temperedly, but with an underlying respect beneath his show of anger. 'So then . . . Do you take the harvest?'

Nokes glanced around his company, eyebrows raised in silent question. Each man nodded, their smiles showing their pleasure at the terms their Harvest Lord had won for them.

Davy held out his hand. 'I'll take the harvest, Master Blascomb.'

The two men slapped palms, and the agent produced a handful of silver shillings from his pocket.

'Then here's the Earnest Money to bind you with.'

He moved round and handed a single shilling to each man.

'We'll start the bottom meadow at break o' light tomorrow,' Davy announced.

'Good!' Now that agreement had finally been reached, the agent relaxed and his manner softened almost to joviality. 'Take the company across to the inn, Davy

Nokes. I'll buy a round of ale . . . But only one, mind. It would have been two or three, but I'm giving too much drink allowance as it is.'

The company roared with laughter at his sally, and encouraged by this Blascomb continued. 'I can't think for the life o' me why you want to get drunk tonight, Nokes, now you've got that pretty young maid staying with you . . . I know if she were mine, I'd find a better use for my parts than to piss through them all night.'

A flash of resentment crossed Davy's face, but knowing that the man meant no offence, he replied civilly. 'I'm afraid Mistress Tildy is no more than a friend to me, and only shares my roof as a sister might. So I'll need to keep you to the full ale allowance, for that's my sole pleasure these days.'

'Ahr, and mine as well, I'll tell thee true!' Old Jas Tolly cackled, and laughing and joking the company went off towards the inn, leaving the agent to notice and greet Dick Suffield.

Even as Suffield talked prices for his nails, his mind was dwelling upon what he had heard Davy Nokes say about Mistress Tildy.

Fatty Bunegar reckoned that Tildy Crawford had been taken in by someone hereabouts, Suffield pondered. Could be her that's living wi' the young cove? There's only one way to make certain, arn't there? I'll have to get a look at the wench myself . . .

173

Chapter Nineteen

Tildy stirred the stew of salt-beef, onions, carrots and potatoes in the iron pot and sipped a little of the rich gravy from the large wooden spoon. Its taste was savoury and good. Satisfied, she left it to simmer above the small fire. From a shelf at the side of the ingle-nook she took a big, leather-bound Bible and sat with it open before her at the table. Slowly, she turned the pages admiring the ornate, beautifully-coloured patternings that surrounded the printed matter, and wishing with all her heart that she could decipher the tiny letterings.

'Davy can read and write. Mayhap when the winter comes and we've more free time, he'll teach me my letters.'

Even as the thought of Davy crossed her mind, so the memory of their lovemaking simultaneously delighted and tormented her. All Tildy's natural instincts were now driving her towards a happy acceptance of a continuing full physical relationship with Davy Nokes. 'Why must I live the rest of my days without love, now that I have found a man who truly loves me?' she asked herself half in anger, half in anguish. But the long years of mental indoctrination, of insistence that sex without marriage was a mortal sin, still held her in bondage.

'Why cannot I forget my uncle's teachings? He wasn't a good or kind man. He showed no tenderness to anyone in his life. Why should his teachings still influence me, why shouldn't I give way to my own desires? I could bring great comfort and happiness to Davy . . . And in all truth he is the only man in the world who has ever shown me real kindness and real regard!'

She tried to concentrate on the pages in front of her, to immerse herself in the intricate illuminations, but it was an impossibility. Again and again her thoughts came back to her troubled, conflicting emotions. Finally she replaced the Bible on its shelf and, snatching up a besom broom, swept the already clean floor. Even this physical activity failed in its purpose, and so she decided to take the baby and go to the Plymouth Arms.

'Davy told me to come there. Mayhap the outing will soothe my restlessness.'

She tied a flat-crowned sunbonnet over her glossy coiled hair and slipped her feet into the painted wooden clogs that Davy had bought for her. She examined herself in a broken piece of mirror, and was pleased with what she saw. Her grey dress was clean, and neatly darned where the brambles had torn it. Her eyes were lustrous, and her skin toned to a sun-tinted creaminess.

I'll not disgrace him by my looks, she thought, with a touch of vanity.

Lifting the cradle she slipped her arms through the carrying straps so that it rested comfortably against the small of her back, and left the cottage.

The shadows of the trees lengthened as the sun dipped towards the western horizon, but the heat of the day still hung heavy above the land. Drink had loosened tongues and clothing. Men's hard-calloused hands crept stealthily beneath girls' petticoats and bodices, searching for the soft warm smoothnesses of breasts and thighs. Here and there in the seclusion of the hedgerows coupled writhed together in passionate struggle, muted voices panting protestations of love, fervent pleas, outpourings of mingled ecstasy and pain.

Around the Plymouth Arms family groups ate, drank and talked, while their swarming children ran hooting and screaming in play, and tail-swishing horses munched nose-bags of oats and hay and whinnied for their masters.

Tildy sat near to some of the men and families of Davy's company at the rear of the innyard and contentedly listened to the jokes and gossip, while idly watching Davy and his friends playing the game known as Bumble Puppy.

An ancient flat-topped tree stump, some three feet high and two feet in diameter formed the block, on which a dozen wooden skittles were standing. The players stood on a mark ten yards away from the stump and tried to knock the skittles over by skimming thick round discs of iron at them. Each man took three shots in turn. Both players and spectators wagered money on the play and excitement could rise high as the games progressed and the bets increased. A sizeable crowd were watching now, and betting was fast and furious.

Davy was at the mark preparing to make the final set of throws for the current game. His calico shirt was unbuttoned, displaying his bronzed throat and chest. His thick hair was tousled and a faint sheen of perspiration moistened his flushed face. He turned, his eyes searching for and finding Tildy, sitting some distance away. He smiled at her, and waved, his teeth a flash of white between his lips. At that moment he looked like a young boy. Tildy smiled and waved back, and was flooded with a surge of loving tenderness towards him. In that split second of union her mind was made up. This night she would share Davy's bed. Be his wife in the flesh, if not in legality . . .

He winked broadly and swung to face the block.

'Order now! Let's have some order!' a self-appointed

steward bawled loudly, and the excited crowd hushed and waited expectantly.

'How many skittles must he knock down to win?' Tildy whispered to Jas sitting next to her, the baby's cradle set between them.

'He mun take eight,' the old man told her. 'Hush now, and watch. He's a rare skimmer, is Davy.'

'Come now, make your casts.' The game referee held up his hand, and as he dropped it to signal the throw, Davy moved with fluid grace. As fast as the eye could follow one, two, three discs flew from his curled fingers, exploding against the skittles, hurtling them across the block to bring others tumbling down with them.

'Nine!' the referee bellowed. 'Nine fallen! Game to Davy Nokes!'

The winning gamblers cheered uproariously, and the losers booed their disgust.

Tildy clapped and cheered, then suddenly felt a hand clamp roughly on her shoulder. In fright she jerked and looked up and sideways. A stocky, smock-clad, swarthy-featured man was leering down at her, his teeth black and rotting in his beer-reeking mouth. He crouched and thrust a tankard of ale towards her face.

'Here, sweetheart, tek a cup,' he urged, in a harsh north-country accent.

Tildy shook her head. 'No, I thank you. I've got a drink already.' She pointed to the leather-jack of cyder on the ground before her.

'Nay, sweetheart, I'll not tek no for answer,' he persisted, and tried to push his tankard against her lips. 'Thee'll tek a sup o' mine.'

Tildy's initial fright had passed, and now annoyance caused her to push hard against his thrusting hand. 'No! I don't want it!'

The tankard tilted and ale spilled onto the ground. Beneath the shapeless hat the man's forehead creased, and his bleared eyes reddened.

'Tha'rt a snooty bitch, arn't tha . . . Well, where I come from we dunna tek kindly to snooty bitches.' His voice was a hoarse growl.

'Leave the wench be, Cully,' Old Jas intervened. 'Her man's over theer, and her's waiting for him.'

'Who rattled your chain, monkey?' the north-countryman snarled. 'Dost want a smack in the chops, tha nosey old bastard?' He rose upright and stepped to stand directly over the old man. 'Dost hear me, monkey?' He exuded an aura of threatening violence. 'Bist tha looking for a smack in the chops?'

By now the altercation had attracted the attention of the people surrounding them, and others got to their feet and gathered around the trio.

Old Jas swallowed hard, and quavered nervously. 'Look, Cully, we'em just having a quiet sup, and the young 'ooman has not spoke to you, has she? So why canna you just leave us be?'

'All I did was to invite her to tek a sup from me pot!' The north-countryman's voice rose as his drink-inflamed temper fuelled on itself. 'I were just being neighbourly, that's all. And the bloody slut knocked me drink all over the ground. Does she reckon she's too high and mighty to tek a drink from a Lancashire lad? Be that it? Arn't us Lancashire men good enough to tek a sup of ale from? Bist that what tha'rt trying to say, monkey?'

Other northerners were in the crowd. Half-drunk, conscious of the latent resentment their presence aroused in the local people, they were more than ready to egg on the aggressor.

'Gi' the owld sod your clog in his chops, Darky!' one of them shouted.

'Aye, that's reet! Show him 'ow we does it back home!'

'Show the bugger our Lancashire Purring, Darky!'

'Aye, kick his arse through his head!'

Davy Nokes and his friend Tommy Gibson pushed through the crowd to stand facing the man named Darky.

'What's up?' Davy demanded.

The swarthy man spat contemptuously at Jas Tolly, and the spittle clung to the old man's white beard. 'This bloody monkey, and that bloody slut sitting there . . . That's what's up, my cocker.'

'Aye, the bloody slut thinks herself too grand to tek a sup from a Lancashire man,' one of Darky's supporters joined in.

Davy tried to soothe the inflamed man. 'Look, Cully, I'm sure no insult was intended. Why can't we let it go, and have a drink together in good harmony?'

Darky's rotten teeth showed behind curled lips. 'Aye opp, lads! We've got a real Creepin'-Jesus come among us. He wants to kiss and mek-oop . . . Mayhap he's a bloody dolly-mop.' The bleared eyes swung to Tildy. 'Is this your man, slut? God rot me! Tha needs a real man, not this bloody dolly-mop . . .'

'You'd be well advised to shut your mouth and get off from here while youm still able,' Davy warned, his face set rigidly, and his only visible sign of emotion the veins pulsing furiously in his temples.

Darky ignored him, and went on speaking to Tildy, who could no more drag her eyes from his rabid face than a terrified rabbit could turn from a stoat.

'Why dost not tha come back to me tent, slut? I'd gi' thee summat between thy legs as 'ud mek thee squeal like a stuck sow.'

Davy's self-control all but snapped, he so lusted to smash the rotten teeth down the man's throat. But he saw the cradle at Tildy's side, and was afraid that if a brawl erupted on this spot, then Tildy and the child could get hurt or even killed. So to draw the other off, he forced himself to laugh loudly and begin to saunter away.

'This Lancashire cove 'udden't dare to meet me in a straight fight!' he declaimed. 'The chicken-livered bugger is only good for blaggardin' women and old men.'

'Did'st hear that, Darky?' a northerner shouted. 'He

reckons tha'rt feared to meet him, man to man.'

The swarthy Darky left Tildy, to follow Davy through the crowd. 'What's that tha says, dolly-mop?' He growled. 'Turn about, and say it agen.'

Davy kept walking until he was sure that Tildy and the baby were well out of reach, then swung to face the other man.

'Right, you foul-mouthed pig, I'll have you now!' he hissed.

'Form a ring! Form a ring!' The cry was taken up by the crowd, who came pushing and jostling to see this free show. 'Form a ring! Form a ring! Do it proper! Fair fight! Fair fight! Form a ring!'

'Reet then, dolly-mop, I'll learn thee thy lessons.' Darky threw his shapeless hat to the ground, and shrugged his shapeless smock over his head. Stripped to the waist he was a fearsome sight. Broad-shouldered, heavily muscled. A mat of coarse black hair covering chest and shoulders. His close-cropped, bullet head set on a thick squat neck.

In his turn Davy stripped off his leather waistcoat and calico shirt. Naked to the waist, he lacked the sheer bulk of his opponent, but his satin-brown body writhed with muscle and carried not an ounce of surplus fat.

A seething ring of eager onlookers coiled the two men, and both had their partisans in the crowd.

'Purr him Darky, purr him!'

'Gi' him the Manchester Kiss!'

'Sicken the bugger, Davy!'

'Ahr, trim his bloody lamps for him, Tardebigge!'

Tildy was still with Old Jas. Trembling and afraid for Davy, she stood on a ridge of high ground that enabled her to see over the heads of the crowd. As the two combatants squared off and circled each other with weaving fists, Tildy's heart seemed to turn over in her body, and she closed her eyes, praying silently.

'Dear God, protect Davy. Don't let harm come to him. Dear God protect him, I beg you, protect him.'

The crowd hushed, then roared as Darky came with a rush, fists swinging, blackened teeth bared in a snarl of hate. Davy ducked and dodged, evading the wild swings with almost contemptuous ease, and the crowd howled their appreciation. Then his own fists moved in short vicious jabs, thudding into the mat of black body hair, jolting Darky to a standstill and driving him back.

Groans of dismay came from his supporters, and cheers from Davy's.

The minutes lengthened and the advantage swung first to one, then to the other. Their breathing grew harsh and ragged, and their bodies ran with sweat. At Tildy's side Old Jas grunted with every blow, as if it were he who fought. Tildy clutched her baby to her breasts, and even in the midst of her fear and revulsion, experienced a glow of pride that Davy Nokes should care sufficiently for her to fight a man who offered her insult.

Then a wild, round-house blow took Davy full in the face, and he staggered back, blood pouring from his mouth, dripping from his chin, splashing onto his smooth chest. Exultant howls shattered the air as the north-countryman sprang for the kill. Another smash into Davy's face, the scarlet blood flying out like a fine rain under the impact, and a wave of sick faintness engulfed Tildy, so that she swayed and nearly fell.

'God help him now . . . ' she begged piteously. 'Oh God help him now . . . '

More soggy-thudding impacts and Davy was staggering back and back, blinded by blood, excruciating agony splintering his senses, only his courage keeping him on his feet. But courage could not save him now. Darky's fists pounded at him like hammers, battering all consciousness from him, and at last his knees buckled helplessly, and he collapsed.

'Hold my baby!' Tildy thrust the child into Old Jas' arms and ran like a demented woman. She clawed her way through the uproarious crowd until she reached the open circle where Davy lay on his back, arms outflung, blood oozing from the swollen wreckage of his face. Tears threatened to blur her sight, and angrily she dashed them away. Then she tore strips from her petticoats and, kneeling at Davy's head, began to wipe away the lather of blood and sweat. Others came to help her and gradually the panic-stricken thudding of her heart slowed, her shaking hands steadied, and she became engrossed in her work of mercy.

Surrounded by a cheering phalanx of supporters Darky swaggered away, while those who had sided with Davy stood in sullen disconsolate groups, casting resentful looks at the victor's back. And smiling genially, Dick Suffield took his own leave of the scene . . .

With the help of Tommy Gibson and Old Jas, Tildy brought Davy back to the cottage, and put him to bed. The injured man spoke little, only disjointed sentences which made no sense to his hearers. Tildy wanted to have a doctor brought to examine him, but her companions vehemently dissuaded her.

'He'll be alright arter a good sleep,' Tommy Gibson asserted. 'Davy's as tough as old oak, you'll see. In the morn he'll be right as rain.'

Tildy gazed unhappily down at the bruised, swollen features, the torn lips and cut eyes. 'He's sore hurt . . . The doctor should look at him.'

'Doon't talk so sarft, wench.' Old Jas' beard quivered. 'There arn't a doctor breathing who can do as much for Davy as me . . . I'll just goo home and fetch some things to treat him with. You mustn't goo throwing good money away on a bloody quack.'

Within an hour he was back, carrying a wicker-work basket filled with stone jars of differing sizes.

On the bed Davy stirred and lifted his hands to his face. As his fingers touched the fluid-weeping cuts he groaned.

'God blast me! That bugger can hit alright.'

Relief brought a smile to Tildy's lips. 'Oh Davy, you're talking sensible again . . . Thank God for that!' She clutched his hands in hers. 'How are you feeling?'

The torn lips twitched in the semblance of a smile. 'Wonderful!' he told her dryly. 'I feels just wonderful . . . Apart from me yed.'

She felt like smothering him with kisses. 'You're alright, Davy, you're alright . . . I feared you were dying, so I did.'

Freeing one hand he pushed open the swollen slit of his eye so that he might see her more clearly. 'My oath, girl, I'se had worse hidings than this 'un, and I'm still here to tell the tale . . . Fair play to the bugger, though, he had the best of me this day. But he won't next time, that I'll swear.'

'No Davy!' Tildy exclaimed in dismay. 'Don't talk of fighting him again. Leave it lie now.'

'Shift your bones and let the dog see the rabbit.' Old Jas had completed his preparations.

Tildy moved back to give him room, and Tommy Gibson, until now a silent spectator, patted her shoulder.

'Youm a good girl, Tildy. I had me doubts about you afore, but I see now that they was uncalled for.'

His words brought a warm inner glow to Tildy, and for the first time since she had come to Tardebigge parish, she felt that they were beginning to accept her as one of themselves.

The old man dipped his fingers into one of the large stone jars and brought out a wet, black, slug-like leech which he placed on Davy's swollen eyelid. The leech elongated its body as its sucker took hold of the skin, and then began to swell as it voraciously drank in blood. Old Jas deftly positioned more leeches on the bruised swellings and as each one in turn sucked its fill, he plucked the distended bodies from the wounds and dropped them into a jar filled with salt-water. The clear water became a swirling redness as the salt caused the creatures to regurgitate the blood, and Old Jas again replaced them on the wounds.

Despite a sense of revulsion, Tildy could not help but watch in fascination as the swollen flesh visibly lost colour and diminished in size.

After a while the old man returned all the leeches to their stone jar and wiped Davy's face clean. Then from other smaller jars he extracted fragrant-smelling pastes and smeared them thickly onto the skin until Davy's features were hidden behind a thick, greasy, multi-hued mask.

'That'll do then . . . You just rest easy now, Davy, and come tomorrow morn you'll be nigh on as good as new. Here, drink this!' The old man lifted a stoppered ale-horn from the basket, opened it, and made Davy empty its liquid contents. 'You'll sleep like a babe now, so we'll leave you to it.'

He shepherded Tildy and Tommy Gibson from the room and closed the door. Noting the questions in Tildy's eyes, Old Jas chuckled.

'Don't you moither yourself, my wench. It'll be as I say . . . I'm well known in these parts as a witch-man.'

He cackled with laughter at the shock on Tildy's face, and his beard waggled as his toothless gums worked together. 'Yes, my wench, it's naught but the truth . . . I'm a white witch, as was me feyther, and his feyther, and his feyther's feythers down through the ages. I can cure most anything in men or cattle, and lift the Evil Eye from hearthstone or barn or byre . . . Arn't that so, Tommy?'

The younger man nodded vigorously. 'That's so, Tildy. Old Jas has always bin known for it in these parts. You just do as he says and leave Davy quiet in theer, and come the morn he'll be as brisk and lively as a cricket.'

Both men took their leave and Tildy busied herself settling the baby for the night, and making up a bed on the wooden pallet. She tried to eat some of the stew from the iron pot, but found that she had no appetite. The events of the day were now coming home to her with full force, and she felt weak and queasy. She sat by the ingle-nook and stared into the glowing fire. Through the bedroom door

184

she could hear the faint snores of Davy asleep, and an ironic, joyless smile curved her lips.

'And tonight I was going to sleep with him. Bring him comfort and happiness . . . And instead, because of me, he lies there torn and bruised. I've brought him naught but trouble.'

Her mood turned sombre.

'The same way that I brought Tom Crawford trouble. Until he met me he was happy at Ipsley Rectory, and as soon as we married he lost his position and ended in the stocks . . . and now must slave at the nailing. Poor Davy. He could have been crippled or even killed this day, because of me. Dear God, why do I bring troubles onto the heads of those men who become involved with me?'

Her mood deepened to a black-sickness of despair and depression.

'Am I cursed? Am I only ever to bring grief to those who care for me? Even my baby has had the shame of being birthed in a poorhouse . . . If I hadn't gone running into the night like a mad thing he could have been born beneath his father's roof. I brought the shame of a pauper birthing onto his innocent head. Dear God, I must be accursed. I must be . . . '

Through the hours of darkness Tildy remained awake and seated by the fire, occasionally moving to add more wood and dried turfs to the flickering flames. Outside the winds soughed, and clouds moved across the rays of moonlight, creating wavering patterns of light and shadow upon the cottage. Tildy's thoughts were a maelstrom, but one conviction slowly began to override all else. It was her fault that Davy Nokes had taken this terrible beating, and if she remained with him, then she would inevitably bring more troubles down upon his head.

'I'm living in a state of sin,' she told herself with bitter resignation. 'My desire for Davy is a sin. A black, evil sin. I don't belong here . . . I belong where God placed me. At the side of Tom Crawford. No matter what my feelings are towards him, he is my husband in the sight of God, and it must have been God's will that I should wed him. Otherwise it could never have come about . . . '

At last she rose to her feet and tiptoed into the bedroom. Davy slept peacefully, the moonlight lancing through the window and shining upon his face – imparting to the surface of the thick-layered pastes a quality of luminescence, so that he resembled an ethereal being, rather than an ordinary man of this earth.

Tildy lifted his hand and pressed her lips to the warm skin. 'Oh Davy, I'm so sorry,' she whispered, and as if the sleeping man heard her, he stirred and murmured her name, then lapsed once more into deep slumber, only the rise and fall of his chest showing that he still lived. Again Tildy kissed his hand before gently replacing it upon the coverlet.

'Goodbye Davy, I pray to God that you will someday find a woman who is worthy of you.'

Her cheeks wet with tears, Tildy lifted her baby in its cradle and slipped from the cottage. Helplessly in the grip of compulsions that she was unable to deny, or to prevail against, she set out across the fields in the direction of Bromsgrove . . . and the Sidemoor . . .

Chapter Twenty

Tom Crawford awoke reluctantly, dragging himself into the awareness that yet another long day of hard labour stretched before him. Unwashed and unshaven, his thick hair matted with grime and dried sweat, he pulled on his greasy clothes, blinking and yawning in the dawn's overcast light. He suddenly shivered violently in the chill air, and sourly compared his present condition with the relative comfort of Ipsley Rectory.

'God blast my bleedin' luck!' he grumbled bitterly. 'And blast God as well, for bringing such luck on me.'

He shuffled down the steep narrow staircase, and at the bottom came to an abrupt halt. His jaw dropped open and he could only stare disbelievingly.

Tildy sat facing him on one of the broken-backed chairs, the baby asleep in its cradle on the table, which was littered with mouldy scraps of food, soiled plates and empty bottles.

The man rubbed his eyes and resumed his staring. 'God strike me dead!' he swore softly. 'Is it you?'

Tildy had awaited this moment in trepidation, dreading

what might befall her and the baby, but unable to resist the compulsion to return. Now, suddenly, all her fear left her, and she felt calm and strong. When she spoke it was with the eerie feeling that someone other than herself was speaking through her, using her lips and tongue to form words – that in their turn seemed to flow unbidden from a source outside herself.

'Yes Tom, it is me, and this is your son.'

The man continued to stare blankly at her, as if uncomprehending of what she said.

' . . . You have the right to be a full father to him, that's if you so wish. If you do, then I'm prepared to remain here also, and be a wife to you.'

Her voice held a quality of calm strength that, despite his bemusement, Tom Crawford was already sensing.

'You'se changed Tildy . . . Youm different . . . Stronger somehow.' He frowned in puzzlement.

She smiled mirthlessly. 'Mayhap that's so, Tom. But then, I've learned much about myself these last weeks.'

Now the initial shock was wearing off, Tom Crawford was able to take stock of his wife.

'By Christ, but she's looking bonny.' His mind seethed with a tangle of conflicting emotions. Curiosity, anger, jealousy, even sexual desire, all struggled for mastery.

'Wheer's you bin? Wheer did you go that night? I been worried sick as I 'as, didn't you give thought to that?' The questions poured from him.

'Wheer did you birth that babby? Who'se bin sheltering you all this time? Have you bin living wi' some man? Have you? . . . Been playing the whore? Is that it?'

His jealous temper began to flare through, but in place of her customary timid reaction to his anger, Tildy's own spirits rose and flared.

'Don't bawl at me so, Tom Crawford! The days when you could treat me like some poor dumb beast have gone!' She got to her feet, facing him defiantly. 'Have you forgotten why I ran away?' she demanded furiously. 'Have you forgotten how I caught you rutting like an animal with a girl who's still but a child?'

He took a step towards her, his fists clenching. Tildy didn't flinch, only hissed at him warningly.

'You raise your hands to me, Tom Crawford, and I'll bring ruin down on your head. Make no mistake! I'm ready and able to do just that.'

Even as she voiced the threat, Tildy marvelled at her own lack of fear and ability to bluff. For bluff it was. She had no idea of how she could bring ruin down on the man.

For Tom Crawford, however, it was no bluff. A name immediately flashed into his mind . . . Dick Suffield! This bloody hell-bitch was being protected by Dick Suffield! That's why she was facing him now, mouthing threats at him, showing no fear. The cow had come back because Dick Suffield had promised her protection! It must be so!

Crawford's heart sank, and he let his fists unclench. One thing was clear above all else: he could no longer treat Tildy as he had done in the past. As long as Dick Suffield gave her his protection, then she held the whiphand.

For the moment, at least, he was forced to accept his defeat, and he tried to cover it by bluster.

'I've no wish to lift a hand to you, wench. But you drives me to it. Youm enough to make a bloody saint lose his temper. You goes running off, then weeks later turns up as bold as brass wi' a babby, and tells me naught of wheer you'se bin, or what you'se bin doing . . . '

Tildy knew that she had won a victory. But for now, she was at a loss, not knowing why she had won, or how to exploit it. So she decided to blindly follow her instincts.

'Like I said, Tom,' her voice was softer now. 'A baby must have its father. I've seen what can happen to children who have no man to protect them. I'll stay with you, and try to be a good wife . . . But in return you must try to be a good husband and father. If we work together, then surely we can rise above this station in life. We can give the baby some sort of school learning. Fit him for a better station in life than ourselves . . . So tell me, what is it you want to do?'

The man blinked hard. He was puzzled and uncertain. He knew well that he badly needed a woman. Not only for his bed, but more important, for the forge and the house. A man alone in this environment needed all the help he could get to survive, and only a woman could help in all aspects of a man's bodily needs. Even at this moment, Crawford knew that he still desired Tildy sexually above any other woman he had ever known, and he was forced to acknowledge that she was a good worker and housewife . . . But how could he accept the fact that he would be sharing her body with Dick Suffield?

His familiar demon of jealousy roused itself again, but this time he forced it back, sickeningly aware that he had no real choice in the matter. Suffield had sufficient evidence to get him transported, if he so chose, and Tom Crawford could not face the prospect of long years in the penal colonies. He knew only too well that he hadn't the necessary toughness of mind to survive that.

He shrugged, and reluctantly accepted the situation.

'Alright then. We can but try, carn't us?'

Tildy felt neither happiness nor unhappiness at his decision. Only a deep certainty that she was about to trace in another fragment of a predestined pattern she was powerless to alter, and from which there was no escape . . .

The rumour of Tildy's return swept rapidly through the Sidemoor, and drawn by curiosity many of her neighbours came to her cottage to verify the fact for themselves. Hester Lammas was foremost among the visitors, and remained after the others had left. While Tildy scrubbed and swept the cottage, she told the older woman all that had befallen her.

'Bugger me, if you arn't a bloody fool.' Hester's gaunt features were a study of scornful surprise. 'Why in God's name didn't you stop wi' that young cove in Tardebigge?

190

He sounds a hundred times the value o' this bleeder you'se got here.'

The thudding of the Oliver in the forge demonstrated that Tom Crawford was safely out of earshot, but even so Tildy touched her fingers to her lips in mute warning.

'Shhh, Hester. Don't talk so loud. What I've told you of Davy is for your ears alone.'

'Don't moither about that, my duck, I'll tell no one,' the older woman averred. 'But I still reckons youm the biggest fool in Christendom to ha' come back to this bloody dung-heap when you was well out of it . . . What made you return, wench? What made you?'

Tildy hesitated, searching for words to explain reasons that she could not fully explain to herself.

'It's a strange thing,' she said finally. 'But I didn't seem to be able to stop myself returning. God only knows, there is less than nothing to tempt me back here . . . but . . . but it was as if some power had seized my body. I just could not help but return. But I'll tell you this Hester, I'll not stand for a repeat of the treatment Tom Crawford meted out to me before. Things will be differently ordered from now on . . . I intend to rise above this station in life. No matter what I must do to ensure it. My baby was born in the poorhouse because of me. He'll not die there, that I swear!'

Hester Lammas' sunken eyes were kindly. 'Theer's a good many on us hereabouts has made vows such as that, Tildy, my duck. But until now I've yet to see anybody fulfil them.'

Tildy smiled grimly, and spoke with utter conviction. 'Then I shall be the first to do so, Hester. You may be certain sure of that.'

Hester Lammas left to join Ikey, her husband, in their forge, and Tildy went down again on hands and knees to her scrubbings. As she scoured the deep-ingrained dirt from the flagstones she pondered on what had suddenly begun to happen to her as a person. An iron determination seemed to have possessed her soul. A determination that her child should never endure the hardships and humiliations that she herself had endured . . . But how could she achieve this ambition?

She took stock of her strengths, and her weaknesses. Physically she was no match for a man's strength. Mentally, although completely uneducated, she sensed that her intelligence was equal, if not superior, to the majority of men. To her own acute surprise she found that at this moment she was able to consider using her beauty to gain advantage in life. The consciousness of sin that had so distressed her when staying with Davy Nokes, seemed to have lessened a little in its oppressive weight.

'Mayhap that's because I've come back to reality,' she decided. 'And while with Davy, I was existing in some dream-life that bore no relation to what reality actually is.'

She wondered why Tom Crawford had allowed her to better him in their brief dispute.

'What is it that made him feared to hit me? He's never hesitated to do so before. Why did he not use his fists this time?'

Wondering about Crawford introduced another disquieting train of thought. Would he want to possess her body this coming night? She experienced an acute wave of revulsion.

'Could I bear him slavering over me? Forcing himself into my body? Using me as I saw him use young Martha? And yet, if we are to continue as man and wife, then I must allow him to do as he pleases . . .'

A spark of rebellion smouldered, then burst into flame.

'No, I must not, not if I do not choose to. He's yet to prove himself sincere in his intentions to be a good father and husband.'

'But how will you prevent him, Tildy?' the tiny voice whispered in her mind. 'He is so much stronger than you. How will you stop him using your body?'

Almost desperately she cast about for some answer, and then it came to her. She would simply use the same tactics that had served her so well that morning. She would bluff again, threaten him with that still unnamed power that she had undoubtedly exercised over him.

Another priority was to get them both out of the hands of the foggers. An essential act if she was ever to rise in her station in life. A calculating gleam shone in her brown eyes . . . Dick Suffield had aided her before because he desired her sexually. Why should not she utilize that desire deliberately to gain her own ends?

'God forgive me, I'm becoming an evil bitch.' A sudden surge of self-disgust assailed her, and she raised her body, throwing the scrubbing brush into the bucket of filth-scummed cold water. Then her baby wailed hungrily in its cradle, and the self-disgust abruptly became a luxury that she could not afford.

'I'll do whatever I must,' she whispered. 'You'll not die in the poorhouse, my honey. No matter what price my soul must pay.'

'Well now, Mistress Crawford, youm looking the picture of health.' Dick Suffield appreciatively looked Tildy up and down. 'I was real surprised when I heard yesterday that you'd come back to the Sidemoor. Most people that I knows who have ever left it, takes good care ne'er to step near the place agen.'

'That's as maybe, Master Suffield, but I'm not most people.' Tildy deliberately flashed him a coquettish smile. 'But I'm feared that I need to ask your help again. I know I'm already in debt to you for money, but without your help I don't see how I ever will manage to repay you.'

They were standing close-faced in the warehouse, hidden from the view of anyone passing by the half-closed doors.

'You knows me of old, Mistress, I'm always prepared to gi' a helping hand to those I regards as friends.'

His tone injected a veiled meaning into the words, a meaning reinforced by the expression in his small yellow-flecked eyes.

She lowered her gaze to the floor. 'I hope that I may regard myself as one of your friends, Master Suffield, for indeed you have always shown me much kindness.'

'Ohh, I'll always do that . . . Tildy.' He drawled. 'But there's no need for we to be so formal towards each other. Call me Dick, for that's what my friends calls me.'

Slowly she raised her head to meet his regard. 'Very well then . . . Dick, it shall be.'

He grinned his satisfaction. 'Right then, Tildy, how can I serve you?'

'I want to be free of Johnno Dipple,' she told him bluntly. 'While Tom and me are working for a fogger, then we'll never know ought else but hardships. Tom is much better at his work than he was, and now I've come back and regained my full vigour, I'll be able to do much more to aid him at the forge than I could previously.'

Suffield made no immediate answer, instead he let himself feast his eyes.

God rot me, but she's a rare sweet thing. The best-looking wench this side o' Brummagem, wi'out a doubt. I reckon I could keep her wi' me for years afore tiring of her, and that's a fact, he thought. He had already made certain plans concerning Tildy, but her voluntary return to the Side-moor, and this present visit, were unexpected fillips for those schemes, and he could now foresee a satisfactory culmination coming much more quickly than he had dared to hope for. He assumed an expression of doubt.

'Well, my honey-lamb, I'm only too willing to help you, but I can't rightly see how it's to be done. Iffen Tom Crawford works for Johnno Dipple, then he'll not have the time to strike a blow for anyone else, 'ull he?'

Tildy laid her hand on his arm in artless appeal.

'But you know Dipple, well, do you not? I thought that if you would have speech with him about this matter on my behalf, then something could surely be arranged.'

'Like what?' The foreman, susceptible to her beauty though he was, still retained full control of his senses.

'Well Dick, if you would ask him if he could wait a few months for what Tom owes him, and if he were to agree, then me and Tom could again work at the better paid nails for you and Master Sanders. We could pay off Dipple a little each week, after first paying you what I owe you, of course. And so, little by little, we would clear our debts and so better ourselves.'

The man's head bent as though he were considering what she had said. Then he questioned her sharply, saying, 'What will Tom Crawford ha' to say about this, Tildy? You coming to me, and me doing you this favour, if I'm able? Your husband's got a devil o' jealousy in him, as you must well know by now.'

Tildy's white teeth plucked tentatively at her full bottom lip, and Suffield stared at the soft red moistness, hungering to crush his mouth against it, to fill his mouth with its sweetness.

'I'll tell you something that must be for your ears only, Dick.' Her voice was pitched so low that he was forced to strain to hear the words. 'Tom and me are husband and wife in name only. I do not share his bed. I'm become a different person to the stupid wench who married him. We've slept separate since I've come back, and shall continue doing so.'

The brown eyes were limpid and appealing.

'I pray you will not think ill of me for being so undutiful a wife, but I confess that I cannot stand him to come near me. I regard my body as my own, to do with what I will. It is my property, not Tom Crawford's . . . If I ever give myself to any man again, then it will be to someone who uses me kindly. Someone I can have trust in, and regard as a true friend.'

Again she stared at the ground, a deep flush suffusing the sun-tinted creaminess of her throat and cheeks.

For all his experienced cynicism, Dick Suffield was powerfully affected by her words and manner.

'Doon't you worry your pretty head about Johnno

Dipple,' he said huskily. 'I'll arrange things for you . . . and iffen that husband o' yourn tries to force himself on you, or gi' you a hard time on it, then you tell him that Dick Suffield is your true friend.' For a brief instant the foreman let his innate caution lapse. 'Mind, he knows already that if he hurts you he'll have to answer to me for it.'

'So that's it!' Realization came instantly to Tildy. That's why Tom daren't hit me yesterday morning, and didn't argue too much when I refused to bed with him last night. This man was already protecting me, she mused.

Involuntarily she gave the muscular arm beneath her fingers a squeeze of gratitude.

'I can't thank you enough, Master Suffield,' she said aloud, and sincerely meant what she said.

He laughed delightedly, and stroked her cheek. 'Mayhap some day you can, Tildy, and remember, my name is Dick. For you and I shall be good friends from now on . . . Real good friends.'

Chapter Twenty-One

It was the month of February, 1821 . . . Snow lay thick upon the roofs of the Sidemoor, and in the streets and alleyways was trodden underfoot into a filthy slush which soaked through broken shoes, and turned children's bare feet into agonized chunks of freezing flesh.

The tiny Emmanuel chapel was full for the Sunday evening service. A few rushlights created a pathetic illusion of light, and the congregation packed closely to one another upon the benches, each trying to draw heat from the bodies next to their own. There was a continual barrage of racking coughs torn from aching chests, and breath wheezed through inflamed throats and congested lungs. A stench pervaded the air. A stench of cold, of damp, of poverty, of hopelessness.

Wearing only his customary white linen shirt, black tailcoat and breeches, Jacob Ashfield defied the cold and the damp. His face was harshly shadowed as, from the tiny pulpit, he gazed down upon the bare heads of his flock, and saw the grey-white plumes of their breathing jetting from their mouths. For a considerable time he remained motionless, and hands and bodies began to twitch restlessly beneath him.

'Brethren! Brothers and Sisters before the Lord!'

The sudden stentorian onslaught caused some to start in shock.

'The Race of Masters . . . '

All eyes involuntarily swung to where, on the foremost bench, Jonathan Sanders, swathed in a voluminous cloak, sat alone.

The preacher did not look at the nailmaster. Instead, hands tight-clenched on the pulpit rail, he declaimed again.

'The Race of Masters . . . A race whose whole wisdom consists in that cunning which enables them to devise the cheapest possible means for getting out of the workers, the greatest possible amount of labour, in the shortest possible amount of time, for the least possible amount of wages . . . '

A dozen voices gave assent to the preacher's words, and a tangible atmosphere of anger and bitterness thickened in the room.

Jonathan Sanders remained motionless. Sitting bolt upright, mittened hands resting upon his knees. Features taut and grim, but his eyes troubled and sad.

Jacob Ashfield lifted both hands above his head, then smashed his palms down upon the pulpit rail so that the impact cracked out like musket shots.

'The Race of Masters!' He was now shouting in visible fury. 'A race of men of whom Agur would have said . . . ' His voice dropped, and he let each syllable drip from his mouth with loathing. 'There is a generation, Oh how lofty are their eyes, and their eyelids are lifted up to the Heavens. There is a generation whose teeth are as swords, and whose teeth are as knives to devour the poor from off the earth, and the needy from among men . . . '

'Amen to that, Brother Ashfield!'

'Amen!'

'Amen!'

'Amen!'

'Amen to that!'

'You spakes the truth, Brother!'

'Amen! Amen! Amen!'

From all over the room haggard faces shouted, and a woman burst into loud sobbing. Her children, frightened by her grief, screwed up their eyes and added their own high-pitched wails to her shuddering cries.

Jonathan Sanders lifted his tophat from the bench, and rose to walk down the centre aisle to the door, looking neither to right nor left, his bootheels beating loudly upon the smooth flagstones.

Outside in the freezing air, he automatically started towards his home, then suddenly remembering that Carlotta was holding one of her soirées, he turned in the opposite direction. As his boots crunched over the frozen slush Jonathan thought about the preacher's impassioned sermon, and was forced to acknowledge that the bitter strictures were well-founded. The winter had been a hard one. Trade had slumped. Prices had risen. Wages had fallen. And, as always, the greatest sufferers had been the poor. He grimaced unhappily. And if all that were not sufficient to be going on with, only last Wednesday at a General Meeting of the Nail Ironmongers and Masters Association convened in Dudley, it had been unanimously agreed to cut the rates for what diminished amounts of work there were available.

The young nailmaster was himself torn by conflicting emotions concerning that decision, for which he had voted. He knew that it would add immeasurably to the hardships of the nailers. But as a businessman he recognized the necessity for the rates cuts. It was a hard, competitive trade, and in fairness to the masters, they had to be equally hard and competitive, or go out of business.

'But even so, it's cruel . . . Damn cruel!' he muttered. 'We masters live like kings compared to these miserable wretches. We have possessions, and some degree of wealth. They have naught but their strength to offer, and God alone knows, the present harsh conditions they labour under will all too quickly destroy the strength of their bodies. We masters have our Association, so that we may support one another. These wretches are forbidden even that. They cannot by law combine. So they are powerless to negotiate better conditions. And if they resort to violence, why then, we bring the troops and the Yeomanry Cavalry against them.'

Jonathan recalled only too well the affair at Manchester, not two years previously, when a vast crowd of peaceful demonstrators had been charged and sabred by Yeomanry Troopers.

'The Peterloo Massacre, that's what the Radicals term it still . . . ' His footsteps slowed, and he came to a halt. 'Dammee, but it's too cold to tramp the country,' he decided, and retraced his path towards his home. 'I must make the effort to be civil to Carlotta's guests. Little though I have in common with them.'

In the drawing-room, brilliantly lit by scores of tall wax candles, Carlotta was holding court. There were several other ladies present, but in an emerald-green gown cut low to show off her thrusting breasts, and a jewelled and feathered turban perched upon her mass of raven-hair, she was by far the most beautiful woman there, and the men vied with one another to attract and hold her attention. But even while her admirers clustered about her, Carlotta's green eyes constantly flickered towards Captain Edward Cassidy, who stood turning the sheets of music for the young girl playing the pianoforte. Cassidy was resplendent in the uniform of the Worcestershire Yeomanry Cavalry, and the close-fitting scarlet jacket with its heavy silver-fringed epaulettes, gold and scarlet waistsash topping the narrow black trousers with their broad red sideseams, set off his fine figure to perfection.

Carlotta was piqued at the rapt manner in which Cassidy was listening to the girl's indifferent playing, and she found it increasingly difficult to respond to the laboured witticisms of the assortment of wealthy merchants, farmers, and tradesmen surrounding her.

Jonathan's quiet entrance caused little stir among the company. He wore all-black clothing since he was still in mourning for his uncle, who had died some three months previously. Carlotta thought how dour and dowdy he appeared in contrast to the glittering Captain Cassidy.

Carlotta's brother, Jervis Tinsley, saw Jonathan, and malice gleamed in his eyes.

'Lord bless us, Brother Jonathan, have you only now returned from your Seat of Atonement among the Methodys . . . ' The young exquisite languidly raised his long-handled eyeglass and examined his brother-in-law with exaggerated movements of his carefully-curled, pomaded head. ' 'Pon my soul, Brother Jon, you present a most funereal aspect.' He gestured to his own lavender coloured tailcoat and breeches, the lavishly ruffled shirt and cravat, puce silk stockings and satin pumps. ' 'Pon my soul, I feel a veritable peacock in comparison.'

Jonathan's slender face remained impassive. He had long since learned not to give Jervis the satisfaction of any discernible response to his verbal barbs.

'Have you forgotten, Jervis, that my uncle died not three months since,' he replied quietly. 'I merely show respect for his memory.'

'Do you not think that you exaggerate that respect, Brother Jon?' Jervis Tinsley was sneering openly. 'After all, when the Princess Charlotte so sadly died, the Court wore full mourning for only a month. Do you try to appear more sensitive to grief than our beloved Royal Family, that you must continue to appear in public looking like an undertaker?'

With an immense effort Jonathan Sanders suppressed the impulse to crash his fist into the rouged face leering so vindictively at him, and instead moved away to greet the other people in the room.

The young girl finished playing with one last discordant flourish, and the conversation became general.

'Tell me, Captain Cassidy?' fat-faced, pot-bellied Joshua Juggins, Jonathan's neighbour and fellow nailmaster asked loudly. 'You are now commanding the Hewell Troop of Yeomanry, ain't you?'

Cassidy nodded. 'I am, sir. The Honourable Other Archer could no longer continue in that position, he has so many pressing matters to deal with at this time. Therefore I was appointed to the command last week.'

'And a damn good thing too!' Jervis Tinsley interjected enthusiastically. 'Edward is just the fellow that's needed. He fought all through the Peninsula Campaign with the Light Horse, and at Waterloo also, did you not, Edward?'

Cassidy's hard face showed just a hint of contempt for the younger man's brashness. He bowed slightly, and acknowledged. 'That is so . . . I had the honour to serve my country during the late war, but then, so did many gallant fellows, and most of them rendered greater service to British Arms that I myself did.'

A murmur of approbation greeted this display of modesty, and female eyes shone invitingly above opened fluttering fans.

'Well, I for one am happy that such an experienced soldier 'ull be in charge of the Hewell Troop,' Juggins affirmed portentously. 'Because it 'udden't surprise me iffen we warn't to have need of a strong swordarm in these parts afore long.'

'How so, Master Juggins?' Jonathan queried.

His fellow nailmaster stared in surprise. 'How so, you say? Well, I'd think that to be plain for anyone to see. The work people am becoming terrible surly ever since we cut the rates. They was bad enough before, but now . . . why, they'm becoming positively insolent. It 'udden't surprise me in the least iffen they even offered violence towards us.'

202

Two or three of the more timid ladies uttered mewing cries of horrified fear, and Jervis Tinsley was quick to offer his opinions.

'Dammee, Juggins, I cannot conceive that the scum will ever find sufficient courage to offer violence towards their betters.'

Juggins resented the contradiction. 'Oh carn't you, you say.' His loose lips sprayed flecks of saliva. 'Well, they'se bin violent enough throughout my lifetime, and anyone who'se ever had any dealings wi' the nailers 'ull vouch for that. How about the riots here in '09?'

The young exquisite dismissed the argument with a contemptuous flick of his vermilion-lacquered fingernails.

'The nailers are animals, Juggins. Brute beasts who brawl among themselves. But they'll never find the courage to face armed and disciplined soldiers led by gentlemen. 'Pon my soul! Did not the Luddites attempt that, and they got short shrift. They were in sufficient numbers in Peters Square at Manchester to have created a revolution . . . And what happened? A squadron of Yeomanry put them to flight in seconds.'

'You are talking like the fool you are, Jervis!' Jonathan Sanders could finally take no more. 'There was no question of either a Luddite revolution or even a Luddite involvement at St Peters Fields in Manchester. Peaceful men, women and children went to a lawful meeting. They were unarmed and helpless. The Yeomanry behaved like murderous savages. I think that the man responsible for giving the order to charge those helpless people should have been tried and hung for murder. Because that is what it was . . . Bloodthirsty murder!'

'There is much justice in what you say, Master Sanders.' Edward Cassidy was quick to intervene and defuse an argument which threatened to get out of hand. 'I trust, however, that such a sad event as the Peterloo Massacre will never be repeated in this, or in any other area . . .' He paused, and smiled wryly. 'I do assure all present that while they remain under my command, the Hewell Troop will never be ordered to charge against peaceful people going about their lawful occasions.'

Not for the first time Jonathan Sanders found himself admiring the other man.

'I think that to be well said, Captain Cassidy,' he replied warmly. 'And your sentiments do you the utmost credit.'

'Hear, hear!'

'Yes indeed!'

'Well said, Captain Cassidy!'

'Hear, hear! Well said indeed, sir.'

The audience shared Jonathan's own sentiments, and a warning glance from Cassidy ensured Jervis Tinsley's mouth remaining closed.

Carlotta rang a small bell, and maidservants brought in trays of cake and wine. The tense atmosphere that the brief dispute had engendered dissipated in talk and laughter, and after the refreshments the guests began to take their leave until only Carlotta, Jonathan, Jervis Tinsley and Edward Cassidy remained.

Jervis yawned. 'I shall go to me bed.' He could not resist a parting sneer. 'This rural life makes me so confounded tired . . . I think it must be the boredom of it all.'

After Jervis had sauntered away, Edward Cassidy asked to be excused.

'I must rise early tomorrow,' he told his hosts. 'I do assure you that is the sole reason I seek my bed. I do not find the rural life to be boring . . . Quite the contrary, in fact.'

His eyes briefly locked with Carlotta's and for a moment Jonathan fancied the two were sharing some secret known only to themselves.

'Dammee, I'm becoming like some spiteful old maid,' he berated himself. 'Searching for that which is not there, and suspecting wickedness in the innocent.'

'I shall light you to your bedchamber door myself, sir.'

Carlotta rose gracefully to her feet, her olive skin glowing in the soft candlelight. 'For I too am tired, and wish to retire . . . I bid you, good night, husband.'

Jonathan bowed to her. 'I trust you will sleep well, Carla, and you also, sir,' he told Cassidy.

'I'm sure I shall, sir.' Cassidy smilingly bowed in return, and then followed Carlotta, who held before her a double-sconced candelabra, leaving Jonathan to his own company.

For a while he stood gazing into the heaped coals and logs that burned cheerily in the marble fireplace. His thoughts were troubled, and a sense of foreboding depressed his mood. The financial affairs of the Sanders Warehouse & Ironmongery were in a bad way. The slump in trade, allied to Carlotta's extravagances, had all but used up what monetary resources he possessed. Already this year some nailmasters had registered bankruptcy, and Jonathan feared that unless there was some rapid and radical improvement in the trading position, then he could all too easily join those other unfortunates.

He found himself wishing with all his heart that Uncle Samuel was still alive and in partnership with him. He needed the old man's toughness of mind and character to support him now.

A candle guttered and died, and Jonathan bitterly computed the amount of sheer waste for which his wife was responsible. Dozens of the most expensive wax candles were even at this moment literally burning money away, when just a few would have sufficed to light the room.

He shook his head resignedly. 'I should not blame Carla for this waste, or for any other of her spendthrift ways. I should be strong enough to limit her spending at this time . . . But I am not strong enough! Perhaps it is my guilt at being impotent that forces me to let her have her way in all things. But, Dear God, how will it end? How will it all end?'

Upstairs on the dark landing a floorboard creaked beneath

the weight of a slippered foot, and a gentle tapping of knuckles sounded upon the panel of a door. The door opened to disclose Edward Cassidy's hard features smiling in welcome in the gloom. Carlotta Sanders' loose peignoir rustled as she came into his arms and, as he quietly closed the door behind them, she pressed hungrily against his hard body, her lips urgently seeking for his mouth . . .

Chapter Twenty-Two

Despite the lateness of the hour a rushlight still gave off its smoky, guttering light in the tiny living room of Hester Lammas' cottage. The woman was ill, at times burning with fever, at times shivering with cold. She lay on a straw mattress before a minute fire of breeze coke, and Tildy sat by her side on a three-legged stool. Upstairs Ikey Lammas snored and muttered in restless sleep. A restless sleep because his empty belly was not conducive to sound slumber.

The sick woman shifted her head on the coarse pillow and her tongue moved in the hot dry cavern of her tooth-less mouth. Tildy bent and lifted the gaunt head gently forward, her fingers burying themselves in the tangled mass of matted hair. She held a cracked earthenware bowl of water to the thin lips.

'Come Hester, sip this,' she whispered.

The sick woman gulped the liquid, and some of it spilled down her chin and onto the stringy-tendoned throat, to trickle down between shrivelled breasts that were barely covered by the torn bodice. Momentarily eased, she opened her eyes and tried to smile.

'Youm a good cratur, Tildy.' Her voice was cracked and laboured. 'This old fever gives me the gyp nearly every year about this time. But I'll soon be on me feet agen, you see if I arn't.'

Tildy laid down the bowl and stroked the hot, rough, skin of forehead and cheeks. 'Lie quiet now, Hester. Try to sleep,' she urged softly. 'And don't worry. I'll not leave you.'

The red-rimmed eyes closed, and once more Hester Lammas drifted into an uneasy doze.

Tildy straightened, and settled herself as comfortably as the hard seat allowed. Her mind wandered, but she would not release it to dwell on Davy Nokes and the cottage at Tardebigge. That was an indulgence which she could not permit herself, in case the tender memories weakened her present hard-acquired resolve.

The winter had been tough for Tildy, but not a time of unbearable hardship. Dick Suffield had kept his word, and had acted as a good friend towards her. He had given her and Tom Crawford the better-paid work from Sanders' warehouse that she had asked for, and by toiling to the limits of their endurance, they had slowly cleared their debts, and now were free of the fogger, Johnno Dipple. Even now, Tildy still did not know the real relationship between Dick Suffield and the fogger, and for her own peace of mind took care not to enquire too closely into it.

Her life with her husband was that of two people existing in a grudging acceptance of a mutual dependency. To give Tom Crawford his due, he had worked to the best of his ability, and had left her in peace. He made no sexual advances towards her, and offered no violence. There had been sporadic outbursts of verbal insult and abuse, but Tildy was prepared to accept that as part of the price she had to pay to achieve her own ends.

Towards the baby, now named Davy, Crawford

displayed little interest, except to curse if the child cried too loudly. Tildy also accepted this attitude and indeed preferred it so. For in her heart she regarded Davy as hers alone, and Tom Crawford as merely the biological instrument that had initiated the process of conception.

Towards Dick Suffield, Tildy could not help but feel a warm gratitude, knowing only too well that it was his presence in the background that gave her the degree of safety she now possessed. Her concentration now centred on the foreman. She found him a strange man. Although he made no secret of his continuing desire for her, yet he never subjected her to any pressure for consumation. She knew now, of course, that Janey Porter was his woman, and that there were other women who gave him their bodies.

'Mayhap that suffices him,' she told herself. And dismissed the subject from her mind. Tomorrow was Monday, and, and, thank God, they had a bundle of iron in the forge; something that lately was becoming an increasingly irregular occurrence in many of the Sidemoor's workshops. A lot of the nailers and their families were now being forced to apply to the parish overseers for relief.

'And precious little relief do they get.' Tildy frowned. 'Some of the poor creatures are nigh on starving, and this terrible weather increases their suffering almost beyond endurance . . . I wonder how it will end? Will there be violence?'

She had heard the angry murmurs, and the threats issuing from the mouths of desperate men and women. But, as yet, these threats were scattered and unorganized. Nailing was a solitary trade. Individuals and small groups working for themselves in competition with their fellows. Everyone for themselves, and Devil take the hindmost . . . But lately a group had sprung up that might well act in concert, at least, that was Tildy's impression. And this group, strangely enough, were the normally pacifist Methodists who gathered each Sunday in the bleak chapel of Emmanuel. People were saying that the preacher there, Jacob Ashfield, was urging his congregation to act together. To stand united and resist the latest rates cuts decreed by the masters.

Recognizing the injustice of the cuts, Tildy was strongly drawn towards any group prepared to fight against them, but she had Davy, her child, to consider.

'I'll do better for him if I go my own way,' she told herself. But even in the telling, she felt a sense of loss . . .

It was daybreak.

'You stupid little bastard! I'll bloody gi' you the flash!'

The small boy cowered against the workshop wall as the man lunged at him. The long rod of iron whipped viciously down, its glowing tip struck the bricks above the child's head and a rain of white-hot dross showered upon the tender skin and soft flaxen hair. The child screamed as the tiny shards of metal burned deep in a hundred places. The man dropped the rod and, grabbing the flaxen hair, lifted the thin little body right off the ground.

'I'll teach you to muck up the work. I'll teach you, you little bastard!' Spittle frothed at the corners of the man's lips and his great shock of tow-coloured hair fell across his rage-mad eyes.

The child shrieked again and again, the screams blending into a long pealing of agony.

In Hester Lammas' cottage, Tildy almost dropped the bowl of oat gruel she had been feeding to the sick woman.

'What in God's name?' she uttered.

At the table Ikey Lammas lifted his frowsty head from his own bowl of gruel. 'Sounds like Martin Duffil's throwing a bit of a fit.' He grunted unconcernedly.

Tildy's face was white and tense. 'It sounds more as if there's a murder being done.'

Duffil's bellowed curses carried clearly on the still air, mingling with the high-pitched shrieks of the boy.

Tildy placed the bowl she held onto the table. 'I'm going

to see what's happening. That sounds like a child being sore hurt.'

'Keep out on it,' Hester Lammas told her. 'Iffen Martin's thrashin' his childer, then that's his right. It's naught to do wi' anybody else.'

More screams reverberated along the terrace, and in them Tildy could hear all the bitter anguish of a soul in Hell.

'I'm going!' She ran from the cottage.

'Goo arter her, Ikey! For God's sake goo arter her!' Hester urged her man. 'You knows Martin of old. Iffen he's in that mood, he'll as live break her skull as look at her.'

'And what about my skull?' Ikey Lammas blurted indignantly. 'What if he breaks that? Besides, her's got a man of her own, arn't her? Let Tom Crawford goo arter her.'

Bright spots of colour flamed in the woman's hollow cheeks. 'I said get arter her, you great lummox. Her's bin a good friend to us, and I'll not stand by and see that bugger serve her badly.'

Her husband still remained seated, blinking resentfully at her, and losing patience completely Hester dragged herself to her feet and stood swaying, holding on to the table edge for support, fighting against the feverish weakness of her illness.

'I'll go meself, iffen youm too bleedin' feared o' Martin Duffil.'

The man's mouth gaped, and a stream of vituperation flooded from it. But even as the vile words flowed, he was heading for the back door.

Tildy halted outside Duffil's workshop, heart pounding in trepidation, eyes wildly searching for the child. The tiny figure was standing bolt upright, its narrow back pressed against one of the tall, thick wooden posts that held the nail block. His eyes were screwed tight, and from his lips dribbled a continuous hiccuping of sobs.

The next instant Tildy gasped aloud with horror. A six-inch nail had been driven through the flesh of the child's delicate ear and into the post. Blood ran from the wound in a bright scarlet stream, soaking his ragged shirt and already beginning to harden and cake upon the slender neck and shoulder.

Martin Duffil himself appeared at the door which divided workshop from cottage. A lean-bodied, savage-looking whip of a man. 'What the Hell does you want here?' he snarled.

Tildy's horror was fast-laced with hot anger against this human brute who could so torture a helpless child.

'Why have you done this thing?' she shouted. 'Are you a madman? If you don't free the child this instant I'll fetch the constable.'

Duffil's eyes widened in surprise, his face became a study in puzzlement. 'Fetch the constable? What the Hell be you talking about?' He was genuinely mystified. 'Who the bleedin' hell does you reckon you am? Coming into my house and blaggardin' me, and telling me you'll fetch the bleeding constable?'

From behind Tildy, Ikey Lammas reached out and pulled at her arm. 'Come away, Tildy. This arn't none o' your affair. You doon't know what youm about.'

Duffil's wife now appeared from the cottage. A toilworn woman with several little children hanging to her skirts. She glowered at Tildy.

'What's you want here, you bloody whore?'

Tildy pointed at the nailed boy. 'Don't you see what's been done to this poor child?' she demanded incredulously. 'Don't you see?'

The woman pursed her lips and spat a gob of spittle onto the dirt at her feet. 'The bugger deserves it,' she snapped curtly. 'He's a lazy, good for nothing little bastard, so he is. And I'm his mother and knows that best. The bugger messes up the work deliberate, because he doon't want to work wi' us at the nailing . . . So you just pull your nose from out of our business, and get you off from here. Me and me man has got work to do . . . We arn't as lucky as you . . . Dick Suffield wun't gi' us easy money. He only gives that to whores like you as lies on their backs wi' wide open legs for him.'

As the full imputation of the bitter tirade sank into Tildy's understanding she felt an almost physical shock of dismay. A dismay quickly intensified by the growls of agreement that came from the small crowd gathered about the workshop door as avid spectators. Tildy glanced wildly about her, and on all sides grimy, haggard faces glared accusingly.

'They really believe it!' She could hardly absorb what her senses told her. 'These people really believe that I'm Dick Suffield's whore!'

Duffill came forward and thrust his face close up to Tildy's.

'I'll not tell you twice, whore . . . Get off from here, and keep your nose from other people's business.'

She swallowed hard, and would not lower her pride by denying their slander. But she refused to give ground.

'What about this child?'

'God blast me, Tildy! Come away, 'ull you!' Ikey Lammas grabbed her arms and pulled her from the workshop by sheer force; and Tildy was powerless against his massive strength. As he dragged her with him he kept up a continuous barrage of speech, overriding and drowning out her protests.

'Listen to me, you silly cow. Listen, 'ull you!' He was becoming angry himself. 'What's happened to that kid is naught but what's happened to nearly every nailer when we'se first bin put to the trade. Look at me own bloody lug-holes. I bin hammered to the post more times nor once, I'll tell you.'

She could not help but examine his ears, and see the small indented scars that liberally bespattered their hairy red surfaces.

'But it's barbaric!' she argued vehemently. 'Just because it happened in the past is no reason why it should continue to happen.'

He halted at his own doorway, and when he replied his eyes were gentle. 'Tildy, my duck, you'se proved a good friend to me and Hester, but you doon't belong here in the Sidemoor. Youm not, nor ever 'ull be, one of us. Why doon't you goo back to your own place, and dwell wi' your own people? You'll ne'er understand our ways, and you'll ne'er be accepted here. Youm a foreigner, my duck, and you allus 'ull be.'

His words, although spoken in kindness, immeasurably saddened Tildy, and she sighed heavily, as she replied.

'I'd hoped to be regarded as one of you, Ikey, and I thought that perhaps I was becoming accepted as such. But if even you and Hester think me still to be a foreigner, then that must be so. But then, no matter where I go, I am still regarded as a foreigner. I don't seem to belong to anywhere . . .'

He released her arms, and slowly she turned from him, to meet Tom Crawford's hostile glare. He had watched the altercation from the doorway of their forge, and now hatred shimmered in his black eyes.

'Be you coming to strike a few blows this day, or not, whore?'

Chapter Twenty-Three

It was the first Sunday in the month of March, and Jacob Ashfield had spent the day in fervent communion with his God. He had walked the mean, rutted, mud-thick environs of the Sidemoor for long hours, breakfastless, dinnerless, supperless, his eyes seeing in the ramshackle cottages and tenements a people whose rulers treated them worse than the black slaves on the plantations of the Americas.

A people who were hungry, in the midst of a land of plenty. A people who shivered at fireless hearths, in a land that held beneath its surface fuel in massive abundance. A people who toiled from dawn until dusk and still were clothed in rags in a land whose wealth was the envy of the world. A people in whom hope had been crushed and who knew no real freedom, in a land that boasted of being the Great Bringer of Hope and Freedom to the world . . .

Now he mounted the pulpit of Emmanuel chapel, recognizing and understanding the essence of despair that saturated its atmosphere. Serried ranks of beseeching eyes stared up at him, and he swept his own gaze backwards and forwards across those ranks. Willing them to draw from him the strength and fervour and trust that his God had so bountifully bestowed upon him that day, in answer to his prayers.

'Brethren! Brothers and Sisters in the Lord!' His voice rolled sonorously above their heads. 'The Race of Masters are determined that we shall work for the cut rates . . . ' He lifted both clenched fists above his head and brought them smashing down upon the rail of the pulpit, and the rail quivered beneath the blow. 'Let us, the people of the Sidemoor, with the help of Almighty God, find within our hearts the determination that we shall not work for those accursed rates. Stand together, Brothers and Sisters! Stand united! Each one helping the other to so stand. Each one sharing with the other, what they have. Each one determined to die if necessary, rather than give in . . . '

He paused, and again his eyes burned into his flock.

'Will you so stand, Brethren?' His voice was a whisper. 'Will you stand?'

His voice became a shout.

'IN THE NAME OF ALMIGHTY GOD . . . WILL YOU STAND?'

For a moment all was hushed, and then a roar shook the flimsy rafters.

'AMEN! AMEN! WE'LL SO STAND, BROTHER ASHFIELD! WE'LL SO STAND . . . '

The best bar parlour of the Golden Lion Hotel in Bromsgrove was a smallish room, and the local members of the Nail Masters Association filled it to capacity. Roper, Tinsley, Juggins, Hobbs, Rutter, Sanders, Brighton, all the district's warehouses were represented. James Brighton was in the Chair, and now in an atmosphere redolent of port, claret, brandy and tobacco fumes, he called the meeting to order.

'I'll not waste time on niceties, gentlemen.' His florid features were grim, as were the features of the men before him. 'This refusal to work at the new rates is doing me no good. What I want to establish first of all today, is the extent of the harm it is doing to we local concerns as a whole?'

George Hobbs, the oldest man present, held up one liver-flecked hand and, receiving the Chairman's nod of assent, said in tones that quavered with age, 'I reckon I con spake for all on us, James.' His broad, uneducated accent contrasted oddly with his fine suit of broadcloth and expensive lace-ruffled linen. 'Larst Weigh-in day, I took but a third o' me normal quota. Now like the rest on us, I arn't bin carrying but a few pecks o' stock, what wi' the state the trade's bin in lately. So iffen next Weigh-in day I doon't tek in a full quota, then theer's a pair o' contracts I'll not be able to meet; and that's pretty well the sitooation we'em all afacing, I'm dammed sure.'

A chorus of assent proved the accuracy of his judgement.

'What is to be done then, gentlemen?' James Brighton questioned, and a babble of conflicting suggestions filled the room with noise.

Jonathan Sanders remained silent, his face impassive. But behind that mask of calm, he was a desperately worried man. Only three weeks had elapsed since the Methodists, directed by Jacob Ashfield, had refused to take iron from the warehouses for working up at the new rates, and those three weeks had been sufficient to bring him to the verge of ruin.

Thanks to Carlotta's wild extravagances, he had no financial reserves left to carry him over this bad period. He could, if it became necessary, still command an extension of credit, and perhaps take out a loan at crippling rates of interest. But even using those resorts he was still forced to face the inevitable fact, that if this present situation continued for only a few more weeks, then he was finished as a nailmaster.

The babble of voices died away, and in the ensuing silence George Hobbs' quavering tones came again.

' 'Tis my thinking, that we should pay the full rates agen.'

'How the Devil can we, sir?' Joseph Rutter prided himself on his genteel accents and bearing. His aristocratic beak of nose was, he felt secretly convinced, an inheritance from undoubtedly noble ancestors. 'Speaking for myself, I will never surrender to the insolent importunities of the rabble. Besides, the decision to cut the rates was taken by the Association as a whole, and we are honour-bound to uphold that decision until such time as the Association as a whole rescinds it.'

'I says Bollocks, to being honour-bound!' George Hobbs had always disliked Joseph Rutter, and now welcomed this opportunity to clash with him. 'It's all very well for you to prate about bloody honour, Rutter, but it's squarely on us this bloody trouble has fallen. The boggers across in the Black Country arn't suffering. Their bloody nailers am still working, arn't they? It's only the boggers hereabouts that am refusing to take the iron.'

'Order, gentlemen! Let us have order, if you please!' The Chairman asserted his authority, and Old George Hobbs closed his mouth with visibly bad grace.

'What I propose gentlemen,' James Brighton went on, 'is that we call an immediate General Meeting of the Association . . .'

'But that 'ull tek a month o' bloody Sundays,' George Hobbs interrupted irritably. 'Them Black Country boggers be laughin' up their sleeves at us, no doubt about that. The longer this trouble goes on, the better business they con do. They'm freed of our competition, arn't they? They con bid for the contracts we'em alosing . . .'

'Goddamm me, George, keep silent for a moment, won't you.' The Chairman's temper was becoming strained, and his florid complexion was taking on a purplish hue. 'We are all of us rowing in the same boat, are we not? This dammed refusal to take the iron is affecting all we local masters equally badly. But all we can do is-to place

218

our case before a General Meeting, and demand the assistance of the Association. Without doubt, they will be happy to render that assistance. Because if this defiance by our workers spreads to their districts, then it will spell ruin for the entire industry . . . And make no mistake, gentlemen, if the nailers demands are seen to succeed here, then that defiance will most surely spread. What say you, gentlemen?'

He appealed to the room in general, and with some individual reluctance, the room agreed with him.

'But what are we to do in the meantime, until the General Meeting can be convened?' one man wanted to know.

James Brighton gave some thought to the question before answering. 'The people involved are, for the most part, the Methodys. Dammed Ranters! They have carried a large number of others with them. We must endeavour to isolate the Ranters from the rest of the community.'

For the first time that day, James Brighton smiled.

'I fear that we have been forgetting that in point of fact, gentlemen, we hold all the trump cards in this particular game of Hazard . . . ' His smile instilled some hope in his audience, and they eagerly urged him to explain what those trump cards consisted of. He was happy to comply, drawing pleasure from his dominance of the assembly. 'Many of the cottages the nailers live in are owned by our families. If they refuse to take our iron and work it up, then what is to prevent us from evicting them from our own properties?' He saw the doubt gather in certain of his more humane listeners, and moved swiftly to allay that doubt. 'Naturally, this would only occur in a situation of the utmost extremity, but nevertheless, we are surely entitled to use the threat of eviction, if by doing so we are enabled to avoid our own ruination.

'Also, we have the virtual control of the Board of Parish Guardians. Some of us actually sit on that Board. Therefore we are in a position to direct the poor relief given out in this parish. I, for one, would be prepared to refuse any relief whatsoever to the families of those nailers who wilfully and maliciously refuse to take our iron.'

His audience was visibly perking up as he spoke, renewal of confidence tentatively burgeoning within them.

'We can also insist that the present laws governing our trade be implemented to their fullest extent. Any offence, by any nailer, against the legal code of practise must be prosecuted and dealt with, with the utmost rigour the law allows. We have all of us in the past been guilty of misplaced kindness in this respect. We have all allowed the nailers to escape penalty for breaking those laws. Now see where our leniency has led . . . The nailers have contemptuously and insolently cast our previous benevolence back into our teeth.'

His hearers muttered resentfully about the wickedness of the depraved nailers, and felt badly wronged.

Jonathan Sanders held up his hand, seeking the permission of the Chair to pass comment on what he had heard.

'I cannot help but wonder, Mister Chairman, that if we were to implement these suggestions you have made, would we not in doing so, be in great danger of provoking outbursts of violence in this district?'

The Chairman gravely nodded acknowledgement. 'I admit, Sanders, that I share your anxiety on this point. But, as we all here present know, we are, sad to say, living in a violent society. The respect for law and order that our fathers and grandfathers were accustomed to, tragically does not exist in this modern age. The younger generations have become increasingly disrespectful to their betters, and uncaring of the morals and mores of a civilized society.

'As true-born Englishmen, and loyal subjects of His Most Gracious Majesty, I feel strongly that we should not allow any fear of provoking violence, to prevent us from doing our duty. The continuing prosperity and wellbeing of this nation depends on trade, Gentlemen. Trade is our very lifesblood. We owe it to our country as patriotic Englishmen to maintain the free flow and stability of trade. Nothing must hinder that object . . . If violence should come to this district – and I most heartfully pray that it will not – but if it should, then we must stand prepared to meet and deal with it.

'We have the Law behind us, gentlemen.

'We have the constables.

'We have the Yeomanry Cavalry.

'And above all else, gentlemen . . . We have the right!'

The meeting was declared closed, and Snagee Porter, waiter at the Golden Lion, and brother to Janey Porter, slipped away from his listening post at the passage door.

'I'm just going on an errand,' he called to his employer, and left the building.

In the back room of the Mitre alehouse, he related all that he had heard to the attentive Dick Suffield. The foreman's genial smile shone out, and Snagee Porter gave profuse thanks for the half-sovereign pressed into his hand.

'Remember now, Snagee, mum's the word,' Suffield instructed.

'Just so, Dick, mum's the word,' Snagee Porter agreed, and went back happily to his place of employment.

'Johnno, bring in a drop o' gin when you come,' Suffield shouted, and re-seated himself on the wooden bench before the fire. He was well satisfied with the information Snagee Porter had brought to him. He knew already that Jonathan Sanders was facing bankruptcy, but he now also knew that none of the local masters were in any position to help Sanders. He realized that the man's own pride would prevent him from asking his wife's family for help. Besides, from what the maids had told him, that loose-living whore was about to run off with the gallant Captain Cassidy. The Tinsley family could therefore be safely disregarded.

Suffield's own covert fogging operations had also suffered from the effects of the rates dispute, but it had only meant a loss of profit for Suffield. After all, he and Johnno Dipple had no expense of premises, or taxes, or stock, or licenses to meet. His smile widened in satisfaction. The way things were going he would soon achieve his life's dearest ambition.

Once Jonathan Sanders was declared bankrupt, then he, Dick Suffield, would move through agents and buy up the Sanders warehouse and business for a fraction of its true worth.

'Soon it'll be Richard Suffield, nailmaster.' He spoke aloud, relishing the sound of the title he was so near to gaining. 'I'll ne'er again have to swallow insult and abuse from anyone. Ne'er have to bow and scrape to weak little puppies like Jon Sanders. It'll be Master Suffield to all then, to the nailers *and* to the gentry . . . '

The hulking menace of Johnno Dipple loomed over him, the stone bottle of gin nearly lost to view in one great hand. Suffield grinned up at his lieutenant.

'Right, Johnno, there's summat needs doing that's right up your street, my buck. I reckon it's time that the Belly Hoggers went awalking through the Sidemoor. What d'you say?'

The shaven-head bobbed with pleasure. 'I says yes, Dick.'

'So be it, then.' Suffield chuckled. 'Let's do it this very night, shall us? Let's bring on the Belly Hoggers!'

Chapter Twenty-Four

Pump the bellows, turn the rods, swing to the block,́ tap off the scale, smack smack smack with the hand hammer, bent rod into die bore and break the rod free. Smash! with the Oliver. Tap the paddle. Pump the bellows, turn the rods, swing to the block, tap off the scale . . .

Tildy moved like an automatum, her lithe body operating independently of her mind.

On the opposite side of the flaring hearth Tom Crawford moved in concert, and their shadows swayed and dipped upon the filthy walls in an eerie ballet of toil. Outside, the cold wind and rain drove both man and animal to seek shelter. Inside, the heat and fumes brought sweat streaming and caused man and woman to shed all superfluous coverings.

Davy's cradle hung upon the pumping handle of the bellows, the Teasers, level with Tildy's head, and in the cradle the infant gurgled and waved chubby arms and legs with pleasure as he swung to and fro, and up and down.

At the sides of the nail blocks the hot heaps of blued

nails rose higher and higher as the night progressed, and Tildy took satisfaction in their growth, and drove herself to work ever faster, ever harder, for those expanding heaps represented her baby's well-being . . . And perhaps, if all went well, would be the foundations upon which his future education could be built.

The three weeks since Jacob Ashfield's flock had begun their stand had been a period of much bitter controversy within the Sidemoor. Fathers had clashed with sons, wives with husbands, brothers with brothers, sisters with sisters, families with families. Until now, however, there had been little physical violence, no more than was commonplace in the Sidemoor.

Tildy had kept her tongue silent, and her own counsel, when those of her neighbours who followed Jacob Ashfield had tried to persuade her to stop working. When persuasion had failed, insults and threats had followed, but Tildy, although in sympathy with their aims, had steadfastly refused to join in their fight. Her allegiance was to her child. He must be fed, and clothed, and sheltered, and only she could ensure those things. As long as work was available, then Tildy was determined to do it. But that determination had also brought a great sadness to her. Hester and Ikey Lammas had sided with Ashfield, and Tildy's refusal to follow suit had created a rift in their relationship which now, as the bitter feelings were intensifying, seemed unbridgeable.

'I am friendless, once more,' she realized miserably. 'But what else is there to be done? My baby must be cared for.'

The Crawford family as a whole had refused to stop work, and for Tildy that was one small blessing. At least, for once, she and Tom Crawford were in agreement. He enjoyed drink, and tobacco, and a willing whore too much to let any point of principle stand between him and his appetites . . .

'When you'se done that, bring me some water,' Tom

Crawford ordered peremptorily. Tildy completed the nail she was fashioning and, replacing her rod in the fire, went to refill the empty jug.

At the well-housing in the centre of the square she drew a bucket of fresh water and refilled her utensil, then paused for a moment to let the wind and rain beat on her over-heated flesh, cooling and refreshing her body. She glanced about her at the four rows of workshops which bordered the square. Not many were lit by the flames of the forges. More than two-thirds were dark and silent, their bi-sectioned doors closed. Tildy pondered briefly on the terrible want and sufferings those closed doors' represented, and yet again experienced the urge to join in their struggle – yet again realized the futility of that urge.

'I must go my own way, and think only of my baby.'

The top half of Martin Duffil's door was wide open, the glaring light of the hearth shining through it and the ringing of metal on metal sounding from within. The cloud-covered sky and the mists of rain made the square almost pitch-black and Tildy fancied, rather than saw clearly, the obscure shadows issuing from the covered passageway that led into the small confined area of the Tinyard. She stared harder, but still her eyes could not penetrate the gloom sufficiently for her to discern what the shadowy mass was that now moved so stealthily towards Duffil's doorway.

'Tildy? Be you bleedin' well fetchin' that soddin' water, or not? God strike me, a man could die o' bloody thirst here.'

Her husband's bawling sent her scurrying back, the jug held between her hands. He scowled and took it from her, gulping noisily and ending by tipping what water remained over his thick black hair, so that it streamed down his sweaty, grime-smutted head and naked torso.

As Tildy resumed her work she heard shouts from outside, but paid them little heed. Shouts were constant companions to life in the Tinyard by day, and by night.

She pumped the long bellows handle and the draught hissed through the burning breeze-coke, sending tiny blue-tipped flames shooting up through the surfaces of the bed of fuel. The end of the iron rod glowed white-hot and she was about to recommence the work sequence, when the closed bottom half of the outer door came crashing inwards. A grotesque, giant-statured figure filled the doorway wearing a shapeless gown and hood of rough sacking. All that could be glimpsed of its face were the glint of eyes through the small holes cut into the hood. In one hand the figure brandished a length of thick rod-iron, in the other a long-bladed knife.

Tom Crawford blanched in fright. 'It's the Belly Hoggers!'

Before Tildy could fully comprehend what was happening the giant figure had stormed into the workshop and she glimpsed other sack-swathed shapes following the first. A blow from the iron rod sent her husband sprawling, blood spurting in black gouts from his forehead. Tildy screamed and a fist hammered into her belly, and even as she doubled over another heavy blow sent her smashing against the wall and she jackknifed down onto her knees, her forehead colliding painfully against the swarf and dirt of the floor. She lifted her head and looked sideways to see the long blade of the knife glinting in the fire's light as it slashed backwards and forwards behind the hearth. As air reached her straining lungs she was able to straighten up. Two of the sack-clad figures moved jerkily above Tom Crawford's sprawling body, and she heard the dull thuds of heavy, iron-shod boots against flesh and bone and the howls of agony coming from her husband.

In the cradle the baby added his wails to the pandemonium. Tildy dragged herself to her feet and the sack-clad figures disappeared from the workshop as suddenly as they had materialized. She saw that Davy was unhurt, and left him to wail, while she painfully shuffled over to where Tom Crawford lay groaning. He was dazed and helpless, face bloody, his naked torso welted with raw swelling scrapes where the boots had landed.

'Can you move, Tom? Can you?' Tildy tried to lift the upper half of his body, and he shouted out, cursing savagely at her.

'Leave me be, you stupid bugger, leave me lie here for a bit. I'm soddin' well broke up, so I be. Broke to soddin' pieces!'

'What were they, Tom? Who were they?' Her voice betrayed her, and she choked back a sob.

'Ohhhh, God strike me.' He moaned, as he gingerly moved himself until he was sitting with his back to the wall.

'Why have they done this to us?' Tildy managed to steady her voice, and hold in check the rising hysteria that shock, pain and fear had engendered.

'Who be they?' Tom Crawford panted out. 'They'm the Belly Hoggers. Come to make sure that we does no more work . . . Look theer!' He flung out one arm.

Tildy stared at what he indicated, and suddenly understood the reason for the long-bladed knife. The leather belly of the big bellows had been slashed to ribbons.

'Oh Dear God!' She breathed in distress. 'It'll cost a fortune to mend them.'

Despite his bodily pain, Tom Crawford vented an ironic chuckle. 'That's only money. Next time, you stupid bugger, it'll not be the bellows' belly that the Hoggers 'ull rip out. It'll be our'n . . . Yours and mine . . . ' He groaned as his arm rubbed against the raw-scraped flesh over his ribcage. 'That's the finish for us, wench. We'll not strike another blow until this trouble is done wi' . . . I likes my belly-button wheer it is.'

By morning Tildy's shock and fear of the previous night had dissipated, and a stubborn anger against the Belly Hoggers was burning in her brain.

'Why should I allow them to defeat me?' she asked herself again and again. 'I've done harm to no one, and

227

yet they came like wolves in the night to destroy my means of existence. I'll not let them beat me . . . I'll not.'

When Tom Crawford rose from his bed she attempted to talk with him about getting the bellows repaired, and continuing to work. His handsome, bruised face resembled that of a petulant boy.

'Be you gone crazed? Does you want your belly ripped out? Because I bloody doon't . . . I'll not strike another blow until it's safe, I'll tell you.'

'But what about Davy?' she questioned.

Crawford's right hand grabbed and painfully squeezed one of her full breasts. 'The bugger can suck on this, carn't he? At least he'll get that comfort . . . And that's summat I'se never got from you, arn't it? I never gets to suck on your tits, or block you, does I?'

'Take your hands from me!' She struck his grasping fingers away.

The black eyes became rabid. 'Not good enough even to touch you, am I?' he shouted. 'You bloody fine-mouthed whore! Youm glad enough to open your legs for that bastard Suffield!'

'That's not true, and you know it's not!' She made vehement denial. 'I'm no whore, and never was. No man beds me.'

Crawford's own voice dropped to a low growl. 'Youm worse than a whore . . . Youm a bloody witch, an evil witch. You'se brought naught else but misery to me e'er since the day I first met you. I curses the day I married you, and I reckon I'll not know any good fortune until youm alaying in your grave.'

This suddenly revealed intensity of hatred sent an icy shiver through Tildy's body. 'Dear God, am I truly evil?' The concept jangled in her head. 'Am I cursed to bring evil on those who mingle with me?'

Their few remaining shillings were in a small pot on the mantelpiece above the firegrate, and Tom Crawford now emptied them into his hand.

'Does you know what I'm going to do, whore? Does you know, witch? Well, I'll tell you . . . I'm agoing to walk out on this house and leave you to it. Dick Suffield can take you, and welcome.' He stamped back upstairs to reappear some little time later, carrying his scanty possessions bundled up in a sheet from the bed.

'Goodbye, whore!' He swung his free hand in a parting blow that rocked Tildy's head back. Then he was gone.

Stunned by the suddenness of events, she stood unmoving. The baby began to cry for food, and mechanically she lifted the tiny squirming body in her arms, and gave him her breast.

'I'll not let them beat me.' The refrain beat ever louder through her brain. 'I'll not let them beat me.'

Chapter Twenty-Five

At the very end of Broad Street, where it joined the road
that led from Bromsgrove to Stourbridge, stood the smithy
of Isaac Crane. Who, for a penny would repair a tool, and
for three pennies fashion a cold chisel or hammerhead, or
block-die. When Tildy, cradle strapped upon her back,
entered the smoke-infested smithy, Isaac Crane, a man as
spindle-shanked as his feathered namesake, rang out in a
tuneful tenor.

'Tell me, pretty mai--den . . . What may I do for
youuuuu?'

She could not help but smile at his droll manner and
appearance. His nose and chin were long and narrow, his
arms and legs like sharp-angled sticks. Yet he wielded the
heavy smith's-hammer with an ease that exhibited
immense bodily strength. His bright eyes twinkled.

'Ahh me! As a poet I must confess that your beauty
moves me beyond all manner of understanding. But can
you speak, I ask myself?'

Tildy giggled, he was a tonic for her depressed spirits.
'Please, I wonder if you could repair my bellows?'

The twinkling eyes became wary. 'Bellows? You did say bellows, did you not?'

She nodded. 'I did.'

He laid his hammer on the huge anvil, and wiping his hands on his fringed leather apron came to stand facing her.

'I take it that you are one of the unfortunates on whom the Belly Hoggers called last night?'

Again she nodded.

His long nose twitched erratically, and he smoothed down his straggle of grey hair with both hands. 'Well, I could of course repair them, possessing as I do a consummate mastery of my craft. But . . . ' He dropped his hands, then lifted one very long, very dirty finger up before his face. 'But? Pretty maiden . . . There's the rub.'

Thinking that he was mocking her, she snapped curtly, 'Are you afraid to mend them?'

He scowled ferociously, and drew his skinny body up to its full height of more than six feet. 'Afraid?' he declaimed theatrically. 'Afraid? I? Isaac Crane, late fugleman of the Bromsgrove Volunteers of most glorious memory. I, who stepped forward ready to fight the hordes of Napoleon Bonaparte should they have ever dared to descend on my native Bromsgrove. I, Isaac Crane, afraid? Did I not march to Redditch when the Bread Riots took place in that sinful town. Did I not stand on the foremost rank to receive their dreadful onslaught. The Siege of Redditch, I was there all the while . . . '

He started to recite, waving his long finger in circles to keep the time.

'With nothing to eat, but the piece of a tile.
Men, women and children, with trade all alive.
Clods, pebbles and brickbats sent at us full-drive.
Sent at us on purpose to batter our pates;
Tongs, shovels and pokers, and cheeks of old grates . . . '

Abruptly he broke off in full flow to demand pugnaciously! 'Afraid? I? Who has stood firm under such a bombardment as that one? I trust you now have your answer, pretty maiden?'

Once more Tildy felt an overpowering desire to laugh, but with a struggle she controlled it. 'Will you then repair my bellows?'

'But of course. Isaac Crane is at your service. For a trifling fee only,' he added as an afterthought.

'Can I pay you on the coming Weigh-in day?' she asked timidly.

His white teeth were as long and as thin as the rest of him.

'Of course you may. Beauty shall always find credit at the smithy of Isaac Crane. But the work will not be done today. I have a previous engagement with this plough-share.'

Tildy's dismay showed clearly, and the man laughed kindly.

'Fret not, pretty maiden. I shall come tomorrow, be assured on it . . . '

Even while Tildy was meeting with Isaac Crane, another meeting was taking place in the best bar-parlour of the Golden Lion Hotel.

The Reverend, Lord Aston, clergyman and magistrate was in the Chair, accompanied by his fellow magistrate, the Reverend Mark Pyndar MA (Oxon) and their clerk, Joseph Blackwell Esq.

All the local nailmasters were present, as well as Captains Edward Cassidy and John Emmot of the Worcestershire Yeomanry Cavalry, respectively the officer commanding the Hewell Troop, and the corps adjutant.

Reverend the Lord Aston, a bulky-bodied, dyspeptic man, who always wore the full-skirted coat, black breeches, stockings of his calling and a white, short-queued clerical tie-wig upon his bald pate, brought the meeting to order, and then addressed Joseph Blackwell.

'Be good enough to read out the account of last night's outrages, Mr Blackwell.'

232

The clerk, a fussy-mannered, pedantic little man, whose clothing was layered with the dust of his ledgers, cleared his throat nervously.

'I'm honoured, My Lord . . . It appears that last night, between the hours of eight and nine of the clock, a group of ill-disposed persons wearing disguises of hoods and gowns fashioned from sacking material, entered some nine workshops in the district of the Sidemoor. They assaulted various of the nailers who were engaged upon their lawful callings in the said workshops, and using sharp-edged instruments, the trespassers did so cut about the bellows contained within the said workshops, as to render those said machines incapable of being used for the purpose for which they are so intended, to whit . . .'

'Goddammit Blackwell, you rambles like an old maid. Why carn't you spake plain and simple?' Old George Hobbs irascibly interrupted. 'The damm Belly Hoggers was out last night down the Sidemoor, and that's well known, and why we'em all on us here. What we wants to know is what's to be done to stop the boggers from splitting every bloody bellows in the parish?'

Reverend the Lord Aston knew George Hobbs of old, and realizing the impossibility of conducting this meeting in the formal manner, signalled for Blackwell to remain silent.

'What measures would you have we, the magistrates take, gentlemen?' he enquired frostily, swallowing a belch and inwardly asking his God yet again, why His humble servant was so doomed to martyrdom by indigestion.

'We wants the Belly Hoggers stopped from doing any further damage.' George Hobbs answered, having been deputed as their spokesman by the other nailmasters before the meeting.

'We can swear in special constables, and have them patrol the streets,' Aston offered.

Hobbs pshawed his contempt for that idea. 'Bloody useless, they'd be . . . No good at all . . . The Belly Hoggers 'ud ate 'um for breakfast. No, we needs the Yeomanry down theer on Sidemoor. Hot lead and cold steel is the only thing as 'ull stop them Belly Hoggers . . . I'm old in the trade, and I'se sin this sort of thing more times than enough. When men be desperate enough to goo Belly Hogging, then words and ash-staves wun't stop 'um, only bullets.'

'Unless there is actual riot and bloodshed taking place, then I am not empowered to call out the Yeomanry. The lord lieutenant of the county must do so, and you know that full well,' the Chairman countered huffily.

'How far is bloody Worcester town from here? Not fifteen miles? You could goo and see the lord lieutenant, get him to issue the orders, and be back in your own bed be nightfall.'

George Hobbs had never been overawed by any magistrate or clergyman, titled or not. 'What in 'ell's name is the use o' you being a bloody Beak, iffen youm just agoing to sit theer bleatin' and puffin' like an old ewe? Tell me that, My Lord!'

'Gentlemen, gentlemen, let us not be heated, it is not Christian.' The Reverend Mark Pyndar's voice was as soft and oily as his well-fed face. 'All necessary steps to maintain the public order and rule of law will be taken, I do assure you. But all in good time, gentlemen. All in good time.'

Outside, Snagee Porter kept his ear pressed to the keyhole and willed the meeting to end quickly. His knee-joints were killing him . . .

That same night the Belly Hoggers came again to the Sidemoor, this time striking at some of the families who lived and worked in the Providence Street and Square, the Troths, Kings, Lloyds and Taylors. Once more men bled, women wept, children shrieked in terror, and bellows were left slashed to ribbons.

Tildy heard none of it. She had barred her doors and spent the long hours of darkness sitting by the tiny fire in her living room, too tense and nervous to go upstairs to her bed. She was enduring a terrible loneliness. A loneliness so intense that at intervals tears of misery fell without any conscious volition, and it seemed that a tangible substance was crushing against her throat and chest and stomach. Her thoughts were sorely troubled by nameless fears that she couldn't identify with certainty. Many times throughout that long, lonely night she considered taking the baby and leaving the Sidemoor there and then.

'I could go back to Tardebigge, to Davy. He'd shelter me. He'd comfort and protect me . . .'

Yet always, just at the point when she was about to rise and go, a stubborn refusal to submit would intervene, and cause her to remain seated. 'I'll not give in, I'll not let them beat me . . . They'll not drive me away like some stray cur-dog.'

She did not attempt to identify and isolate 'They' as individuals. To her mind 'They' were all that amorphous mass of troubles and personalities that seemed to have combined against her.

She evaluated what resources remained to support her. She had a half-loaf of bread, some cheese, some onions, some potatoes, some oats. A third of a sugar-cone, and a pot of mutton broth which had been intended for yesterday's supper and today's dinner.

'I've food and enough,' she told herself with a degree of satisfaction. There was also sufficient breeze-coke in the forge to enable her to complete the working-up of the rods remaining in the sixty-pound bundle of iron from Sanders' warehouse.

Determination steeled her. 'If I work all the hours God sends, then I can finish the bundle by myself and draw wages. That's if Isaac Crane comes to mend the bellows. Please God, let him come . . . Let him come early . . .'

Isaac Crane arrived at Tildy's door just after dawn. A fine drizzle was falling and the day threatened to turn gloomy and depressive. He, however, sang gaily as he worked, cutting the pigskin to shape, hammering the brass studs, stitching seams with tough waxed thread.

His gaiety cheered Tildy's spirits, and she was sorry when he had finished and was leaving. His eyes twinkled down at her.

'There was a deal of excitement up in Providence Street last night, pretty maiden. Another seven bellows slashed by the Belly Hoggers. There's not a single forge being worked this morning in the whole of the Sidemoor . . . You are either very brave, or very insane, if you begin to strike nails this day.'

'I am most certainly not brave, Master Crane,' she told him quietly.

He threw back his straggly-haired head and laughed uproariously, his protruberant Adam's apple jolting up and down in his long stalk of a throat.

'Then you've naught to fear, my pretty. For as I know from my own experience, the Good Lord protects the crazed and drunkards . . . I suggest you double your own protection by taking a few drams of strong spirits afore you commence your labour. By the way, you owe me eight pence ha-penny. Pay me when you can, there's no rush. Goodbye now, and may good fortune shine on you.'

Tildy watched his ungainly figure stalk away, and a lump came to her throat. 'He's a good man,' she acknowledged. 'Truly a good man.'

Attracted by Crane's songs and loud laughter, the people of the Tinyard had come to their doors and windows, drawn by curiosity. Now little knots of men and women coalesced, talking in low tones and casting suspicious glances towards Tildy. She turned her back on them and went into her workshop to light the hearth fire.

'What be you doing, Tildy?' It was Hester Lammas.

Tildy's heart gladdened. She was deeply fond of the Lammases and had no wish to continue being estranged from them.

'I'm going to strike my nails, Hester.' She smiled tentatively. 'I know you think I'm wrong to do so, but I've no real choice.'

The older woman sniffed noisily. 'Ah well, my wench, we must agree to differ on that point. Wheer's Crawford?'

'He's gone,' Tildy answered bluntly.

'For good?'

'Yes, for good . . . At least he said it was for good.'

Again the noisy, expressive sniff. 'Good riddance if you arsks me.'

'Yes, well, that's as maybe.' Tildy deliberately kept her tone non-committal, and went on arranging the scraps of wooden tinder.

'Tildy?' It was Hester Lammas who now smiled tentatively. 'I knows we 'as a difference of opinion between us, but I 'opes we 'em still friends.'

'Oh yes! Indeed we are.' Tildy answered warmly. 'I trust we'll always remain friends, Hester, no matter what temporary differences may arise between us.'

The harsh lines etched deep into the older woman's face softened.

'Then let me tell you this, as a friend, Tildy. Youm sadly mistaken if you begins to work today . . . You must know what happened larst night? Three o' the Troths got real badly hurt atrying to fight off the Belly Hoggers. Iffen hard-chaws like the Troths got beat so sorely, then what chance does you have?'

She saw Tildy's lips set into a stubborn line, and spoke with greater urgency.

'Listen girl, I'se sin the Belly Hoggers walking the Sidemoor afore now. Nobody can ever put a name to 'um. So the bloody constables and the Beaks 'ull do naught agen 'um. Oh yes, I knows that iffen I cared too, then I could make a few good guesses as to the faces under the hoods, but some on 'um arn't from these parts at all. They comes in for the money, and they arn't fussy about what they must do to earn their wages. We 'em strangers to 'um.

There's no ties o' kith or kin to hold 'um back from crippling, or even killing us, and mek no mistake, my duck, that's what the buggers 'ull do, iffen you keeps on defying 'um. They'll either cripple or kill you . . . Mek no mistake about it!' Her voice throbbed with utter conviction.

Through Tildy's body the now-familiar tremors of fear began to shiver. Every sense of self-preservation clamoured at her to leave what she was doing, and accept the advice given to her. But from somewhere she could not place, a stubborn determination drove her on.

'No Hester, I'll not give in. It's useless you trying to persuade me, I just cannot help myself. I'm not going to let them beat me, not even if it costs me my life!'

The sunken eyes before her flickered shrewdly to the cradle hanging on the bellows handle. 'Ne'er mind your life, my wench, what if it corsts your babby's life?'

For a moment Tildy wavered, and then she replied, 'Hester, if his life is going to be dominated by fear of Belly Hoggers, nailmasters, starvation, poverty and all the other curses we labour under, then he'd do better to lose it now.'

Hester Lammas looked long and searchingly at her friend, and accepted. 'Then God help you, my duck. For He 'ull be the only one able too . . .'

'So, Tom Crawford's cut and run, has he!' Dick Suffield grinned. 'Well, that doon't really surprise me.'

'No! And it gets him nicely out of the way, doon't it?' Janey Porter's fine breasts heaved agitatedly as the jealousy bit into her. 'You'll be able to have a clear run at his bloody smarm-faced missus now, wun't you?'

The man's grin did not falter. 'Now Janey, youm not my wife. It don't concern you.'

'Oh yes it does!' Her eyes flamed at him, and her raised voice brought malicious pleasure to the warehouse-hands working in the yard.

The foreman was well aware of the sniggers of laughter

being directed at him, and his tone hardened. 'Keep your voice down, my wench, or I'll do summat to close up that big mouth o' yourn.'

For a moment it seemed that she would defy him, but that moment passed, and when she next spoke it was in little above a whisper. 'Well what about me and my babby, what's to happen to us?'

The man hissed impatiently. 'I'll see that youm alright, Janey. Arn't I always done so?'

Tears glistened in her eyes and she bit her lips. 'You knows I loves you, Dick. Why does you torment me so? If you married me, like you promised, then I'd be a good wife to you.' A spasm of hatred twisted her mouth. 'I'm twice the woman that that whey-faced bitch is! I doon't know what meks you so bloody randy for her . . . Be her tits firmer than mine? Be they?' She lifted her fine breasts towards him with both hands. ' 'As I ever refused you anything in the bed? As I?' She was begging now. 'I'se never turned from you in the night. I'se always done anything you'se wanted me too . . . I always pleased you well enough afore that bloody Tildy Crawford come on the scene. Since she's come here, you'se not gi' me so much as a pat on the arse. You'se gi' me naught!'

'You've not gone short o' goods, I've seen to that,' Suffield told her roughly.

'I'm not saying that you arn't seen me alright for food and shelter, Dick.' Janey Porter's misery was a miasma emanating from her, as her pride crumbled. 'But you'se not gi' me any loving, as you, Dick? You'se took me into your bed, but that was only to ease your balls, warn't it? There was nothing loving in it, I was just like a bloody shilling doxy for you, warn't I? A bloody shilling doxy?'

Suffield's seething impatience boiled over. 'A bloody tanner doxy, my wench! You was ne'er worth a shilling . . . Now listen, I'se got work to do, and I'm not agoing to stand here with you bletherin' in me earhole any longer, so leave me be.'

The girl's gutter-devil flared out. 'I'll tear the eyes out o' that bitch's head, you see if I wun't.'

The man's hand clamped on her arm like an iron band. Yellowed teeth bared in a ferocious snarl. 'Keep right away from Tildy Crawford, you poxy whore, or you'll be picked out of a ditch one bright morning wi' no eyes in your own head. Now get off from here, and leave me be . . . '

He half-threw her from him, and she stumbled and nearly fell, to dejectedly trudge from the yard, smothering her sobs with her hands.

Suffield remained looking after her, and spoke loudly and evenly so that the three men in the yard would hear him clearly.

'Iffen any word o' what's happened here gets out, then you three 'ud be well advised to pack your traps and leave the Sidemoor.'

Not one of them looked up from their tasks, only the stiffening of their postures showed that his threat had struck home. Satisfied, Suffield swaggered out into the Broad Street.

The afternoon was grey and overcast, but despite the chill air there were groups of men lounging apathetically against walls and on corners, while their women and children went to the wastelands to search for twigs and to cut turfs for fuel to keep their miserable hovels warm. An atmosphere of desolation hung over the village, which Suffield, as he slowly walked along, recognized and rejoiced in. Not a forge glowed, not a hammer rang, not an Oliver thudded. The Belly Hoggers had done their work well.

The foreman's breathing quickened as the exultation of power filled him. 'I've done this! I've brought this place to a standstill . . . And at a standstill it'll remain, until I say otherwise.'

He passed the bleak Emmanuel Chapel and heard the strains of hymn-singing coming from within. He was feeling well-disposed towards Jacob Ashfield and his flock.

'If that bloody Ranter hadn't acted as he did, then I'd never have bin able to succeed so quick.' A smile tugged at the corners of his lips. 'Ne'er thought the day 'ud come when I'd feel kindly towards any Methody pisspot.'

The hymn approached its climax, and the choir of voices thundered out in full-throated paens of praise.

'Hark to 'um.' Suffield's smile widened. 'Filling their empty bellies wi' the Love o' Christ . . . Meself, I'd sooner fill my belly wi' a rare-done beefsteak and a few pots o' porter . . . '

Inside the chapel Jacob Ashfield regarded his flock. Their appearances were mute testimony to the hardships they had been, and still were, enduring. His own stocky body was stripped of all superfluous flesh, and his coat and linen hung loosely on his now bony frame. But as he studied the congregation Ashfield's heart swelled with pride and love. They had indeed stood together, supporting and sustaining each other. Sharing what little they had, and caring for their sick, their aged, their children, with a fierce devotion.

'Brothers and Sisters in the Lord!' Despite his bodily weakness and the constant gnawing of hunger in his body, the preacher's voice was still strong and sonorous. 'The Holy Bible tells us that God moves in mysterious ways His wonders to perform. We've sin the truth o' that this very week, here in the Sidemoor. The Belly Hoggers are walking among our homes and workshops. They are the servants of the Devil, who come in the hours of darkness, those hours in which their Master allus performs most on His evil works, and they come bringing terror and destruction. But yet, Brethren, those wicked men are aiding our cause. Not a single nail is now being struck in the Sidemoor! How long will the masters now be able to sustain their tyranny? How long can they survive now that production has ceased entirely?

'Not long, Brethren! Not long! Soon, soon the masters must give in, and restore the rates to the old levels. They worship Mammon, and without our labour their foul idol is brought crashing down into the dust where it belongs. We have only to endure a little while longer, Brethren, and we shall gain the victory.'

'Amen, Brother Ashfield, Amen!' One solitary man applauded, but the rest were silent, their minds troubled.

The more perceptive did not share Jacob Ashfield's optimism, or his conviction that the advent of the Belly Hoggers was advantageous to their cause. The terror and destruction those Servants of the Devil had brought to the Sidemoor also hovered above their own heads. It was no longer they who controlled the refusal to take iron, the refusal to work. It was no longer they who would be able to decide when they should again resume production. That power of decision had been wrested from them. It now lay in the hands of the men of violence . . . The Belly Hoggers.

Chapter Twenty-Six

In the tender aftermath of passion they lay with arms and legs entwined, soft belly and breasts pressed against hard ridged muscles. It was Edward Cassidy who broke the silence.

'When will Jonathan return?'

Carlotta Sanders nuzzled her lover's throat with moist, love-swollen lips. 'Perhaps this evening, perhaps tomorrow . . . Does it really matter?'

'Naturally it does.' He chuckled fondly. 'It would be most embarrassing if he caught us like this.'

'He'll not do so,' she drawled lazily. 'He never comes to my room.'

Cassidy gently caressed her shapely buttocks and the full, rounded thighs, his fingers tracing whorling patterns upon the silk-smooth skin.

'They will have already seen the lord lieutenant by now then.' It was more statement than question, and he went on. 'I might receive my orders tonight. The lord lieutenant will undoubtedly accede to their requests now that those three nailers have been so badly injured.'

Carlotta pressed her mouth against his, in a bid to silence him. 'Don't talk about such matters, my darling. I've no interest in what the nailers or the masters do, or have done to them. If Jonathan and his cronies must needs go to Worcester and cravenly beg for the Yeomanry Cavalry to be called out to protect them, then it merely proves that they are not men enough to keep order among their own workers themselves. My father would never have needed to call on the Yeomanry to aid him, I do assure you. He would have personally horse-whipped the scum until they begged for mercy.'

Not for the first time, Edward Cassidy experienced a fleeting distaste for this woman who, in his opinion, was the most selfish and self-centred female he had ever possessed in his life. Unfortunately for his peace of mind, she was also by far the most beautiful woman he had ever possessed; and he was beginning to fear that he lacked the necessary strength of will to break off his relationship with her. It was primarily her beauty that held him, but at times she also exhibited a quality of light-hearted, mischievous devilry that utterly enthralled him.

'Do you know, Carla, you are the only woman I have ever known who simultaneously both delights and distresses me.'

Her teeth were a pale gleam in the dark haven of the curtained four-poster bed, as she nestled closer to his warmth, and with her soft hand began to tease and stroke his maleness.

Cassidy's own caresses became more fervent, more demanding, and unable to restrain himself any longer, he spread her thighs with his and drove his body into that warm, sweet wetness that he so urgently craved to enfold him and give his easement. He groaned aloud in the torment of ecstasy, and heard her voice panting in his ear.

'Yes, Edward, yes! This is where you belong . . . This is where you belong . . . '

The deputation of nailmasters had travelled to and from the county town by post chaise, but considered the expense well justified, since they brought back with them the lord lieutenant's warrant that would empower the magistrates to call out the Hewell Troop of Yeomanry for active service. Jonathan Sanders was the sole remaining passenger as the chaise jolted along the Broad Street. The night was dark and only the dull gleam of an occasional candle or rushlight showed that people were still awake in the rows of cottages.

The young nailmaster was not particularly elated about the lord lieutenant's warrant. He disliked the idea of armed cavalrymen patrolling the Sidemoor. Such a happening smacked more of some continental oligarchy, than a nation ruled by a freely elected parliament.

'But what else can be done?' he ruefully considered. 'Those people who are willing to work must be protected.' Another disquieting thought caused him to frown. Old George Hobbs and his clique had decided that as soon as they had obtained the protection of a mobilized Yeomanry, then, they would in their turn reassert their authority over the nailers by all or any means. The young man was deeply saddened.

'I shudder to think what might happen here. I fear that there could be created such a rift between man and master, that I will never see healed in my lifetime . . . And yet, needs must when the Devil drives! I have no other choice but to support my fellow masters. I'm in trouble enough financially as it is. I must help break the backbones of those who stand against us, or go into ruin myself.'

The chaise lurched to a halt, and the cape-muffled driver informed gruffly, 'Here's your house, Master Sanders, and you'se got a visitor by the look on it.'

A big bay hunter was tethered before the main door, and

Jonathan recognized it as belonging to Edward Cassidy. He frowned unhappily, his earlier suspicions that something existed between his wife and Cassidy, had lately hardened into a virtual certainty.

'But what can I do?' A feeling of helplessness flooded over him. 'I have no actual proof that they are committing misconduct . . . And even if I were to obtain proof, what then? Should I challenge Cassidy, and try to kill him? And Carlotta, what of her? Could I bear to live without her? No matter that I'm impotent, I still love her above all else in this world. What would my life be without her? Nothing but a miserable desert! But could I bear to continue to live with her, knowing for certain that she is cuckolding me?' He seemed to hear the rasping voice of his dead uncle. 'Theer's nobody so mocked and jeered at as him who knowingly wears the horns his missus puts on his yed, boy . . . '

Jonathan shook his head hard as if to physically expel that rasping voice from his mind, and went on into the house.

His wife and Cassidy were playing chess in the drawing-room, and Jonathan could not help but study them keenly as he came in. A self-torturing search for some token of illicit love by which they would betray themselves. Cassidy rose to his feet, his hard features smiling a welcome. For a brief moment Jonathan felt intense self-disgust.

'I must be mad!' he silently castigated himself. 'I should be in Bedlam with the rest of the loonies. This man is a gentleman, and a King's officer. He'd not seduce another's wife under her husband's very roof.' Aloud, he greeted the visitor pleasantly. 'We are well met, Cassidy. I have urgent news for you. The Hewell Troop is to be embodied immediately for service in this district.'

'Fie on you, Jon!' Carlotta pouted prettily. 'Could not your news have waited until we had finished this game. I'm enjoying it so.'

Jonathan's love for her was a sickness in his soul, as he

visually devoured the beautiful face surrounded by the mass of raven-black ringlets, and the enticing, tantalizing curves of breasts and hips revealed by the low-cut, form-clinging gown of white satin.

'Pray forgive my interruption, my dear,' he apologized, and nodded to the other man, so elegant in his dandified grey riding clothes and knee-boots. 'Please, Cassidy, be seated and continue the match. My news can wait.'

Cassidy bowed gallantly. 'Indeed I will, sir, but I fear that your lady wife has the measure of me in this particular battle.'

From a crystal decanter standing upon a side table, Jonathan poured himself a glass of Madeira wine, and stood sipping it while he watched the play. Unable to help himself he found that each time the protagonists glanced at each other across the board, he was seeking for some sign to confirm his suspicions – and each time he so sought, he felt unclean and sick at heart.

At last Edward Cassidy smiled triumphantly and moved his knight. 'I think that is checkmate, Mistress Sanders.'

Carlotta studied the board for some moments, then mock-scowled. 'I fear I am defeated by that final onslaught of the white horseman, Captain Cassidy . . . ' Her black eyes glinted mischievously from beneath lowered lashes. 'But then, that seems to be my fate in life, does it not. Always to succumb to the horseman . . . '

To Jonathan her words struck like a physical blow, and the blood drained from his face. 'I'm imagining it!' he told himself vehemently. 'There is no hidden meaning in her words . . . They were said in jest only. I'm reacting to them like a stupid, jealous fool.' He turned to the side table to hide his distraught emotions, and fumbled with the decanter and wine glass until he had himself under control once more.

'I suddenly have a headache. I shall go early to my bed, and leave you gentlemen to your talk,' Carlotta announced. Her lips barely touched Jonathan's cheek, but the fragrance of her body filled his nostrils, even after she was gone.

He forced a smile to his trembling lips and turned to the other man. 'Will you take wine with me, Cassidy, and then I'll relate the day's happenings in Worcester . . .'

Chapter Twenty-Seven

The blast of the trumpet echoed along the Broad Street, and the small column of cavalry came to a halt. Saddlery and accoutrements creaked and jingled as the horses moved restlessly, snorting through widened nostils, hooves pawing the muddy ground; and black-shakoed, scarlet-jacketed troopers stared about them, sibilantly cursing the wind-driven sleet that chapped their faces and hands, and soaked their uniforms and saddle-cloths.

The natives of the Sidemoor stood in their doorways and peered from windows, louring at the Yeomanry Cavalrymen in sullen silence. Only a few excited children and dogs ventured out into the wind and rain to caper about the mounted men.

Jonathan Sanders came out from his warehouse yard, his tall hat pulled low on his forehead, and his dark cloak flapping in the wind. At the head of the column, Edward Cassidy saluted the nailmaster.

'A foul morning it is, to be sure, Sanders. I trust we have arrived in good time for you?'

Jonathan nodded. 'Indeed you have, Captain. It still

wants almost half an hour until the Weigh-in.'

It was the first Weigh-in day following the visitations of the Belly Hoggers, and the nailmasters had requested that sections of the Yeomanry be concentrated at each warehouse in the district, to give protection to those nailers prepared to bring in what work they had completed before the total stoppage. For the last few days and nights small parties of Yeomanry had patrolled the Sidemoor, but still no one had dared to do any more work . . . No one except Tildy Crawford . . .

Even as the trumpet blasted out, she stamped out the final nails to complete the working-up of the bundle she and Tom Crawford had begun. Grey-faced with exhaustion Tildy laid down her hammer and went into the cottage living room. She dared not allow herself to sit and rest, knowing that if she did so, she would not be able to rise to her feet for hours.

'I'll rest afterwards, when I come back from the warehouse,' she promised herself, and blessed the fact that Davy was sleeping soundly in his cradle, and not wailing for his food. For three days and nights Tildy had slaved at the forge, snatching brief hours of sleep when her body was too tired even to pump the bellows, taking mouthfuls of food only when her head throbbed and her sight swam giddily through hunger, laying aside the hammer and iron rods solely to feed the baby, replenish the hearth, or ease bodily needs. She had worked behind bolted and barred doors, scraps of sacking covering the windows so that no light should show. Listening constantly for the coming of the Belly Hoggers, her heart pounding with fright at every sudden noise that came from beyond her doors.

Now, as she drank some of the musty-smelling water from the wooden bucket on the table, she felt a sense of pride.

'I've done it! I've done what I set out to do . . . Completed the task.' With that pride there also burgeoned an increasing sense of self-respect. 'I'm not the weak, stupid creature I've been called by Tom Crawford and others like him, am I? I've proved that to myself.'

When the nails had cooled she gathered them into a thick sack bag, and lashed a length of rope around it to form a crude sling, so that she could carry the heavy weight more easily. Lifting a corner of the sacking from the forge window she saw that it was now full daylight.

'I'll go early to the warehouse. Davy will be safe enough here for a while. Mayhap he'll sleep until I get back.'

A sudden wave of weakness and nausea assailed her, bringing cold sweat starting from the pores of her skin. She closed her eyes and held onto the support-pole of the Oliver until the attack had passed.

'It's only tiredness and hunger,' she reassured herself. 'Naught else . . . When I've rested and eaten I'll be alright.'

There were barely a third of the usual number of nailers queuing up at the great brass scales of the warehouse, and their sacks contained only a fraction of the normal amount of nails. Half a dozen cavalrymen under the command of a sergeant sat their horses at the big double-gates of the entrance, and Jonathan Sanders stood in his customary position a little behind and to the side of Dick Suffield and his two helpers.

Outside on the roadway a large crowd had gathered, muffled in their threadbare coverings against the weather. All was unnaturally silent, only the occasional whispered comment, or yelp of a trodden-on dog, issuing from the group.

Tildy trudged to join the queue, her head held high, and her gaze set forward. A murmur of surprise at the apparent weight of the sack she laboriously carried greeted her appearance, but no one spoke to her, and she could sense the waves of hostility directed at her. She fought to maintain an air of calm, but shivers of apprehension coursed through her body, and her breath was drawn in shallow, rapid gasps.

As the nails of the people in front of her were weighed, she noted the deepening despair of Jonathan Sanders's expression, and she wondered why Dick Suffield retained his customary geniality as nailer after nailer refused to take the bundles of iron rods offered to them for the coming week's work. As each man or woman left the warehouse yard empty-handed the crowd buzzed excitedly, and all eyes were directed at the small group of strangers standing in the forefront of the mob. Roughly-dressed, tough-looking men, who glowered ferociously at each departing nailer, before nodding in satisfaction at their lack of burden.

Tildly stepped up to the pans and Dick Suffield affected an air of surprise at the amount of nails she proffered.

'My oath, Tildy, you'se toiled hard, arn't you?' His lips smiled, but his eyes held a curious mixture of warmth and warning. 'That's nine shillings and four pence you'se earned, my honey-lamb.' He took the coins from the cashbox at his feet and handed them to her. 'Make your mark here.' His spatulate finger indicated the place.

As she lifted the quill pen from the open ledger he held before her, his lips almost touched her ear. 'Just take your money and go now, Tildy. Doon't bother wi' any more iron.'

At first she could not believe that she had heard him correctly, and swung her head to face him fully.

'What do you say, Dick?'

His bloodshot eyes hardened. 'Just goo wi'out taking iron,' he gritted.

Jonathan Sanders was watching closely. 'What is the delay, Suffield?'

The foreman didn't turn, only spoke back over his shoulder. 'A query as to the rate, Master Jon.' To Tildy he hissed angrily, 'Get off now, weneh.'

'But I must have some more iron,' she said quietly, still not fully understanding why he was behaving in this way.

'Doon't talk like a bloody fool.' The man's harsh whisper propelled a gust of stale-smelling breath into her face. 'Iffen you takes more iron, you'll bring the Belly Hoggers down on you agen, and they'll not let you away so lightly next time. It's only thanks to me that you'se bin let finish this lot wi' out hindrance.'

Tildy's heart fluttered, and for a moment her fear of what might happen to her caused her resolve to falter. Then she screwed up her courage.

'I'm grateful for that . . . But I still want more iron.'

Jonathan Sanders caught the last sentence. 'You want more iron, Mistress Crawford?'

She met his sensitive, dark-shadowed eyes.

'Yes, I do, Master Sanders. I want more iron.' She spoke out clearly, uncomfortably aware of Suffield's angry scowl, and the exclamations of surprise from those who had heard her.

The nailmaster regarded her intently for several seconds, then smiled warmly. 'You shall have more iron, and welcome, Mistress Crawford.'

'My thanks to you, sir.' Tildy swallowed nervously, and steeled herself to face the rabid fury glinting in Dick Suffield's eyes.

'Please . . . will you give me the bundle?' she requested hesitantly.

His yellowed teeth clenched together, and he jerked his head at one of his helpers. 'Gi' it to her.'

Tildy took the heavy bundle of rods from the man and balanced it across her shoulder. Then, eyes downcast, she walked out into the street.

'Her's took iron! . . . Her's took iron!'

The news ran through the crowd like wildfire, and the goup of hard-faced strangers glowered and spat at the slender figure passing between the jostling, avid-staring onlookers. From the rear of the crowd a clod of muddy earth came hurtling to crash against the side of Tildy's head. She cried out in shock and pain, and staggered, but managed to retain her balance and walk on, eyes still firm-set to the front.

The sergeant shouted orders, and the troopers drew their sabres and kicked their horses into motion, driving them between Tildy and the crowd surrounding her to form a living shield.

'Any more throwing, and you bastards 'ull be getting a taste o' this!' the sergeant bellowed, brandishing his sabre menacingly above his shako.

The troopers escorted Tildy right up to the Tinyard, and only trotted away when she had entered her cottage, and bolted and barred its door.

As their hoofbeats faded, Tildy let down her bundle, and dropped onto a chair. A trembling began in her hands, which spread and intensified until her entire body was shaking uncontrollably. Tears scalded from her eyes, and she moaned aloud in misery: 'Oh God, I'm so alone . . . so alone . . . so alone . . . '

Jonathan Sanders did not stay long at the weighing pans. He left his foreman to finish the tallying and retired to his office. The nailmaster could not dismiss the image of Tildy Crawford's white, drawn face from his mind.

What courage she has, he thought in deep admiration. 'To take iron in front of a crowd which undoubtedly contained Belly Hoggers . . . The only person brave enough to take iron, and that a woman. Not even a woman yet, only a slip of a girl . . . Husband a runaway, she with a baby, already attacked by Belly Hoggers once, yet still defies them. By God, she is a most remarkable person! We masters should be doing everything in our power to aid people like her. Not grinding their rates down, and forcing them into rebellions that in the long run they cannot hope to win.'

His train of thought was broken by the entrance of Dick Suffield. The foreman's expression was unreadable, but there was an inflection of satisfaction in his tone, as he made his report.

'It's the worst yet, Master Jon. We arn't took but a

quarter of the quota. And that's our lot for God knows how long to come, ceptin' for that silly wench who took a bundle. But one bundle next Weigh-in day wun't do us any good at all. I knows wi'out even lookin' in the books that we'em not able to deliver to Jenkins, or to Taylors, or to the boatyard. We carn't even make up what we was short on larst week wi' Smailes and Sons. So I reckon it's a safe bet we'se lost all that lot's custom once and for all. And you knows what that means, doon't you? We arn't got the wherewithal to pay the iron factors. We owes for two deliveries already. They'll not gi' us any more on tick, that's a fact . . . . '

He shook his head mock-dolefully, and now a jeering note entered his voice. 'Youm all but bankrupt, Master Jon. It doon't look as there's anything can stop you going Ponto, does it?'

'You do not seem unduly perturbed by the prospect?' Jonathan's customary dislike for the man was aggravated by the relish with which the foreman had spoken such unpalatable truths. 'Does it not cause you concern that if I go bankrupt, then you also, as a matter of course, will lose your employment?'

The foreman let the mask drop. 'I care not a cow's-fart for this poxy job, Sanders, nor what happens to you and yourn. I'se always known you for a weak fool . . . But Dick Suffield's no weak fool. He'll always mek his way.'

Jonathan's overstrained patience snapped. From his pocket he fished out a sovereign and a crown-piece, and tossed them on the desk in front of the other men. 'If that's the case, Suffield, then take your pay and go. And do not ever set foot on these premises again!'

The man laughed jeeringly. 'Many thanks, master, many thanks! I'll goo now and gladly . . . But it'll not be the last time I sets foot on these premises. You may lay odds to that.' He lifted the coins and swaggered away, slamming the door so hard that the nails rattled in their showcases on the walls.

The nailmaster sighed. 'You must not give in to your temper like that, Jonathan,' he reproved himself, and then smiled with satisfaction. 'But I must allow, it was rare enjoyable doing so.'

His smile faded as he began the perusal of his ledgers, and understood the melancholy story they told. After a time he stepped from his high stool.

'So I am to all intents and purposes, a bankrupt.'

He started to pace up and down the narrow room, lost in a reverie, and while the minutes lengthened and became hours, still his heels tapped the floor in a rhythmic march. All the while, the image of Tildy Crawford's white, drawn face constantly superimposed itself on his mind.

At last he stopped by his desk, and with a sudden upsurge of feeling, slammed the ledgers shut. 'Dammee if I'll let that slip of a girl shame me with her courage! It's time I took true stock of my own life, and showed a courage to equal Tildy Crawford's . . . I must also stand alone, as she did this very day - and if needs be suffer the want and hardship that she suffers, if I judge her appearance aright . . . Because of my impotence, I have allowed myself to excuse my own cowardice in refusing to deal with my wife and her lover. Bedammed if I'll continue to do so. And I'll not allow this business to crash, because I've been behaving like a dammed fool all these years . . . '

Pulling on his cloak he went from the office, shouting to the yardman to saddle his horse . . .

Chapter Twenty-Eight

While the rest of the Tinyard slept Tildy laboured hard behind barred and bolted doors. Driving her aching muscles on as their over-strained tissues cramped and threatened to falter. It was well past midnight when a loud knocking on the solitary small window of the forge caused her to halt in fright, her hammer suspended head-high in mid-lift.

'Doon't be feared, Tildy Crawford. I mean you no harm.'

The sound of Martin Duffil's voice caused Tildy a shock of surprise.

'What do you want with me?' she asked nervously, and lifted the sacking from the window, barely able to glimpse his unshaven, wolfish face peering through the filthy glass.

'I only wants a word wi' you . . . Doon't be feared, I means no harm to you,' he reiterated.

'Then speak,' she told him, and saw his fangs of teeth as he chuckled huskily.

'God rot me, missus! I'se told you twice I means no harm to you. But open the door and let me spake plain and open wi' you. There might be someone watching, and I've no wish for them to think me a Peeping Tom.'

Tildy hesitated, then unwillingly unbolted the workshop door, and retreated quickly to stand by the side of the glowing hearth, gripping her hammer as if it were a weapon.

The flickering fire cast reddish, ever-shifting gleams of light across Duffil's features, revealing the black dried-up cuts and swollen bruises left by the fists and boots of the Belly Hoggers.

'Speak your piece,' she told him, her voice edged with dislike and tension.

'It's easy spoke.' He stared intently at her and pointed to the hammer she held. 'But first, Tildy Crawford, let me tell you yet agen . . . I means you no harm! You'se got no need to be feared o' me.'

She nodded doubtfully. 'That's as maybe. But what is it you want?'

'I wants to work wi' you at your forge,' he stated baldly, and, seeing her instant reaction of rejection, hurried on. 'I'se got a bit of iron, and I'se got breeze; and I needs to finish me task, because I'se not got a penny-piece in the house to feed me 'ooman and childer wi.'

Suspicion was heavy in her. 'Why must you work here with me? Why not just get Isaac Crane to mend your bellows?'

The man grinned, but that grin bore more resemblance to the snarl of some feral beast. 'The bloody Belly Hoggers warn't content just to slit me Teasers. They smashed 'um to bits, and all me poles and tools besides. The Teasers arn't able to be repaired, and wheer can I get the money for new 'uns, and new tools as well . . . Tell me that, missus?'

'But why do you choose me to work with?' Tildy's curiosity was overlaying her initial fears. 'We are enemies, are we not? I think you to be a brute, for what you did to your boy; and you revile and despise me, because you think I am Dick Suffield's whore!'

The man spat onto the hearth, and the burning coals crackled and hissed. 'Happen I said things that I shouldn't ha' done, missus . . . But said 'um I did, and I'll not crawl on me belly like some cur dog now. The thing is, none o' the other buggers hereabouts 'ull stand up to the Belly Hoggers. Most on our neighbours supports 'um anyhow. Theer's only you as shows courage enough to goo on wi' your work . . . And theer's me! Four hands be a sight better nor two for the nailing. Together we can earn more, and let's face it . . . You got more chance o' being let alone to do the work iffen you'se got a man wi' you in the forge. By yourself, you'll not finish your task.'

'Oh but I will, Martin Duffil,' Tildy interrupted spiritedly. 'For I'm determined that nothing shall stop me.'

But even as she spoke, she was realizing the advantages of his proposal and tentatively added, 'How would we share?'

He visibly relaxed, sensing that he was near to gaining her agreement.

'Why, we'll share like and like,' he asserted positively. 'For the time we works together, we'll split all costs, and all earnings, straight down the middle. I reckon that's more than fair, missus. I'm a good fast blow, and I can get more iron to work up as Spikes for George Hobbs, fust thing tomorrow.'

Tildy knew that Spikes were among the highest paid types of work, being also among the heaviest types of labour.

Duffil pointed to the heap of tacks she had made. 'I see youm striking out Fine Flemish. Well, I reckon that iffen we puts our backs into it, we can earn more nor twenty-three or four shillings wi' the iron we'll have between us . . . So? What d'you say?'

Tildy only hesitated for a second. 'I say yes, Master Duffil.'

The man's snarling grin reappeared. 'You'd best get used to calling me Martin. We doon't need masters in the forge here. Theers more than enough of them buggers outside.'

Now it was Tildy's turn to relax, and secretly admit that it was a profound relief that for the time being, at least, she would not be standing completely alone against a hostile world . . .

The next morning Tildy had a visitor before dawn. It was Dick Suffield. She faced him across the table in her living room, a sense of guilt at having taken the bundle of iron against his will making her feel ill-at-ease.

He was not his customary, genial-smiling self. Instead, his expression was as dour as his rusty-black clothing. He did not remove his tall hat, and made no attempt to put her at ease, only remained grimly staring at her, until she nervously broke the silence.

'What is wrong, Dick?'

He frowned. 'Why did you tek iron yesterday, when I'd told you not to?'

Puzzlement puckered her smooth brow. 'But why should you tell me not to? Until now you've always encouraged me to take my work.'

'It's none o' your concern why I told you nay,' he hectored. 'You need only do as I tells you.'

'But you know that I must work,' she protested. 'I am alone in this world. I have my baby to care for. I must work. You have not the right to deny me iron, if Master Sanders says that I may have it.'

'A pox on bloody Master Sanders!' he cursed roughly. The hunger to possess her was fast building in him, and he felt a thickening in his throat and a throbbing in his loins . . . Deliberately he tried to soften his manner. 'You'se no need to tek iron ever agen, Tildy. You'se no need ever to strike another nail. I'll see to that. All you needs is to be nice to me . . .'

The sickening awareness that he had finally come to claim his reward for helping her flooded through Tildy.

'I've every need,' she flustered, aware of the embarrassed flush spreading through her throat and cheeks.

For the first time he grinned, and began to move around the table.

'Now, honey-lamb, youm a married woman, so there's no need for you to colour up like some silly virgin. You knows well why I'm here. Youm agoing to be my woman, like you always knew you'd be. I'll tek care o' you . . . You'll live well . . .'

Desperately she sought for words to keep him from her. Answers that would give him rebuttal, without provoking him to anger, but no words would come. He took her silence as acceptance and suddenly grabbed her arms and pulled her to him, feverishly talking to her.

'I'se bin good to you, Tildy, arn't I? Ever sin you first come to the Sidemoor . . . This is one o' my houses youm aliving in now, arn't it? I stopped that bastard you was wed to from ill-using you, didn't I? I'se treated you real well . . .'

His breath filled her nostrils and she could taste its rank foulness even in her throat. He moved his head forward, trying to find her lips, and she jerked back from him. He chuckled huskily. 'Doon't try being coy wi' me, honey-lamb. I bin patient long enough.'

Abruptly his right hand clamped on the back of her skull, holding it like a vice, and his mouth trapped hers. He grunted deep in his throat and his left hand moved to grip the firm roundness of her buttocks and pull her lower body hard into his own. Tildy felt his swollen hardness against her belly through the thin layers of cloth that divided them, and a wild terror welled up in her. His wet mouth muffled her screams and her hands pounded unavailingly against his thick shoulders.

His lust exploded and he dragged her down to the floor, pulling her skirts high on her hips, while she fought frantically to prevent him. She felt his fingers brutally exploring her intimate body, and with a surge of desperation she clawed with both hands at his face and eyes. Raking with her fingernails, digging deep, tearing skin and flesh, leaving ruts of blood-welling rawness.

. 'Aagghhh!' Howling, he rolled away from her, and she scrambled up, searching wildly for escape.

'What's happening here?' Martin Duffil had come to work at the forge. 'What be you playing at, Suffield?' he growled, and went to lash out at the man on the floor with the hammer he carried.

'No! Don't hit him, Martin!' Tildy screamed, and Duffil held back.

Suffield, snorting with pain and rage, came to his knees. 'You bastard whore!' he bawled at Tildy. 'Tom Crawford was right about you, warn't he? You brings naught but evil to any man.' He snatched up his hat from where it had fallen in the scuffle and rose to his feet. His fingers tenderly explored the bloody streaks criss-crossing his face.

'Evil bitch!' he spat at Tildy. 'You'll pay a hard price for this day's work . . . You evil bitch!'

'Bugger off from here, Suffield.' Duffil again lifted his hammer in threat. 'Bugger off, afore I buries this in your bloody yed.'

With a last flurry of curses the man went. Duffil hawked and spat after him contemptuously, then said gruffly, 'Come on, my wench, dry your eyes. You arn't the fust, and wun't be the larst 'ooman as a man's got a bit rough wi', when he wanted some loving. Let's get some work done . . .'

Chapter Twenty-Nine

It was late afternoon when Janey Porter came to the Mitre in search of Dick Suffield. He was sitting by the fire in the back room, nursing a bottle of gin, and a foul temper.

'And what does you want?' he snarled, as the young woman came into the room.

She saw the long scratches, still oozing fluid from their deepest parts, and made no attempt to hide her satisfaction.

'I heard about what happened this mornin, and so 'as all the bloody Sidemoor, by now.'

'You'se sin to that, no doubt!' he shouted.

'Yes, no doubt!' she shouted back, and for a moment it seemed that he would lunge at her. But then, he deliberately relaxed back into his seat, and lapsed once more into a morose silence. The girl's fierce jealousy would not allow her to leave him alone, however, and once more she taunted him.

'So, Tildy Crawford near tore the bloody eyes out o' your yed. That was a shock for you, warn't it? A bloody doxy from the Tinyard turning down the great Dick Suffield . . .'

He refused to rise to her baiting, only kept staring into the fire.

Driven almost to madness the girl sprang at him and raked her own fingernails down his face.

'You bleedin' hell-bitch!' he roared out in pain and fury, and punched her violently in the face. As she fell back he came after her, gripping her long hair in one fist to wrench her towards him, pounding at her face and body with his other fist. Kicking and stamping at her legs and feet. Her screams brought Johnno Dipple dashing into the room, and strong though he was, Dick Suffield could not match the giant strength of his lieutenant. The big man wrestled the pair apart, and held Suffield in a bear-hug.

'Leave her, Dick. You'll kill the soddin' cow! Leave her!'

Suffield, powerless to move, hurled filthy insults at the sobbing girl as she slowly collapsed to huddle on the floor.

Blood trickling from the fresh and reopened wounds on his face, Suffield calmed a little, and told Dipple, 'It's alright, I'll not touch her. Now goo and get me a bowl o' water. I'll need to clean what this whore has just gi' me.' He roughly prodded the sobbing girl with his boot. 'Goo out of my sight afore I breaks your bloody neck.'

She clung to his boot as though it were a caressing hand. 'I'm sorry, Dick! I'm sorry . . . Doon't send me away. I only come here to help you.'

'Some bloody help!' he exclaimed in disgust. 'You tries to blind me, and then tells me you'se come to help . . . what soddin' help is that?'

'I loves you, Dick. I loves you.' She hiccuped between her sobs. 'I come to tell you what's going on up the Sidemoor right now.'

Johnno Dipple returned with the bowl of water and some rags. Suffield bathed his face, and then soaked a rag in gin. He pressed the rag against the red weals, wincing at the savage bite of the raw spirits. Fully calmed now, he reseated himself by the fire, and took a long swig of gin from the bottle. Then belched loudly, and turned to address Janey Porter.

'Spake out, then . . . What's agoing on theer?'

'It's all the fault o' Tildy Crawford!' she burst out. 'Because her and Martin Duffil are working, some of the others be going to tek iron from the warehouses tomorrow. They'm saying that if the Belly Hoggers be too feared o' the Yeomanry to bust up that cow, and Martin Duffil, then they'll be too feared to bust up anybody else . . . '

Suffield's face remained impassive as he assimilated this unwelcome news, but his mind raced. He could not let this happen. The total stoppage had brought him to within touching distance of his goal. He must keep the nailers from working! All he needed was another week or two, and he would win. A startling change came over his demeanour, and he smiled genially, and gently lifted Janey Porter to her feet.

'Youm a good wench, honey-lamb, and I'm sorry iffen I'se hurt you.'

Her teary eyes stared wonderingly at him. He kissed her tenderly.

'I knows I arn't bin too loving wi' you lately, Janey. But I've a lot o' burdens on me at present. Tildy Crawford meant nothing to me, I just took a silly fancy to her, that was all . . . My oath, it's happened afore, arn't it? But I always comes back to you, doon't I?'

Again he kissed her, and this time she returned his kiss with a fervent longing.

'Does you still want to be my 'ooman?' he whispered softly.

Her forehead creased, and she burst into fresh weeping. 'You knows I does? You *knows* that!'

'Theer now, theer . . . ' He cuddled her, and stroked her hair and cheeks. 'Then let's forget our differences, and start afresh, honey-lamb.'

'Oh, yes! Yes, Dick,' she choked out, and thankfully sagged against him, burrowing her face into his chest and clasping him tightly in her arms. Over her head he winked at Johnno Dipple, and dismissed him with a flick of his eyes.

When they were alone he began to unbutton the girl's bodice, releasing her big, delicately-veined white breasts and taking the thrusting nipples in turn into his greedy mouth.

'I'll gi' you some loving now, honey.' He crooned the words. 'I'll gi' you what you wants . . .'

More than an hour later, Dick Suffield called Johnno Dipple back into the room. Janey Porter had gone, happy in the knowledge that her lover had come back to her, and ready to do everything that he had asked of her, no matter what that might lead to.

'We've got trouble, Johnno.' Suffield was brusque and businesslike. 'We'll have to stop them buggers in their tracks, else they'll have more people working, and then we'll lose everything.'

The massive shaven-head moved slowly from side to side, and Suffield spoke with angry urgency.

'It's no use you saying nay, Johnno. Them two bastards has got to be stopped from working, no matter what the odds be agen us.'

'But the Yeomanry . . .' the big man started to demur.

'Bollocks to the Yeomanry!' Suffield swore viciously. 'We can't let a bunch o' clod-hoppin' farmers on horseback stop us now . . . The Belly Hoggers must walk this very night. And this time I'll goo wi' you . . . To mek sure the job's well done.'

'But . . .' Dipple had only time to utter the single word before Suffield overrode him.

'But, nothing! You'll do as I say . . . Or mayhap you'd like the climate in Van Diemen's Land?'

Brief moments later the big man capitulated. 'Alright, Dick. It shall be as you say,' he muttered disconsolately.

Chapter Thirty

Edward Cassidy reined in his mount at the door of the Sanders house, and before dismounting sat for some time, deep in thought. The written request from Jonathan Sanders, asking him to call, had given no indication of the reason the nailmaster wished to see him so urgently.

The afternoon was dry, and the sky held only a scatter of clouds. Two girls came out from the yard, and stared admiringly at the dashing uniform of the horseman. They whispered and giggled together, eyeing him hungrily as they did so, and Edward Cassidy grimaced. He knew that it was common gossip among the Sanders' household staff, and throughout the Sidemoor, that he was Carlotta's lover.

'Surely Sanders himself must have heard that gossip?' Cassidy wondered. 'But then, it is a true saying, is it not, that the wronged husband is always the last to find out that he is being made to wear the horns.'

The wind gusted, causing the long hanging white plume of his shako to twitch as if it were a live thing, and Cassidy shivered involuntarily, despite the protection of his black regimental riding cape.

The door before him opened and Jonathan Sanders appeared, a funereal figure, his face as shadowed and sombre as his clothing.

'Please, do come in, Cassidy,' he invited grimly.

A fire burned cheerfully in the drawing-room hearth, but Carlotta, sitting to one side of that fire, did not reflect its cheer. Her face was pale, her posture tense, and her fingers continuously twined and twisted upon her lap.

She did not return Cassidy's greeting, and kept her gaze fixed downwards, refusing to meet his enquiring eyes.

'I'll come straight to the point, Cassidy.' There was none of the usual pleasant diffidence in Jonathan Sanders' manner. Instead, he was grimly uncompromising. 'I know that you and my wife have been cuckolding me for some time past.' He held up one hand to forestall any protest of denial. 'Please, do not exacerbate an already sufficiently unpleasant situation by denying that fact. Carlotta has fully confessed, but that was really only a formality. I have known for some time what was between you, but refused to accept the evidence of my own senses; or rather, was too much of a moral coward to do so . . . ' He lapsed into silence, while Edward Cassidy attempted to marshall his own shocked and scattered thoughts.

'Very well, Sanders,' he answered at last. 'I can only confess that it is true . . ' He deliberately struggled to maintain a neutral and inoffensive tone. 'I make no excuses, for that would be pointless. I realize that I have wronged you in the cruellest manner, and that I have behaved in a way totally unworthy of one who is termed a gentleman. I take full responsibility for what has occurred. Carlotta is not to blame, I am.'

The nailmaster's eyes clearly showed the torment he was undergoing, and Edward Cassidy experienced a surge of pity, and real remorse, for what he had done to the other man.

'I am truly sorry, Sanders,' he muttered, and glanced at Carlotta, who kept her own gaze still firmly averted, then went on hesitantly. 'Of course, if you decide to call me out, then as a gentleman, I am honour-bound to accept your challenge. But I would beg you to consider well before you do so . . . I have no wish to inflict further injury upon you, and I do possess a skill at arms engendered by long service as a soldier, that I fear you may lack yourself. Please, I beg of you, do not read into my words anything of the brag or threat. I am merely trying to spare us both . . .'

Jonathan laughed joylessly, and waved his hand in negation. 'Dammit, Cassidy, I'm no duellist. I have not the slightest knowledge of pistols or swordplay. Also, even if I were able to outshoot or outthrust you, I have no desire to kill or wound you. For reasons which my wife has undoubtedly already made clear to you, I feel that I bear a great deal of the blame for this unhappy state of affairs myself.'

Despite the obvious mental agonies he was enduring, Jonathan Sanders was fully in control of himself, and of the situation.

'I have decided that my wife shall leave my house. I intend, in due course, to seek a legal annulment of our marriage. If possible, on grounds that will not cause any further unpleasant focussing of the world's attention upon any of us.

'As of this moment, my wife is free to do whatsoever she wishes. If you intend to give her your protection, then do so, because she must leave my roof this very day. I have already sent for a post chaise . . . I have nothing further to add, Cassidy, except that the moment you have completed your arrangements with Carlotta, I expect you to leave my home, and never again attempt to impose yourself upon my company. I bid you goodbye, sir.'

The nailmaster went from the room with a quiet dignity that impressed Edward Cassidy, and deepened his remorse. He stared at his lover, and said with considerable feeling, 'Do you know, Carla, I find that I have a great respect and admiration for your husband. He puts us both to shame.'

269

She lifted her head, and with a shock of surprise he saw hostility in her face.

'And me? What is to become of me?' Her full lips pouted petulantly. 'I found it grossly mortifying to be discussed as if I were some piece of trade-goods, by the pair of you. That half-man I'd wed to proposing to evict me from my own home, and you standing there like some pimple-faced schoolboy prating about honour.'

Cassidy found himself once again seeing beyond Carlotta's flamboyant beauty, and not enjoying what he saw: her selfishness, her self-centredness, her lack of any pity or remorse for the wrong that she had done her husband.

Do I really want to share my life with this woman? he asked himself and found himself strongly doubting that he did. But what choice do I have? I must in all honour stand by her and give her my care and protection . . . Aloud, he tried to placate her. 'Carla, let us not quarrel. Let us instead decide what is to be done for the best.'

'Be done?' Her tone became shrewish. 'Be done for the best, indeed? I fear that all the harm and damage possible has been done to me already. Do you not see it? Perhaps, like all men, you are too dull-witted to perceive what lies before your face. You have ruined me. I can never return to my family, or hold my head high in decent Society for the rest of my days. I am being proclaimed a whore! That is the degradation to which you have brought me.'

Cassidy felt the impulse to tell her to go to Hell and be dammed! But he knew that in the final analysis he was bound to this woman, and could never bring himself to desert her.

A confusion of emotions pulsed through him. Distaste and desire. Dislike and infatuation . . .

'You must go to my house in London,' he told her. 'I shall join you there as soon as I am able. When your marriage is annulled, then we can legalize our union.'

A glint of satisfaction entered her black eyes . . . London!

That was much to her fancy . . . London! With its theatres, its shops, its balls, and its men . . . London!

She smiled brilliantly at the unhappy man before her. 'Very well, Edward. I shall obey you and go direct to London. But I shall need money for when I arrive there, shall I not? You surely do not expect me to remain cloistered in your house like a nun, until you are able to join me. I shall need to buy suitable clothes, and so many other things.'

'I shall give you a letter to my bankers,' he answered. 'You shall be provided with money enough . . . ' Even at this early point in their new relationship. Edward Cassidy was experiencing the forebodings that in binding his future with this beautiful, capricious woman, he had voluntarily entered a honey-trap which would eventually consume him . . .

Alone in his office, Jonathan Sanders poured out his grief in anguished tears. When he was finally wept-dry, he discovered that a curious numbness had pervaded his emotions.

'I know that I will sometimes hate Carlotta, and sometimes love and yearn for her,' he told himself. 'But I know also, that I shall slowly heal. That someday I will be able to think of her without grief, or bitterness. And without yearning . . . Until that day comes, then I must learn to endure my torment.'

Now that he had clarified and given verbal substance to his tangled emotions, the nailmaster was able to consider his immediate future with some degree of detachment. He was expecting a visitor, and depending on that visitor, he would be able to put in train the course of action he had decided upon. 'And once I've done that, then what becomes of me will rest in the hands of fate . . . ' he muttered aloud.

Chapter Thirty-One

Mr Saul Shibco dismounted from the yellow-varnished body of the Tally Ho stagecoach in the foreyard of the Golden Lion Hotel, and looked about him with a jaundiced glare.

'The Ordinary is now being served, gentlemen, please to take your places. The Ordinary is now being served,' Snagee Porter shouted from the open doorway of the large dining room where the long table was laid with plates and cutlery, and great bowls of assorted steaming viands for the refreshment of the passengers.

Saul Shibco turned his back on the open door. He had no objections to eating non-kosher food, but his hunger was overlayed by a greater need.

'Here, boy?' He beckoned to a ragged urchin. 'Lead me to the Sidemoor, there'll be a penny for you when we reach there.'

The snub-nosed urchin took in the curled, oiled ringlets that fell from beneath the brim of Shibco's high beaver hat, and the luxurious fur-collared greatcoat.

'Corst you more nor a penny to goo to the Sidemoor,

master,' he bargained. 'It's a long walk for a little 'un like me.'

Shibco's fleshy lips pouted aggressively. 'Tuppence then, and not a ha-penny more.'

'Alright, master, I'm your man.' The diminutive figure stretched out a grimy paw.

'You'll get the money when we arrive,' the man snapped.

The shock-haired head wagged from side to side. 'Oh no I wun't, master. I'll get the money now, or I'll not tek you.'

With bad grace the man proffered a single thick heavy coin. 'I'll give you one penny now, the other when we arrive, and that's final.'

The long walk did nothing to soothe an irritability inflamed by the cold and uncomfortable jolting sustained during the stage journey from Birmingham, and Saul Shibco determined to extract a full measure of recompense for the myriad discomforts of the day.

At last, boots, trouser bottoms and overcoat skirts saturated with the mud of the road, the traveller reached the Sidemoor.

'Where exactly is the Sanders warehouse, boy?'

'Down theer, at the end.'

'Be off with you then, I'll make my own way from here.' The man walked on, and the urchin ran after him.

'Wheer's me other penny? What about me money?' he screeched indignantly.

His shriek of anger became one of pain as the man cuffed him heavily at the side of his head.

'Get away, you little heathen. You'll get no more from me.'

'Dirty Jew bastard! the child howled. 'Dirty Christ killer!'

The Broad Street was empty and foreboding in the dusk, and the boy's courage failed him. He had heard too many horror stories of what the Jews did to Christian children, to risk letting the man lay hands on him.

'I 'opes your balls rots off, dirty Jew bastard!' With a final defiant screech, he ran back towards the town.

A light shone from the windows of the warehouse office, and Shibco knocked on its door. Inside, Jonathan Sanders rose to open the door to his visitor.

Jacob Ashfield was sitting in his fireless cottage reading aloud from the Bible by the light of a solitary stub of candle. Around him assembled in the gloom were his wife and some neighbours, all sitting on the stools or chairs they had brought with them, their whole attention focussed on the gaunt, grey-faced preacher.

' . . . thus saieth the Lord, the God of David, thy father . . . I have heard thy prayer, I have seen thy tears, behold, I will heal thee . . . And on the third day thou shalt go up into the house of the Lord . . . ' Ashfield's sonorous voice faltered as he was forced to take a clean rag from his pocket and wipe his watering eyes.

He looked at the thin, worn faces of those with him, and experienced a terrible sensation of guilt. 'I've brought them to his,' he told himself sadly. 'Through my pride, and my stubbornness, I have brought my people to the very edge of destruction.'

'Please, Jacob,' his tired, ill-looking wife urged him gently. 'Please go on reading.'

Gruffly he cleared his throat, and was about to continue when a loud knocking sounded on the outer door. Motioning his companions to remain seated, Ashfield rose and answered it. His painfully halting gait was a witness to his bodily weakness, and the privations he had undergone in denying himself, to feed those even worse off than he.

'Good evening, Brother Ashfield.' It was Jonathan Sanders, hatless and without a cloak. 'May I enter, I wish a brief word with you?'

Ashfield nodded assent, and the nailmaster walked into the dank, cheerless room.

'What is it you want, Master Sanders?' Ashfield was polite, but unwelcoming.

Jonathan swept his gaze around those present, absorbing the miasma of misery and defeat that emanated from their bowed figures. Dear God, why must Your servants inflict such sufferings upon each other? Why must Man and Master forever be in conflict? He asked silently, and then addressed those present.

'I want to tell you that all who wish to do so may take iron from my warehouse tomorrow morning, for working up at the old rates . . . ' He had not known what reaction his news would bring, but certainly was not prepared for the numbed silence that greeted it. Made uncertain, he went on, ' . . . I'm no longer the sole master of the warehouse. I have taken a partner, a Mr Saul Shibco of Birmingham . . . However, it will be I who deals with the day to day business. Mr Shibco is a man of many affairs, and perforce must spend most of his time in his native city . . . ' Again he stopped speaking to await their reaction, and again was greeted by absolute silence. Only their eyes moved, flickering to each other, then to him, then to each other.

Puzzled and irritated, Jonathan snapped curtly, 'Do you not understand what I am saying to you? I am reverting to the old rates . . . You have won! I am defeated, and you have gained the victory!'

Tears wet upon his lined, hollow cheeks, Jacob Ashfield moved to confront the nailmaster. 'Let us not talk of victory or defeat, Brother Sanders. Let us instead give thanks to Almighty God, that this trouble between us is now at an end. Join with us in a prayer of thanksgiving, Brother Sanders . . . Join with us . . . ' The preacher slumped down onto his knees, followed by his wife and neighbours, and then, by Jonathan Sanders . . .

Chapter Thirty-Two

The Belly Hoggers met in the deserted burial yard of St John's Church some two hours after the moonless nightfall. There were five of them. Dick Suffield, Johnno Dipple, and three brawl-scarred ruffians recruited from the Birmingham slums. All had brought hoods and gowns of sacking, and in addition Dick Suffield carried a long-barrelled pistol and a heavy sack bag that clinked dully as he laid it down on a convenient gravestone, while Dipple held a sledgehammer in one huge hand.

The great clock of the church tower chimed the hour and Dick Suffield cursed softly. 'That bleedin' wench is late coming, God blast her.'

'Give her time, Cully, her's probably prettifying herself . . . Arter all, no 'ooman loikes to goo to the ball wi'out her finery!' one of the men quipped, and next moment vented a choked cry as Suffield's hands clamped upon his throat.

'Just shut your stinkin' mouth, you,' Suffield growled threateningly. 'All you'se got to do is to keep quiet, and obey my orders . . . Understand?'

'Alright, Cully, alright. No need to lose your rag,' the half-strangled man forced out.

Suffield released him with a final vicious squeeze of hooked fingers and thumbs. 'Good! Just you remember it.'

In the dull starlight Janey Porter was a shapeless moving shadow as she threaded her way through the crosses, carved figures and tombstones that packed the churchyard.

'Wheer's you bin 'til now?'

Her lover's anger caused her to falter and babble explanations.

'Shut your bloody rattle.' He brutally cut her short. 'Be the patrols out?'

'Yes, Dick. There's two lots on 'um. One resting in Sanders warehouse, and the other riding through the Side-moor. There's five or six on 'um in each lot.'

The unwelcome information brought instant protest from the Birmingham men. 'I doon't fancy it!' 'Nor me neither!' 'Nor me!'

Suffield's yellowed teeth bared in a sneering snarl. 'God rot my balls! We'se got some hard-chaws here, arn't us just . . . Scared of a bunch o' bleedin' yokels on plough-horses be you?'

'Ne'er mind the blaggardin',' one of the trio rejoined. 'We arn't come here to fight no battle o' Waterloo. I was at the real 'un, and stood in the square agen the Frog cavalry . . . So doon't you go calling me no yellow-gut, Suffield.'

Sensing that there was a danger of losing them, Dick Suffield moved swiftly. 'Lissen, I knows well youm a man o' courage, Sam Snow. So I'll tell you what I'll do. I'll pay you double what we agreed . . . And all you needs to do is to draw off the Yeomanry, so as to gi' me and Johnno here a clear field to do our business in. What d'you say to that?'

The three exchanged glances and withdrew a small distance to argue vehemently in low whispers.

Suffield bit back his impatience, and asked Dipple, 'What's up, Johnno? Youm uncommon quiet.'

The man shook his head. 'I arn't happy about what you

intends doing, Dick, and that's a fact. I doon't mind breaking the yeds of man or woman, but I draws the line at what you . . . '

'For Christ's sake, shurrup!' Suffield ordered sharply, aware of Janey Porter's curious stare.

'What does Johnno mean?' the girl questioned, a sudden anxiety gnawing at her. 'What is it you intends doing to Tildy Crawford and Martin Duffil?'

'Naught to bother your yed wi', girl. You just do as youm told, and leave everything else to me!' he told her sharply.

She relapsed into an unhappy silence, and Dipple also appeared to have swallowed his doubts.

The trio came back to Suffield.

'Well?' he demanded.

Their leader nodded. 'We'em on.'

'That's more like it . . . Johnno, give me them bags.'

Suspended from a cord slung around his waist, Dipple was carrying several linen bags, and these he now handed to Suffield, who in turn distributed them among the trio. He smiled genially, his spirits again rising high.

'These are what you'll stop the bleedin' clodhoppers catching you wi'.'

From one of the bags he extracted a four-pronged piece of metal which resembled four nails joined together by a single head. He grinned savagely.

'We calls this a Tisasitwas. Whichever way you drops it . . . ' He tapped one of the long viciously-pointed prongs with his finger. ' . . . then one o' these beauties 'ull be sticking up. You throws 'um in front of the horses, and the spike 'ull slice up into the hoof-frog like a hot knife going into butter.' He sneered at the old soldier. 'You should have had a few o' these at Waterloo, my buck. The bleedin' cavalry 'ud never ha' got near to you, iffen you'd chucked a few bags o' these in front of 'um . . . Now, let's waste no more time. The sooner the business is done, the sooner you draws your pay.'

Led by Suffield, the party stealthily made their way

towards the few dull flickers of light that was the Side-moor . . .

Sergeant John Edkins swayed in his saddle and thought longingly of his soft warm feather bed, and his wife's soft warm body back in his farmhouse at Alvechurch village. Behind him his section of troopers ambling along the Broad Street were also immersed in their individual reveries. The sergeant reluctantly dragged his awareness back to his present cold, bleak surroundings and peered sourly about him.

'What a miserable hole it is . . . Like the buggers who live here . . . Wun't even give us a civil word, and looks at us as if we'em dirt, so they does . . . And us giving up all our bodily comforts to protect 'um while they lies stinking in their beds. Ungrateful bastards!'

From the shadowed eaves of a terrace of cottages a woman suddenly darted out into the roadway, causing the sergeant's horse to shy and snort.

'Sergeant?' She came straight up to him, one hand reaching for the bridle of the horse to bring it to a halt. 'Shhhh!' She pressed her fingers to her lips. 'Keep as quiet as you can.'

The patrol reined in, craning their necks and bodies to try and hear what the woman was saying.

'What is it you want, young 'ooman?' the sergeant stared suspiciously down at her.

Janey Porter drew her shawl more closely about her head, so that he could not see her face clearly. 'It's the Belly Hoggers, Sergeant.'

'What? Wheer?' His voice rose, and again she begged him.

'For God's sake, be quiet. Iffen the Belly Hoggers was to hear or see me talking to you, they'd slit my throat . . . They'm down theer a ways.' She pointed to a narrow lane some forty yards ahead, angling off from the Broad Street. 'I reckon they'm getting ready to do some mischief.'

'How many be there?'

'Only a few, but you might need more men than you've got with you, iffen youm to be sure o' catching them all.'

The sergeant reacted quickly. 'Trooper Thompson, ride back to the warehouse. Give Cornet Farlane my compliments, and ask him to bring the rest o' the lads up here. Tell him we'se got sight o' Belly Hoggers.'

As the man galloped off, the sergeant dismounted. 'You and me 'ud best goo and take a closer look at these buggers, my wench . . . Lead on.'

The NCO felt tremors of excitement coursing through him, assailed by visions of fame, even promotion and reward, should he be instrumental in capturing a party of Belly Hoggers. These thoughts were already shimmering tantalizingly in his mind.

Together the man and woman crept into the lane entrance and along its length, keeping close in to the blank brick walls and wooden sides of the sheds and storehuts that lined both sides. Janey Porter suddenly halted and laid a restraining hand on his caped shoulder.

'Theer they be,' she breathed in his ear. 'Further down along theer.'

By straining his eyes and ears Edkins was just able to distinguish a clump of moving shadows, and hear a susurration of voices.

'Is there any other way out from here?' he whispered.

'No, all the sheds be kept locked . . . And there's only the big gates o' Juggin's warehouse at the bottom. If you comes in fast, they'll not have the chance to climb over them gates . . . They'm powerful tall, so they be.'

Satisfied, he drew her back with him, and leaving her at the corner hurried back to his troopers, as the cornet and the rest of the section from the Sanders warehouse came cantering up.

Quickly Sergeant Edkins explained the situation, and the boyish young officer laughed excitedly.

'Good work, Sergeant. Dammee if we won't have some

rare sport this night! Right men, draw swords!' he ordered, and steel whickered on leather. He drew his own sword, and was barely able to restrain himself from whooping aloud with joy. This was what he had joined the Yeomanry Service for . . . High adventure, and the chance to show his mettle on any sort of battlefield.

'Dammee,' he told himself happily. 'What a tale I'll have to tell . . . Please God, let the buggers put up some sort of fight. Please let them.'

He tried to speak in a gruff, manly voice. 'Section will advance in column of threes. Section, walk march!'

Bits and snaffles rattled and saddlery creaked as the small column moved off.

At the entrance to the narrow lane, Janey Porter vented one long low whistle, then shouted at the top of her voice. 'Quick! Be quick! They'm trying to get away.'

'The Devil they are!' The boyish Farlane lost his head completely. 'Charge men! Charge!' he howled, and using the flat of his sabre, lashed his mount into a bolting gallop.

'Charrrgggge! Charrrgggge!' Howling maniacally, hooves thundering, the troopers came headlong after their officer, down the Broad Street and swept into the entrance of the narrow lane. 'Charrrrgggge! Charrrgggge!' They cannoned into each other, horses infected with the madness of the riders, hooves slipping and scrabbling madly upon the wet ground, showers of mud and stones flung up to mark their crazed rush.

Halfway down the lane the cornet's horse suddenly screamed, stumbled and bucked wildly as the cruel prongs sliced into the soft frogs of its hooves. The young man lost his seat and went hurtling over its head to thud to earth. The following horses smashed into the cornet's mount and a mass of squealing animals and screaming men toppled jarringly, bones cracking and breaking, muscles and tendons tearing. Other horses squealed and bucked as they hit the carpet of nails, lashing out with hooves, biting savagely in paroxysms of agony. Men shrieked and fell, sabres clanging against walls, and the narrow space became a black, boiling maelstrom of noise, terror and pain.

Janey Porter ran swiftly towards the Tinyard. Dick Suffield, waiting in the dark arch of the entrance passage saw her coming, and as soon as she gasped out her news, he addressed Johnno Dipple.

'Right! Let's get to it, and you get home and stay there, Janey. Remember, you've not bin out the house this night.'

Rapidly the two men donned hoods and gowns. Suffield checked the priming of his pistol, and hefted the clinking sack in his hand. 'Come on!'

They ran through the covered passage and came out into the yard. All was silent, except for the thudding of the Oliver in Tildy Crawford's forge. Dick Suffield glared at the barred and bolted doors, and the small sack-shrouded window.

'You thinks youm safe behind locked doors, Tildy Crawford!' he growled beneath his breath. 'But the gates of Hell 'udden't keep me from settling accounts wi' you . . . You stinkin' whore!'

Unseen by either of the men, Janey Porter had disobeyed Suffield's instructions and crept along the passageway to watch what they were doing. She was desperately worried about her lover's intentions, and sorely afraid that he would go too far in his attempts to stop Tildy Crawford working.

'You could get yourself hung, Dick, if youm not careful,' she muttered. The thought made her shudder.

Crouching at the end of the passageway, she cautiously peered into the Tinyard Square. Her eyes now accustomed to the darkness, she could see the two men as they moved towards the only workshop where the Olivers thudded and hammers rang on iron.

Suddenly Dipple swung his sledgehammer against the rag-shrouded window. The glass and frame shattered inwards, dragging with them the sack curtain, and the fiery red glare of the forge shone out. Suffield sprang forward, hurling the bottles of lamp-oil taken from his sack through the gaping hole. Glass smashed and flames exploded from the hearth.

Tildy Crawford screamed in frightened shock, and Martin Duffil howled in agony as flaming oil splashed and clung to his naked chest and shoulders.

For a split second Janey Porter couldn't comprehend what was happening, then horror hit her like a physical blow.

'He's trying to burn them alive! Dick's burning them alive!'

Dipple was smashing the double-tiered door even as Suffield hurled another two bottles through the window to smash and explode in shooting flames. Choking and gagging on the thick smoke, her skin blistering as flames licked at her clothing and flesh, Tildy tore at the hanging cradle where her baby shrieked. She crushed the child into her breasts, trying to shield it from the leaping flames, and blindly stumbled into the cottage. Martin Duffil had preceded her, crawling on hands and knees, coughing and retching, blinded by the clouds of oily smoke.

Outside in the square Janey Porter ran screaming towards the two men. The forge door flew from its hinges and Dick Suffield raised the pistol he held and took aim into the flaring interior.

'No Dick! NOOO!' Janey flung herself at him, knocking his arm as the pistol cracked and jerked.

'You stupid cow!' he bellowed, and swung the long heavy barrel, whipping it backwards and forwards across the girl's head, beating her to the ground.

The impact of the lead ball smashed the breath from Tildy's body and sent her cannoning forward. Her forehead hit the wall and her baby shrieked as she let it fall, only to fall in turn across the tiny, helpless body. She made a despairing effort to lift her weight up from the screaming child, then sudden blackness descended, and everything ceased . . .

Chapter Thirty-Three

The merry month of May had come again, and once more house martins darted among the chimneys and eaves of the Sidemoor, and larks sang from sunlit skies. Tildy sat on a stool outside her door, basking in the heat of the afternoon sun, and listening contentedly to the gurglings and chucklings of her baby, kicking his chubby legs in the cradle beside her. Her hair, burned and frizzled by the fire, was growing and fast regaining its previous lustre. Her flame-scarred skin had also healed, and only a stiff weakness in her shoulder, and a deep-pitted round scar on the tender flesh of her back, reminded her of the gun wound she had suffered.

Around her the forges of the Tinyard glared fiercely, and men, women and children toiled and sweated, white-hot showers of sparks flew, hammers rang on iron, and the thudding of the Olivers pulsated through the air.

Hester Lammas came to her working door and smiled toothlessly at the young girl. 'Enjoying the sun, be you?'

Tildy returned her smile. 'Indeed I am, Hester.'

'When I got wed I thought the sun shone out of Lammas' arse.' The woman cackled with raucous laughter. 'It warn't long afore I found out that it warn't the sun at all . . . It was the bloody forge!'

' 'Ull you come and strike a few blows, you lazy cow?' Ikey's indignant bellow came from inside.

Hester Lammas winked broadly at Tildy. 'Arn't he lovesome and tender towards me, my duck. Iffen I leaves him for only a moment, he gets fritted that I'se run off wi' one o' me fancy-men! I'm coming, you bastard!' she shouted back into the doorway, and winked again. 'I'll see you later, Tildy.'

Alone once more, Tildy let her mind wander . . . Dick Suffield and Johnno Dipple were gone into the Maidstone Hulks, waiting to be transported to Van Diemens Land. Janey Porter had turned informer and King's evidence, and taken a terrible revenge on her brutal lover with her testimony.

Jonathan Sanders, that much-wronged, gentle man, lived a solitary life. Smiling rarely, attending to his business and praying to his God. Gossips in the Sidemoor asserted that he pined for his faithless wife.

No one had seen anything of Tom Crawford since he had run off. Rumour had it that he was in service in London as a footman. Tildy smiled wryly. That would suit Tom better than the nailing.

Davy Nokes? This time Tildy's smile was tender. 'My sweet Davy . . . Mayhap some day we'll meet again. I truly hope so . . . '

'And I'm here in the Sidemoor still . . . Living on parish relief. But very soon I'll be strong enough to work again, and to give my baby what he needs to grow strong and tall. The neighbours have been kind to me since that night, and accept me as one of their own. Why, I owe my baby's life and my own life to Martin Duffil. He got us both away from the fire. Hard and savage man he may be . . . But then, we have to be hard to survive here. But I'll not stay here as a slave to the masters all my days. I'll find some way of rising in this world. I'll find some way of raising my baby as a gentleman . . .'

She suddenly laughed aloud, and thought fancifully: It's true, isn't it? I really am become like the Iron Duke. I really am become unbeatable . . .